In Transit

Previously published books by Brigid Brophy:

Novels
Hackenfeller's Ape (Cheltenham Literary Festival Prize for a first novel)
The King of a Rainy Country
Flesh
The Finishing Touch
The Snow Ball

Drama
The Burglar (play with preface)

Non-Fiction
Black Ship to Hell (London Magazine Prize for Prose)
Mozart the Dramatist
Don't Never Forget
Black and White, A Portrait of Aubrey Beardsley
Fifty Works of English Literature We Could Do Without (in collaboration with Michael Levey and Charles Osborne)

BRIGID

BROPHY

IN TRANSIT

an heroi-cyclic novel

G. P. Putnam's Sons, New York

This pious memorial is dedicated to

SAINT SEXBURGA

(abbess of Ely, *c*.679–*c*.699)

Contents

... καὶ ἐπυνθάνοντο τί

ἐστί ποτε ὁ Ἔρως,

πότερα παῖς ἢ ὄρνις ...

... and they asked 'What is this Love, then? Is it a boy or a bird?'

LONGUS

SECTION ONE
LINGUISTIC LEPROSY
Allegro non troppo

1

Ce qui m'étonnait c'était qu'it was my French that disintegrated first.

Thus I expounded my affliction, an instant after I noticed its onset. My words went, of course, unvoiced. A comic-strippist would balloon them under the heading T H I N K S — a pretty convention, but a convention just the same. For instance, is the 'T H I N K S' part of the thought, implying the thinker is aware of thinking?

Moreover — and this is a much more important omission — comic strips don't shew whom the thoughts are thought *to*.

Obviously, it wasn't myself I was informing I had contracted linguistic leprosy. I'd already known for a good split second.

I was addressing the imaginary interlocutor who is entertained, I surmise, by all self-conscious beings — short of, possibly, the dumb and, probably, infants (in the radical sense of the word).

Consciousness: a nigger minstrel show in which you are forever grabbing a disembodied buttonhole and gabbling 'Pardon me, Mister Interlocutor'.

From the moment infant begins to trail round that rag doll, mop-head or battered bunny and can't get off to sleep except in its company, you know he's no longer infant but fant. Bunny is the first of the shadow siblings, a proto-life-partner. Mister and Missus Interlocutor: an incestuous and frequently homosexual marriage has been pre-arranged. Pity Bunny, that doomed child-bride.

I have known myself label the interlocutor with the name and, if I can conjure it, the face of someone I am badly in love with or awe of. But these are forced loans. Cut short the love or awe, and the dialogue continues.

Only death, perhaps, breaks the connexion. Perhaps it is Mister Interlocutor who dies first, turning away his head and heed.

The phantom faces of the interlocutor are less troubling than the

11

question of *where* he is. I am beset by an insidious compulsion to locate him. When my languages gave their first dowser's-twig twitch and I conceived they might be going to fall off, I still treated that matter less gravely than the problem of where I was addressing my account of it.

The problem was the more acute because I was alone in a concourse of people. After a moment I noticed that my situation had driven me to think my thoughts to the public-address system, which had, for the last hour, been addressing me — inter aliens — with commands (couched as requests), admonitions (a tumble of negative subjunctives) and simple brief loud-hails, not one of which had I elected to act on.

Whichever language it might be I should be left with a few words of when all the rest had dropped off, at least public-address would be equipped to understand my halting thoughts. Comforted, I set myself again to enjoying the refuge I was deliberately taking.

Yet it's imprecise of me to call the public-address system the location of my interlocutor. As a matter of fact, I had not managed to spot where the voice came out — only the three points where it could go whispered in (to a microphone like a hose), murmurings of an uniformed snake-charmer to her phallic love.

The voice did not seem to emerge anywhence. It was loosed upon and irradiated the vast lounge, the top nine-tenths of which contained only air and light, the people being mere shifting silt at the base. From time to time public-address commanded 'Pass the silt, please'.

The voice was mechanical. Mechanical equals international.

'Bay uh ah annoncent le départ de leur vol six six six, à destination de Rome.'

Italian place name, Frenched, spoken with an angliccent: its mutations made me diagnose my linguistic leprosy as a fallout disease. The unlocateable loudspeakers were bombarding me with linguistic Beta Eta Alpha rays.

At the recognition, my German dropped off, PLONK, its wing swiftly severed by an invisible-ray buzz-saw in mid-flight.

I addressed back to the public-address system my macaronic plaint, with that brilliant apostrophe in *qu'it* through which I sobbed

12

on an indrawn breath — a plaint which, because it both stated and illustrated my leprosy, constituted a rebus in language.

I had decided to refuse to follow the hint of 'destination de Rome' — and equally of 'destination: home'.

My internal eternal city, *my* capital Home, was founded by Romulus and Rebus.

The interlocutor whom child-*I* used to trail to bed was a punny.

I sprang out of the tweed-suited chair which, sloped backwards, was designed to let you rise from it only as a very slow Venus from the foamrubber, and began to stroll. I would have liked to brisk-march but, alone among strangers, you simply *cannot*, unless you are sure in the possession of a purpose which, if stopped and asked, you could declare as to the Customs. It makes no difference that you know no one ever *would* stop you and ask.

I strolled, as if not noticing where, towards the wall of glass through which you could look out on la piste/die Startbahn/the apron, whereon it was forbidden to smoke/rauchen/fumer.

I had not succeeded in leaving the interlocution behind, trapped like drained nectar in the valley of the chair slope. Caught without an answer at the ready, I merely repeated: Ce qui m'étonnait . . .

Hearing this for the second time round, the interlocutor demanded why it was already in the past tense.

I explained. I cruise, my jaws wide to snow-plough in the present tense, the plankton of experience. This I then excrete rehashed into a continuous narrative in the past tense.

Naturally the process is imaged according to bodily functions. That is an old habit of fant's (fant, the feu infant), so much of whose childtime is preoccupied with them. Even adult fant, book-learned enough to know about metabolism, doesn't feel it happening. You eat; you excrete; but you never catch your cells in the act of creating themselves out of your food and never hear the pop of sugar-energy released into your service from your laden corpuscles.

No more can you detect your personality and its decisions in the course of being created by your experience. You know only that you ingest the present tense and excrete it as a narrative in the past.

History is in the shit tense. You have left it behind you. Fiction is

13

piss: a stream of past events but not behind you, because they never really happened.

Hence the hold fictional narrative exerts on modern literate man. And hence the slightly shameful quality of its hold.

I knew as I statelily rose from the tweed and rubber launching pad that my stroll, ostensibly towards the glass wall, would soon conduct me to the bookstall.

Go daily to stall. Or do you want, enquires nanny-interlocutor, to spend a punny?

And hence the disesteem in which authors of fictional narrative are held – and hold themselves. *Don't*, says nanny, hold; don't touch. That's where fantasy and fiction begin. How authors squirm, how they sidle from foot to foot, to avoid that compulsion to narrative. They poise their shears over the wire, threatening to cut the connexion. They say they are seeking to alienate you. They take aim to fling you an open-ended fiction: the book lands legs akimbo, pages open at the splits, less a book than a box of trick tools, its title DO IT YOURSELF KID .

Kidding myself, I run my fingers through the fringes of para-printed-matter. Tartan holdalls (for smartie knowalls), purses impursonating sporrans (is that sporran forran? no, tartan has become the livery of internationalism), sets of dice endicing your fingers to set them a-chatter in memory in advance of the knucklebones your fingers may become on a wired skeleton; penrings, keyknives, paper-screw-openers; snow cosies, egg weights, thermo-timers, paper storms, crystal towers and eiffel palaces; fabergé in lurex: I riffle an eiffel and edge, shamefully, nearer to print.

With a push I revolve and at the same time rock an octagon-tower whose every storey racks storied postcards, every layer a rack and ruins; pastcards single, pastcards in concertinas or twinsets (history

herstory), a trivial fond ricordo di the bay/the hay/the major-duomo outside the sun-bronzed swing baptistery doors. Long stood Sir Bedivere revolving many mementoes.

But if I am to stay here some hours I must disencumber myself of that compulsive interlocution. Let me still it, let me blot, pad, plug or drug it out with other peoples'. I sidle, furtively, towards books.

14

2

Though I believe everyone subject to it, I am prepared to consider that the interlocutory injunction rides me more rigorously than it does most people. Perhaps I have to explain myself twice as hard to stay where I am. Perhaps I am double-pedalling in order to counter that rush to be misunderstood which is a fatality that has impelled me since my early childhood.

At summer weekends my parents would take me on expeditions: sometimes in the Howth direction, sometimes towards Dalkey. The purpose was either to stand on the coast and look out to sea or to stand on a promontory of coast and look back along the coastline towards another bit of coast.

For its size, Ireland has a remarkable quantity of coast.

And, perhaps for want of an alternative, a remarkable quantity of Irish time is spent in pointing out bits of coast from which another bit of coast can, on a not too drizzly day, be seen. On days of good visibility something like ninety per cent of the population must be standing about the island, arms extended like signposts, pointing out coast to the rest of the population.

That afternoon we went, if I remember, du côté de chez Mrs Donovan, who kept a sweetshop on the road to Dalkey. (Proust was not the only child who had a choice of two directions for his expeditions, any more than he was the only child to have a grandmother. To be impaled on a which-of-two-walks dilemma must be a very highly-incident metaphor of children's bisexuality, for there must be very few children living in a house so placed that it doesn't, when you go out of the door, offer you a choice of which way to turn − just as most children have two parents.)

I was three. It was windy on the cliff top. I remember agitating up and down in the outgrown-its-strength, reedy grass: 'I want me da to lift me up, I want me da to lift me up'. ('Don't call him that, dear; only slum kids say that; call him my daddy.')

It must have been thought I had already acquired the local taste for looking at and/or from the coastline of my native land. In fact I wanted my father to lift me up because at three I had just become

15

comfortably tall enough, if he perched me on his hip in the manner of an Augustus John gypsy woman, to look down on the bald spot which the top of his head wore like a tonsure, an egg-cosy or the acorn-size skullcap of a Jewish elf.

He handed my mother the camera and the bar of plain chocolate to hold (motorists in those days fed continuously on chocolate like cross-Channel swimmers), and hoisted me. With his free arm he played the signpost game. We all three stood − or, at least, I stood in the stirrups of his hip − looking. We made a wind-wrapped group. My mother's hair wept out to sea like the thoughts of an Irish myth miss yearning to rejoin her seal lover.

We all followed with our gazes where my father's arm urged: a hard dark blob wallowing in the sea.

'Ireland's Eye', he informed me.

I bounced on his hip. 'Ireland's Eye', they thought I repeated. And who should blame me if I did? For in this Irish conversational habit of pointing places out no provision is made for a witty riposte. No doubt that is why most of the population is so set on getting its pointing out in first.

My father faintly patted me with the hand I was in fact sitting on − a stunted pat. My mother, hampered by the camera case's straps, was scarcely less faint in the pat she gave my bare leg, whose gold hairs were, in the cool of the wind, standing a little more upright than was natural; my legs were in a pre-gooseflesh condition.

My parents were glad enough that I parrotted the information but perhaps at heart disappointed that, at three, I could do no better. Perhaps they secretly expected me to invent the riposte Irish conversational mores have not yet hit on.

But in fact I had not just been repeating the name of the landmark. When I bounced on my father's hip it was in a grand access of either − I can't now recall which − egomania or patriotism. What I cried out was 'Ireland's I'.

It was from the faintness of their pats that I knew I hadn't made myself understood.

That night I wept in punny's arms. I placed his soft secret little hands one on each of my cheeks and whispered 'Paws, bunny, pause'.

16

On our next expedition bunny fell irrecoverably off a bit of Ireland's coastline and I experienced widowhood (widow widower widowest) or perhaps the thrills of sibling-spouse murder (well, criminal negligence at the least).

Six months later I was no longer temptable to the identification Ireland equals I, my parents having been killed in a plane crash and I transplanted across the sea they had so often bid me gaze out at.

3

My decision to remain in the Transit Lounge might or might not be connected with the manner in which my parents died. I was not to be prepared to discuss that till later; for there was another relevant fact which I had not yet disclosed to the interlocutor – which, indeed, I hadn't yet been able to bring myself to disclose.

In itself, however, the decision was reasoned, bold and neatly-scissored-off. I simply did not catch my next plane. Yet my decision had about it that faint unnaturalness which attends any decision made and taking effect entirely inside your own head at a time when you happen to be in public.

Here, too, I will believe the phenomenon is more intense in me than in others. But again I believe everyone liable to it. Suppose you are walking alone along a crowded town street when you suddenly remember an errand in the opposite direction. Are you capable of just, without loss or increase of speed, turning about and walking unconcernedly up the pavement you've been walking down? Felicitations if you are. But I'll bet you aren't, even though you rationally point out to yourself it's no one's business but your own. What *do* I think you do? Cross over. That's if you're the skulking kind. Dodge in and out of the traffic a little, to place obstacles between you and any eye that might be idly taking in your course (Before I swung the coupé across the intersection and onto the boulevard, I doubled up and down the sidestreets for a while so as to shake any tail Murphy might have put on me). To walk back along the pavement on the *opposite* side is a far more possible act: and in any case you might have crossed the road to inspect something suddenly spotted in a shop window, whose nature (Gone Home To Fetch Cash) might have changed your mind and direction. If you're *not* the skulking kind, I imagine you dramatise your decision. You halt as if the next pavement stone had opened into a pit of hell. You tut-teeth; you swing your racquet arm up and then punchingly down, as though you were one of a hussar-caped old-fashioned musical-comedy chorus vowing vengeance on its white-tight thighs; you possibly even click castenet-fingers. Your dramatisation is, of course, a benefit performance: for the benefit of potential readers of your sign language. Not one of these actions would you commit were you, alone at home, to remember something in the kitchen as you walked through the hall. There are no pits of hall. When, on the pavement, you at last accomplish your turnabout, your shoulders are held a little more square than sits easily on you, you perhaps loose a whispered whistle over your own propensity to forgetfulness, and your face, turned up as if to the sun, wears a great, rueful, wide-to-all-the-world, Gary Cooper grin . . .

I click my fingers, bite my castanet thumb at you. *Got* you. *That's* what I think you do, hypocrite (let me alienate you) lecteur/interlocutor.

4

What has impelled me to bite my $\left\{ \begin{smallmatrix} (nn) \\ thumb \\ (vb) \end{smallmatrix} \right\}$ my nose at you so rudely, interlocutor, is, of course, sheer envious muscular frustration on my (retrospective) part.

For *my* decision could not take immediate muscular issue in either skulk or dramatics – for the simple reason that I was at the time sitting, alone but in public, in front of a coffee I had not so much as sipped because it was still much too hot.

Nothing of a technical nature held me. It was my chair which, weighted by one of those loaded metal bases, was as good as stuck fast in front of the bar. But I was affixed by social usage. You cannot publicly abandon a coffee to wither in its cup unless you can brandish a whither by way of pretext – unless you can dramatise

18

your explanation by bustling ostentatiously towards Departure Gate tal-dei-tali: and my decision was, precisely, *not* to.

I decided calmly. I was in high spirits. Only, perhaps, one tiny symptom of anxiety nattered through my euphoria. I felt a compulsion to demand of the interlocutor, which I did with grand good humour, why idiom insisted on placing me in the high spirits when the high spirits, whether you conceived of them psychologically or demonically, were so patently in me.

With fluency and confidence I explained why I was going to sit on and just let my flight be called.

An airport, I told my interlocutor, is one of the rare places where twentieth-century design is happy with its own style. (The outside of aeroplanes is another, but though an instant's kinaesthetic fantasy places me there every time I glance through the airport plate glass and see a plane landing, you can't in practice cling to a wing.) And the result is that there are few places where modern life is, simply, as *nice* as it is in airports.

Inside the plane, you are narrowed to the purpose of getting somewhere. The cabin's style is cramped by passenger-load-frequency economics, yours by your seat belt. You are, indeed, belted-up. Even when she stoops over you, uniformed nanny can scarcely hear what you say for engine-noise.

When your belt doesn't rein you in, you're trapped by your pull-down table.

There you are: fixed in your high (by several thousand feet) chair or wedged into your push (by jet engine) chair, dependent on h $\left\{{a \atop u}\right\}$ rried n $\left\{{u \atop a}\right\}$ nny's finding a moment to play attendant to you.

You wave your arms: she's already glided past up the aisle, with her gait of a streamlined nun. (You can, if you've memorised the Air-Hostess Recognition Book, distinguish which order she belongs to by her habit: the blue nans of Blessed European Airways, the black nans of Lifthandstaheaven, the grey nans of Pan-Immaculate.) Despairing in her slipstream, you bang with your spoon on your pull-down table. It turns out to be a plastic spoon which, by a stroke of nightmare horrifics, makes no discernible sound. You have been rendered dumb. While retaining the expectations, the needs and the thought-processes (these last directed to the interlocutor, who

19

signals his reply by switching on his smiling light, F A S T E N
Y O U R   C E I N T U R E S) of fant, you have been amputated
down to the status of infant.

Suppose, however, you don't let yourself go so far as to get into
the plane. Suppose you retard yourself at the stage of waiting to get
into it.

Here, at the airport, you are already within the ambience of the
exciting architecture of getting somewhere, but your nose is not yet
pointed towards your destination and held hard to it. You're not yet
bound waist and chest. You don't yet need nanny's hand-and-foot
attentions. But already you are cared and catered for. It's not the
limitless anarchic space of everyday life, where you must scrabble a
living. It's circumscribed. It's newer, cleaner and smarter than
everyday life; and services wait to spring to the salute when you
press the button. You are free to supply your own wants, but all the
sources of supply are within stroll.

An airport is a free-range womb.

It's not *just*, of course, that the amenities are within stroll. So
they are at Milan station − a building which nonetheless makes a
caryatid of you, piling its hollow-classic monumentality on your
stooped shoulders and loading you with the guilt for Mussolini.

In my moment of decision I was, it's true, counting up the
airport's amenities. But I took more account of the upper
nine-tenths of the fishtank construction, a nine-tenths filled out only
by light, air, and the fishtank bubbles of speech which, as though
complying with another comic-strip ideogram, were infiltrated into
it from no specifiable source by mon semblable, mon frère, the
public-address system.

Twentieth-century architecture, excusably frightened off imagination by the whimsies of the architecture of the century before,
demands a function to be cantilevered from. (Naturally, therefore,
it's lousy at cathedrals.) An airport is functional − *is* a function. But
a fraction of its function is the seemingly non-functional intention
of preventing you from feeling scared at take-off. It must make you
feel cared for; lapped about; upheld − so that you will not scream
when the wheels leave the ground.

When my interlocutor objected that as much non-functional
20

pleasantness could be predicated of a modern hotel, I didn't need even to raise my internal voice to put him down. Hotels are posh. They exclude, by invisible chips of glass along the tops of invisible wall, rowdies. The even repress the potential rowdy in the client they admit. Their dimmed indirect lighting censors your shouting voice. The absorption that sucks your footfalls into the superfluously deep pile of their carpeting is an admonition, to be read in a braille of the feet: get drunk discreetly.

Twentieth-century hotels have carpeting, not carpets, and lighting, not lights. Their entrance halls are dark as a plush-lined pistol-case. Their way back to the womb is fitted with a silencer. You may commit (registering a false name) but not mention incest.

Airports are smart but not posh. They do not keep you out, proletariat. They raise you, too, to the peerage.

Your feet may clack on their functional floors but the noise is dissipated with your cigarette smoke in the upper nine-tenths. Airports don't awe. Go through the departure gate, and you'll soon be looking down on *them*. They play no cathedral tricks of isolating your footsteps into staccato and then setting them reverberating round the clerestory. Tread softly because you tread on the dead. Shuffle lest God is within earshot. WHISPERS: Where might he be? In that lamp vestally renewed above that altar? Is that his Real Presence? Is the flame tended by a Real Person who has to go to the lavatory, nanny? Shush. Even-swan-song-vesta-vespers is about to begin. Skirt the sacristan. His skirts are sacrosanct. Clack-clack, shoes; but it would have been irreverent to come wearing plimsolls. Or shoes are sucked down deeper than their plimsoll line, slurped over the galoshes-line down into the posh plush. But you would be improperly dressed did you arrive to register in carpet slippers. Lush not admitted. Plush only. Our receptionist would turn unreceptive. Our staff's faces would and our lavatories wouldn't flush for you.

I am incensed (I swing my savage indignation at you: aspertions ad te: bad on you: ego absolvere te nolo) by the cinemorgan design of twentieth-century cathedrals, all of which look as though they had risen out of the ground in a play of coloured-icecream lighting (but Fool-stop the organist has broken the mechanism which should, and would it would, cause them to sink down again). Aware, but too piously euphemistic to admit, that god's a daydream, our architects can dredge their imaginations no deeper than to fetch up a half-gurgitated memory of the essoldos and ritzes that cossetted their own adolescence, a memory they reassemble into liturgical perspectives for the re-enactment of that meaty melodrama (hoc est enim meat meum) whose protagonist is the great J.C. (translate:– Joan Crawford).

And by the twentieth-century's *domestic* architecture I am driven clean up the curtain wall.

Democracy has racked domestic design on a neurotic dilemma: have you the *right* to differ from your neighbour?

By this nag the architectural nerve is worn down to threadbare.

Request them to house the population, and the utmost twentieth-century architects can do is box clever.

We have nowhere to reside. And yet we arrive and depart through airy palaces. Airport alone vindicates our century.

In a social democracy only airport dares raise its tower high and be a palace. It need not flaunt – because it has no occasion for shame. No selfish rentier asserts squatters' rights. All all are peers of the airealm.

Airport:airpocket. Dwell here in a droplet of the twentieth century; pure, isolated, rare twentieth century.

Have you noticed how little of twentieth-century life is in fact conducted in twentieth-century surroundings? There are precious few places where you can glance uninhibitedly round you and be sure of never clapping eyes on an artifact that's an anachronism. Indeed our century hasn't yet invented its style – only a repertory of cliché motifs which aren't in fact functional, since they can be stuck on anywhere, but which imitate the machine-turned and stream-lined and thereby serve the emotional purpose of signalling that our century prefers function to style.

Perhaps our whole century is in transit – a century whose suctions and pressures seek to dislodge you, its inhabitant, from it; a wind-tunnel of a century, on whose sides we sit insecure, scarcely able to snatch breath for the vacuum-force gale sucking us towards the sci-fi-futuristensce and the gritty, soiled, brickdusty, industrial-city-Zephyr sand-blasting us back to the Glasweg-Edwardian rose-red

22

soot-gothi-stone tenements which our own architecture can't/hasn't-time-to think up a replacement for.

What's the nearest to a twentieth-century style? Why, that sort-of-pop-brutalistic tabbying, those curds of canned plum-juice declining to integrate with custard, bits of a jigsaw free-drifting weightless in space: an amateur method of do-it-yourself exterior house-painting, developed out of military camouflage, whose purpose is, precisely, camouflage: to disguise the silhouettes of Victwardian buildings, to break up the outlines of their structure or pseudo-structure (those non-structural Dutch gables, those out-on-a-limb non-buttressing limbs, those non-contributing members), to pretend that the husks of the Great Exhibition of 1851 can be naturalised into today's breakfastfood.

The true pure feel of the twentieth century is a rarity to catch on the wing. Catch it at airport. Sense yourself, at airport, at home; be, for once, in your own period.

Being at an airport is wellbeing. Anxiety is in sight but I'm out of its reach. It's the wind beyond the plate glass walls. Let it claw for my attention. Let it, neo-Gauguin, demand what I'm doing, where I'm going, what I'm wasting. Tough, smooth, ginger-flavoured twentieth-century glass will wear its questions blunt. Obviously I'm going somewhere or I wouldn't be at an airport.

Avaunt, anxiety. Do not disturb. No distractions in mid-enterprise. I am IN TRANSIT.

Nothing more can be done by or expected of me till arrival arrives. Within this pocket, within this fully accounted-for, justified and sewn-up détour in my life line, I can be simultaneously relaxed and efficient. I am on my way yet free to stray — if only my coffee will cool to drinkable. I shall sidle again past pastcards and make for the magazines on the bookstall (did that parental plane's engines, before it DROPPED, stall?). I shall idle past the perfume display case and wanton on towards duty-free alcohol.

The airport's kernel of wellbeing:— You too can be duty-free.

Flatten your claws, windriven hellions, against the outside of the glass.

Furies, conscience, remorse, alarm, slave-driver purpose, super-ego, all that is included in that most onomatopoetic of Italian

23

names, *smania*, word at once smeary and biting, sulphur-fog whose acid drops eat stone and flesh, gnawing the heart and corroding the lungs of monumental statues: you can't get me here. I am super-super-ego, in functional sanctuary. I am the inedible statue in the incorruptible niche.

Wasteful, my argument exclamatorily pursued, and therefore non-functional, that the purpose of this superb functional construct, airport, should be merely to hurry people through.

For here, did you decline to be passed along please with the silt, you could defy the Furies. You could dwell long enough in the twentieth century to notice you were doing so.

Relaxed but not to the extent of sleep or anaesthesia, whetted enough to enjoy but not cut yourself on your own ambition or anxiety, not so intent on the future as to be tensed-up, you could inhabit *this* tense. Your fingers could sink into the very nap and texture of *now*.

It was obvious to me that it was myself whom I had, in my euphoric, light-and-airy boldness, already cast in the rôle of this pioneer who should forever (or at least for some hours) remain in the Transit Lounge and thus perpetually or for a simulacrum of perpetuity remain in the present moment, in at least *semi*-sempiternal transit between departure from the past and arrival at the future.

Yet even as I hectored the public-address system to that effect, the corner of my eye, from its perch on my floor-adhesive stalk before the bar, was casting up the amenities within stroll and including among them the bookstall whence cometh my anaesthesia, in the form of those vertical take-off flights directly out of the present into the never-never tense: fictions.

My present-tense-of-mind was, however, alert enough to be practical. My eye was at the same time calculating that any 'toilet-requisite' that was not already in the attaché case on my bar-hooked knees was promised in several languages by the chemist's/drugstore/farmacia.

One thing my attaché case did, I knew without looking, contain was enough travellers' cheques and cash in several currencies to purchase my 'requisites' in several kinds for my sojourn.

Probably in this air-conditioned tank I would not get very dirty very quickly. If I did become soiled, I could wash in the Toiletten/Toilets/Toilettes downstairs, which I had already visited. If my clothes did, I could actually replace all but the solidest of them. For at the centre of the fishtank there was a smaller fishtank: the only free-standing and the only wholly serious shop in the Lounge, the only one where you could buy things you might physically, as distinct from merely socially, need. From where I sat I could peer through its glass walls as into an aquarium indeed, and its stocks of clothing of a rather woven type looked indeed like underwater reeds or weeds.

I had already noticed that (besides the archipelagos of individual armchairs which stippled the Lounge, each an islanded mosque with its own slim, free-standing muezzin-tower ashtray) there was, backing up against the farthest wall, a classical terrace of soft chairs. Undivided by arm-rests, they could be made to yield me rest. Providing I socially dared (would they mask the lights at night?), I could stretch out and sleep. It would take only a lateral conversion – of me, in this case. Lateral conversion into flats (but here it was I whom I would lay flat) is the economic salvation I have long preached in our century's architectural wilderness, the simple ingenuity that would have saved many and could still save more of the lovely terraces of my lovely Dublin from being razed to desert and replaced by genteel unimaginative boxes.

(I am the bent priest; I work lateral conversions.) (Hedge and ditch priest.)

Clean, clothed, slept: fed would be fixed by the bar, whose hinterland was geographied with tables, half of them for café purposes and half, as their tablecloths denoted in international sign-language, for the rites of a full, sung-and-swung, vestment restaurant. (You like your crêpes flambées with a pinch of incense, yes?)

And when I looked across the channel in which the barmen plied, that ditch between bar counter and the working surface with its splashback cliff of stratified bottles, I saw the tool-kit laid out for the international sandwich. (A port and earl, please.) I could be fed: trilingually and three-deckered.

Not the least of the airport's beauty was, to me, its internationalism. Twentieth-century architecture is no happier with by-jingo than with by-God: we swear bi-lingual.

This airport was the happy ape of all other airports. Its display case cased and displayed the perfumes of Arabia and of Paris, packaged in the style to which they have become acCustomed through the universal Excise of capital letters and full stops in the typography. Every artifact in sight excited me, raised me towards tip-toe. None was everyday. All were exotic. Yet nothing chilled or alienated me, since nothing was unfamiliar. The whole setting belonged to *my* century.

My nostrils caught, drifted down from the invisible wafters of smoke woven across the upper nine-tenths, a Turkish embroidery-thread here and a furnace-blast there of the fierce tobacco of the Métro. A doll evzone danced, his dancing pumps hung about his neck like thieves' hands, among souvenirs of Brussels. The bottles in the cross-Channel cliff facing me outfaced and punt-e-mesed me by their catholicity.

I was in a capsule enclaved not only in the sequence of time but in political geography. I was inhabiting an embodiment come true of such splendid notional diplomatic entities as free ports and extraterritorial territory. (O my pragmatic sanction, my uncle.) (I shall demand at the trilingual bar a hamlet fines herbes.)

I congratulated the airport on its cosmopolitanism.

My aesthetic liked it. Why reproach airports, any more than eighteenth-century terraces, with same-ness? At least it's a sameness of the tolerably handsome. I'll take airportism for a new Enlight'n 'airment.

And my ethic, both politico- (transcend national sovereignty) and socio- (egalitarian), ran out to embrace it. Impalpable comrades Light and Air, my brothers on the barricades, welcome with tears in my eyes.

When we have put aside our several and divisive loyalties to the place where any particular one of us happened to be born, let us unite in loyalty to the time which is the time of us all.

Down with nationalism. Forward to sieclism.

Comrades, create a style for our century to live in.

26

Our internationalism, my comrades, is no sentimentality. Indeed, it is a cynicism — but cynicism raised to an ideal.

We internationalists, we egalitarians: we are simply persons slit, split and filleted on a point of logic of our own perceiving. We noticed one day that it is merely arbitrary to suppose any nation or class superior to the rest simply because we happened to be born into it.

Do we sometimes flap a little flatly up here on the barricades? What do you expect? We are people boned of our norms.

Our programme:— Undo the Normative Conquest.

Some items we have observed:— standard English sets no standard: the *faut* in comme il faut is no logical compulsion but our foe, the faux: Paleface and Black Bottom are interchangeable: what you call the world turned upside down is simply the world to someone who happened to be born on the other side.

Egalitarianism:— the inescapable consequence of noticing that one arbitrariness has no more logical force behind it than any of the others.

The egalitarian manifesto:—

'WHY THIS RATHER THAN THAT?' EQUALS
'WHY THEN, NONE AT ALL'.

Otherwise cut and come again till we've all hacked the liverish lights out of each other.

Fishmonger, fishmonger, with your sharp little life you've spirited my preconceptions away. I'm disorientated to know I'm only accidentally occidental.

Which is my rightsideup?

My rights, my divine rights, my sense of right and strong. Fishmonger, give me my prejudices back.

Which *is* my back?

On a spit I rotate, up here on the barricade rafters.

Reason disallows loyalty to one accident rather than the next. I turn. Give each a turn. Fair shares fair gave me a turn they-did.

Rotating I fillet myself. It would be arbitrary of me to ask you to abrogate your arbitrariness did I not also surrender my own.

I give up my bilateral symmetry (I rotate on a radical axis), because I cannot reinforce it with proof.

I spin; I am spun. I am the sundisk the colours of whose national flag whirl sunnysideup into blinding international white. La patrie? No, le siècle.

NOT HERE, BUT NOW.

Are you Spanish? No, spinage.

Kippered I am, kippered up here in the rafters in the multilingual smoke of my own perceptions, kippered to a fine salty cynicism.

No flip-flop now. I am the flig-flag of all nations, boldly and with only a touch of revolutionary's anger/masochist's desperation/disciplinarian's chastisement nailing itself crucified to the barricades.

Are you Jewish, Scottish, Polish? What, me? I'm punish.

This, then, is my ideological gesture.

I adopt the international airport idiom for my native. Come, be my world-oyster.

I take over this multi-winged building. I resolve to live in in-transit. I move into and occupy my own century.

And internationalism, which suits so well with my ideologies, is also in accord with my personal history.

For when, at three, I ceased to be Irish, I did not become anything else instead.

I am the deep-deep-aboriginal déraciné (a word most English speakers, obsessed with the rat-race problem, derive from the root *race* instead of the root *root*). (And now that French culture is itself becoming deRaciné, who shall sound the rapel à l'ordre?)

('Is it', enquires the French-speaker about the tiny pedigree English dog, 'a race dog?' 'A greyhound, do you mean? Good God no.') (THINKS: The French are not animal-lovers.)

('Will you let me do the washing-up?' enquires the English-speaker after American luncheon. 'Why, of course — second on the left.')

('Do English restaurants', enquires the Italian tourist, 'serve the French kitchen? And wines from French castles?')

('Your famous English publishing house', says the American, '– Château Windus.')

Eyetieresias have fore-sofferto tutto. Take away that Babel.

28

I was, perhaps, ripe for – though this I did not foresee on making my decision – defoliation by linguistic leprosy. I had many branches but no root. Transplanted, I had become derooted and derouted. You can send shamrocks over the sea, but they will not grow outside Ireland.

I have no – I haven't quite a – native language.

But in an airport no one is native. We are all transients. I continued high-spirited. I was in a mood to charge corkage, a buoyancy fee, on Château Windus.

Only two uncertainties beleaguered my plan of sitting on, engaging in a sit-in on the present tense.

I wasn't sure how personal the tabs were that the airline kept on its passengers. If, when my flight was called, I abstained from plunging at the departure gate, would the public-address system page me personally, by proper name?

Trying (in vain I'd better say at once) to assess what information they might have to wield, I unbuckled my attaché case and took out my passport, in which I had for safety interleaved my ticket and boarding card, and put it on the bar counter beside my cup.

The other unknown was this: if I let pass the opportunity to leave the Transit Lounge via the gate to the tarmac and my flight, how, when I did eventually decide to leave, would I go? In a Transit Lounge there is no simple $\left\{ \begin{smallmatrix} \text{uscita} \\ \text{exit} \end{smallmatrix} \right\}$ to the outside world via surface transport to the city centre and town terminal. IN TRANSIT signifies you came by place and by plane must you depart.

I riffled my ticket and then shut it back in my passport. For once I trusted myself to worry effectively when the moment should come.

Only a re-natter about the anomaly of my being in the spirits instead of vice versa caught, a nail jag, hooked on my consciousness. I allayed it with a rebus in action. My coffee was still not quite cool. When the barman bumped alongside, ferry touching its side-slung tyres to my quay, I gently loudhailed him for a double Scotch.

I made my point by pointedly pouring *those* spirits into me.

Let the jocund rebus sound, I soundlessly pledged myself as they went down. As I sink my spirits, so my spirits rise.

My coffee had become, I judged, cool enough. I picked up the cup. Public-address called my flight.

Shock that a much-anticipated moment had debouched into reality; a fore-frisson of angst; or an involuntary flexing of the impulse to express decision in a muscular act of some kind: one or other caused my arm to jerk a millimetre up.

The toast-tan surface of the liquid puckered. A tiny polyp of cappuccino erected itself higher than the rim of the cup.

Down hydra. But a dribble had already leapt out. It splurged, though very small, directly onto my passport. I could tell by the absorbent noise of its landing it had hit not the grained, accounts-book cover but the soft paper heart.

I looked. The drop had fallen into the eye-slit that is cut, with bevelled edges, in the cover. The top slit in the mask of a passport is for your name, the eyedentity of the soul. The lower slit mechanically mouths your number.

It was pale coffee. It made the ink run a little. But it obliterated nothing more vital than my title (or form of address). You are not supposed to alter that document by one tittle. I dried it out by capillary action of my handkerchief as quickly as I could and bundled it and the handkerchief back into my case. Even I am not so alarmist that I truly supposed that little starwort to have bodged the document's or my validity. No longer prisoner at the bar, I left it with a stain only on my handkerchief and a mere freckle, not worth distinguishing as a distinguishing mark, on my passport. My wellbeing was unimpaired. But I decided to go down and wait in the lavatories until my flight should have definitely taken off.

5

Bereavement wasn't too awful at three.

I'm not being heartless or talking out of ignorance. (I'm in fact, interlocutor, edging up the aisle towards the confessional.) I don't recommend orphanhood at three for all children — or indeed for any, if it can be avoided.

Of course the bottom dropped out of my world (PLUMMET, went the plane suddenly in my dreams, nightly at the time, fortnightly till I was grown-up; sometimes still). But so it did when bunny plummeted over my native coast; when I realised, spread flat on slippy grass, that I had lost the sackrace I had been patently about to win; and when, having bought some flowers for my mother with my father's financial help and conspiratorial connivance, I took them into the garden next door to shew to Mrs Rahily (pron. Reilly), who assumed I meant them for her, Mrs Rahily, and supped me like a mouthful of soup into her great moustached kiss of thanks. (PLUMMET went my world: not in loss but in compassion for Mrs Rahily's moustache and ineptitude.)

Orphanhood was overkill. My personality was so thin a substance at three that much smaller blows could sever it clean apart. My parents' deaths couldn't do *more* than destroy me. But equally at three I was, willy nilly, indestructible. Cleft, I flowed together again like ripe, secretly self-moving brie.

Now perhaps I wouldn't *wish* to be healed. Perhaps I fly everywhere in order to offer my parents the opportunity of revenge. I am playing russian roulette by riffling the international flight schedules. But then I was too thin a substance to will my final destruction. I recovered: and when I did so, I was no longer Irish.

The bright side, which no one was tactless enough at the time to bid me look on, I now perceive to be that I was spared alike Irish puritanism and the Gaelic, both of which would have become obligatory on me had I stayed beyond the age of three in my native land.

The only plausible item in Irish legend is that Saint Patrick banished the phallic symbols from Ireland. (Avaunt, I conjure, eyeing that rose-crowned hose-pipe, Mike, from beside my martello tower of pastcards.)

At least, in this deciduousness of my languages, this revocation of the gift of tongues, I have no Gaelic to drop off. My leprous condition is not leprechauny.

For surely those syllables would be as painful as oxygen ice in the severance, refusing to slip off the mind's fingertips except by taking my skin with them. For those are the syllables of what would have been my native language.

Besides, they're tough. Had I acquired them, they would have been hard acquired. To shed them would have pained like shitting

31

icicles or giving birth to a child begotten both by and on oneself.

For don't imagine I haven't, in adulthood and attempts to rediscover my infant patriotism, *looked*. Two first-year courses I've invested in, both of them second-handed-on in a shabbily dog-thumbed state, and both of them by Christian Brothers — to say nothing of the much smarter equipage, consisting of a booklet going four-in-first-hand with a gramophone record, no less, the whole outfit master-minded by a Jesuit attempting to undercut/uppercut the humble Brothers by promising fluency, at a far higher price, within twelve unstrenuous lessons. And still the syllables look irrational to me: seemingly weighted yet only infleighted: dustbins you stoop to shoulder thinking them full that then overturn you and snap your spine because they're empty. Let me counsel you against those smiling parliamentary-bench assemblages of fatuous vowels (wipe that smile off your Dáil, Dóll) emitting in the event only an undifferentiated ugh sound between them. Take my joke upon you and learn of me:

> you will find Dun Laoghaire
> draoghaire
> and should do everything in your power to avoghed a
> visit to Drogheda.

Shamrocks don't grow outside Ireland. Yet I was no clover, either.

There must have been an intermundium, between the accident and my transplantation, in which I was harboured by neighbours. Now that I think of it, I must have been left with neighbours while my parents crashed or I would have crashed too. Memory does, without precision, supply a flurry of nurturing, neighbourly, nannying, more or less goat-bearded Amaltheias, including Mrs Moustache herself. There was Mrs Ní Murteouaigh or some such (pron. McMurdoch), Doctor Ó (and I'm getting this one spelt right) Dubhthaigh (pron. O'Duffy), Father Doyle or conceivably Foyle and Mr Smith who used to excuse his easy pronounceability in that rugger-scrum of mute *e*'s and transmuted *ai*'s by remarking once a day that Smith is a good Irish name. (It appears there are no bad Irish names.)

32

Memory then skips. It next cuts in directly on my acclimatisation, which consisted mainly of re-learning idioms. I was brought up to the logical Irish way of inverting 'I am': 'amn't I?' Here, I observed improbable people improbably asking 'aunt I?'

I took them to be codding — until I observed that that, over here, was kidding. Yet the persons most given to it remained, even here, kids: not cods.

And here you didn't bless but cross yourself — insofar as you did it at all, which did not include when passing a church from the bus.

About the age when I would have begun on Gaelic (was I unconsciously living out a whole shadow, would-have-been life in Ireland meanwhile?), I began on Latin instead; and not church Latin, either.

(Aren't I auntie? I am the logically inverted priest, who wear transvestments and preach Gaylic in hedges and britches.)

I replaced bunny by a mop-head which I found, unused but disregarded, in the downstairs lavatory, and which has bequeathed me a fondness for pom-pom dahlias. Perhaps I was acting-out gratitude for my own adoption.

My adopters were my mother's second cousins by marriage. Her I liked on the instant, because she cuddled me. After a year I found him not the nicer (both were nice) but the more considerable person. He'd chilled me at first, not wanting to put himself forward, knowing he'd already had his share in false-parenthood by putting up the money for my taking-in. I of course at that age had no notion of money, so I failed to appreciate that he had any part in the matter. My infantile sexual ignorance was acted-out in financial terms.

At eight I began to learn Greek and named the mop, which I still trailed everywhere with me, Thermopylae.

My second was a thin man, going bald from a more frontal starting-point than my first father (whose name, as it happens, *was* Adam).

On holidays my second father wore khaki shorts to the knee.

I began to ask him if I might go on holiday to Ireland. When I touched thirteen, it became practical. It fitted-in to other plans. He would take me over on the Holyhead boat (tact, I think, prevented his suggesting we should fly) and would leave me with former neighbours/distant cousins (again memory witholds definition) now living near Rathfarnham; he himself would fly back to London and pick her up, whence they would fly on together to Italy for their first on-their-own holiday since they had adopted me.

I wanted or said I wanted (how could I know?) to visit the west coast: to consult, I said, the omniscient coracle who lived in a cave on Akill in County Mahem, God cross us. (And whereabouts is the County Paris?) But I settled happily for being within car-reach of Dublin. I thought to re-live those walks out towards Dalkey.

(Even now, as a stewardess-sheepdog-sheperdess barks in high heels and grey uniform through the Transit Lounge, lets herself sideways out of the sliding glass, to the disappointment of her silly conglomerated flock who thought *their* hour had come, and advances onto the tarmac pulling out a little fireman's-ladder antenna from the metal box she is carrying, it seems to me that she is operating a walkey-Dalkey.)

Perhaps I even thought to come on bunny's washed-up corpse. Perhaps I was searching for it in the wake of the boat (if I'd found it, would I have given it a wake?) as we bumped into the North Wall and I told my second father, who was shivering in his khaki shorts beside me on deck, in the spume of that sea that is never warm or easy-going, that I felt I was returning to Howth and home.

6

No codding: I think it's because we haven't quite a native language that our tongues tend to trip over their roots.

We speak English as a foreign language, even when we have no other. (This is my foster-mother-tongue, since when I have used no other.) As foreigners we treat the language logically, pronouncing 2d and 3d as two and three separate pence, instead of hiccupy tuppence and thrifty thrippence. It is by foreigner's logic that we ask 'amn't I?', just as it is by foreigner's logic that the Italian when speaking English translates *cuisine* and *château*. How could he logically know

34

that that keep is kept unbetrayed by the traditore? It's idiom that sells the boardingpass and raises the airportcullis. Imperialism gave us Irish/Indians/West Indians its vocabulary, but the idiom wouldn't travel. Imperialism steeped us in its pan-citizenship and receded, leaving us the first non-citizens.

Transplant us further, who are unrooted in the first place, banish us from growth and home, banshe banhe, and we will astonish you by how we run to riot in false flowerings of double-headed counterfeit coinages. Pom-pom.

(Memory won't tell the fate of TherMOPylae. Lay silken dahliance on his tomb.)

Look what became of my distinguished compatriot when, making, with the Irish predisposition to internationalism, for the first handy free port, he was transplanted to windy Trieste, that evocative Avoca where three streams of vocables meet, where everyone is a foreigner and most are anarchist. The wind in Trieste's steep streets lifts the anarchist's soft hat clean off his hard-boiled head. And who compat-pats after it, pounding louder than the Triestine tram, pom-pom-ing more reliably than the anarchist's soft-boiled bomb? Ulysses, the hero who can never accomplish the return of the native, because he isn't one.

We Irish had the right word on the tip of our tongue, but the imperialist got at that. What should trip off it we trip over. Our slips are enlarged into tumbles of petticoats and camiknicks. We pick ourselves up out of their foam, high-camikicking. What begins as endemic lapsus linguae we peddle as precious lapis, with which we illuminate our Book of Sells (an early Book of Ours). We are never knowingly underbold. We are in the grips of compunsion.

Youlysses have fore-suffered all. Before the Jew wandered, jew did.

Is that another of your dog-headed Irish slips?

(Pardon me, ma'am, your mollibloomers is shewin'.)

Cynoscephalae, ladies, sigh no tom-moore.

(We lost Thermopylae, the double pom-pom Bloom.)

I was already at a magazine, but I thought to give warning before firing it. My fantasy steps tiptoed up on that ever-tempting serpent, my compatriot, mike. Should I snatch it and announce to all In

35

Transit my tribute to my great Triestine compalien, the comedi-chameleon, the old pun gent himself? I could loose on the Lounge his obituary: I am the voyce of one crying in the wilderness; reJoyce with me.

I put down the mike in fantasy and the magazine in fact (it contained a page of Irish Tourist Bawdry, soliciting the British motorist to County Caravan), and returned to the turning martello tower to see if Buck Mulligan would come out to play on words today.

A breeze of passage riffled the tiered postcards, snappish as a cardsharper's shuffling.

I glanced round. Four black-and-white puns were being blown, like paper bags down a Triestine street, east-to-west across the Transit Lounge and in the direction of the bar.

A postcard plopped out of its rack, like a suicide fish.

At first I assumed the nuns, as I generally do nuns, to be Italian. But there was a sturdiness about their feet.

'Was it brandy you asked for, Sister?'

'It was, Sister.'

'Was it Rémy Martin for preference, Sister?'

'For preference, Sister, it was.'

(At my acclimatisation I had to learn also the words Yes and No.)

So: Bar Nun. (A Rémy Martello, please.)

(My first father was a spoilt priest. I am his spoilt child, Father. Wise spoilt child that knows its own co-Sister.)

'Kay Oll Om, Royal Dotch Airlines, regrot the delay on their flight to Omsterdom. Possengers presonting boarding cards at the dosk will be issued with loncheon tockets.'

So: now the Duch will flood the restaurant (so easily flooding, those low countries) and, chomping chomp chops, swamp the nuncheon.

Extrapolating from the nuns I surmise a flight is due by my native airline.

(T.C.D., pron. Tay Say Day, the Protestant Irish airline announces . . . To Kells with that. The hierarchy says No.) (We flie hiegher.)

It is not the flight I am booked on, and anyway I am staying here. Do not take flight.

36

I picked up the plopped postcard and propped it in its slot before I should feel obliged to buy it but not before seeing its picture: a golden husky-style dog, black-tongued, captioned Ciao.

A magazine solicited me with a history of filmstars: a cat-show of purrty faces (there are two sexes, masculine and feline) under the blanket-label Lana Pura .

Pura and pura were my thoughts (now that I had suffered the falling away of my always rather literary French, in which they got gautier and gautier), purged to self-denial by the Advent of three palpably unwise men into the Lounge, traders most likely and recognisable on the glance, by the squareness of their rig, for Irish. They too aim at the bar but they're less quick on the chocks-away (liqueur-filled, duty-free) head-into-the-wind up-and-off, -Sister than the Sisters.

They skirt me in a whiff of the mild (like the climate) Irish tobatmosphere. The cardinal Irish fairytale (not that we *have* fairies — not like *that*; *or* tails):— He married (at forty-three) and smoked Sweet Afton ever after.

As they pass, a waft of the native foreign accent accosts me. Genially: 'It's a very daycent class of fellatio you meet travelling Aer Cunnilingus'.

No they didn't. Know they didn't. No by Saint Patherick but they didn't, Horatio (*don't* kiss me, Hardy). Down mike. Down ciao. Bad-cat; hush yo' husky howlin', honey. Down wanton. Down.

7

I had scarcely had time to have pointed out to me more than three items of Irish coast when the news came that my second parents were dead, crashed on their flight to Italy.

Why did I hesitate to disclose this?

For the same reason that when, returned with despatch to England (memory is again not telling how or by whom), I received comfort from a schoolmaster who played sort-of-secular-vicar to the whole neighbourhood and especially my second father, I didn't disclose to him that it was in a plane crash that my *first* parents had died.

Because it's grotesque. It verges on a sick joke. You would want to express commiseration, and hysterico-comedy would rise up your throat. You would swallow back tears, snot and saliva at a singletaneous gulp. My soul would plummet, as it did for Mrs Rahily, pitying your social ineptitude. And at that moment there would erupt up you, unchokeable-down as a hiccup, the black comic peristaltic suspicion that I was a lethal child who made a habit of willing or sabotaging its parents to death by air.

I would be set a little apart, in a black nimbus, a child whose touch fate had touched.

If I were a god, I would be Dionysus, who was twice born.

Or am I not, rather, a successful double Oedipus – an Oedipus who orphaned himself twice? Whenever Freud writes of the double onset of human sexuality, once in infancy and again at puberty, like double-entry book-keeping, I think of myself de-parented at three and again at thirteen.

My vicarious secularist quasi-vicar presently arranged for my lodging (I was a touch too old for further formal adoption) with an English couple (let me point out at once:– they did not die) both of whom taught at a provincial university, she mathematics and he French literature (which is why my French is sound if literary).

More immediately, my vicarious prophetic uncle suggested, as he couldn't in tact have dared do had I told him about my first parents, that I should both recuperate and get my nerve back by going instantly on holiday by air. He accompanied me – to, at my request, Greece.

It is to him I attribute my perhaps in my circumstances anomalous fondness for flying.

This I have been able only lately to indulge in the fl$\left\{ \begin{array}{c} \text{esh} \\ \text{ight} \end{array} \right\}$, for only now is the air-passenger-revolution truly off the ground – though it had begun when my second parents died. What makes the plane crash a bizarre fatality in my life is its second occurrence. But in social history it is the second time round that is easily swallowed – if not, indeed, positively banal and to be expected. The unexpected is that my first parents flew at all, in those motoring-

38

chocolate days when most middle-class people, especially Irish ones, didn't.

Thanks to my pseudo-vicar, I liked models of aeroplanes (in distinction from model aeroplanes – I didn't like them if they could actually fly), aviation fiction (a high-specialised genre), old films about Hurricanes and Messerschmitts, photographs of and from planes, diagrams of aerodynamics, and do-it-yourself guides to the cockpit. I developed a graphic ideogram for depicting propellers in motion by a flat stroke from the side of the lead of a 2B pencil. I gave a framed photograph of the Schneider Trophy the honour of being my bed-head. I nourished my night vision on carrots and, when asked what I proposed to *do* (translate:– by way of métier), spoke of trying for my pilot's licence. But all the time I was taking the utmost care to pick up not the smallest notion of how to work a plane's controls. I had no intention whatever of doing-it-myself. I loved the jargon (LIFT:DRAG:dynamic arrows:TORQUE) purely for the name's sake, like poetry in an unknown language. I never let the names be sullied by a shred of meaning in my mind. Messrs Schmitt: Dear Sirs, please send, on approval, one aircraft guaranteed unable to fly.

8

Key to an historical puzzle picture:– Nelson dying in the arms of Hardy equals Hamlet dying in those of Horatio – Nelson being a Horatio who had always wanted to play Hamlet.

He'd gotten himself mortally shot by prancing histrionically about up there playing prince. When they carried him down he transposed effortlessly into his Hamlet fantasy.

Do people run fantasies while they die? Of course they do. When better? 'I am dying' –Consciousness won't look that one in the eye; consciousness slews and skids off sideways: No, I am Hamlet dying. Kiss me Horatio and flights of angels sing me to my rest.

PLUNGE goes the plane. We regret the delay to flights of angels/parents.

Put your protecting arm round your cuddly wife and fantasise that it lies in that arm's power to save her from fear and both of you from death. This will make it possible for you to die like an Englishman.

Men *would* die, from time to time, in any case. But fantasy makes them *able* to die.

And my first father, who was no Englishman, the wandering jew Adam? I don't doubt he died like an Irishman: on the barricades, on the bar, is anyone in this snug looking for a flight?

He must have transposed himself into the pilot's place. He died at the controls. Solo. Sinn Fein. The single United Irishman. Hold on. For we are going DOWN.

I love you, Nelson.

9

Nelson, Pilar, flamenco singer.

At my acclimatisation I learned that that which is in Dublin a pillar is in London a column.

(*Why* this idiomsyncrasy? Did they fear the Irish would make a phallic cult of it? Pray for us, Saint Colum?) (Ease back that joy-stick.)

(And why did my compatriots lately depillarate him? Puritans: had they just learnt of Lady Hamilton?)

I love you, Nelson. Yours is one of the deaths I have died. They pickled me herring home in your body. Flamingo flames whine at your pyre, prince.

Here is the eternal terminus.

All trams shall turnabout there for him. Buses shall Stepaside. Crowds gawp (I want me da to buy me a stick of Blackrock) while we attend his wake with muffled Dundrums.

40

10

How can I address you, interlocutor, when the only language I so much as half command is one in which the 'you' does not even reveal (stepasiding that problem of *where* you are) how many there are of you and of what sex?

Granted the languages which *can* have partly abrogated the power. Surely it's a bent double till it falls on its arse type of politeness that makes it a mark of courtesy to image you in the plural. *Vous*: how is that polite? It suggests you are not at one with yourself; or that I, hung-over, am seeing you multiplied. Now is that even friendly, let alone polite?

Yet your singularity or pluralism will edge its way through the politeness if we pay complements. Vous êtes belles. Now I know there's more than one of you, and every womanjacqueline of you female.

And *tu*, though it insists also on giving me the information that I know you on intimate terms (or that you are a child or an animal), does also disclose what I want to know. *Tu sei*: at least you are not two or more.

They're sly, though, these romance languages, in this matter of sex. Sly rather than shy, I shurmise; for they sometimes do, sometimes won't, the girlish things. Sometimes the adjectives don't change. Vous êtes triste? Tick:– masc.□ fem.□. Strik(e) out whichever does not apsly. J'en suis content(e).

And o that so demurely flirtatious mute *e* that may be appended to *ami*, where, dimpling, it can be seen but not heard. That's *why* my French is literary. I am so sex-obsessive *I must know.*

They're sexsessive, too, the languages: but unsophisticatedly. I shed them in sheer impatience at the infantility of their sexual curiosity. *I do not want to be told the sex of inanimate objects.*

I don't believe it, for one thing. So why, o latin languages, and not only latin ones (you'd think German would be less fanciful or reserve its neuter gender for things that *are*, instead of dimunitive maids), insist on reiterating what wasn't true in the first place? You are as tedious as trilingual notices (where the eye can't pick out the

41

line in its own language till it's read down to it through the previous ones, with the result that the mind blurs into tri-vocal vision and is staggered by an intellectual hangover; if we're to persist in all this flying and internationalism, and the whole world is not to totter under the effects of a vast bat, we'd better cultivate the ideogram to subtlety). Call yourself a logical language, French? The masculine king Arthur had a feminine table femininely round? I got that it was female first time round, thanks. And anyway it isn't. You're old enough to resign yourself to that. Have you forgotten you're Old, French?

I wonder if Arthur was? (sc. feminine)

I wonder if Guinevere was Bedivere's gay name?

Pleasure, Edward Young promised us, is nought but virtue's gayer name — Ed. Young himself being the name of nothing but a Night Thought, and a night thought being but the bowdlerised name of a wet dream.

I wonder: did Arthur have knight thoughts? Or make ensquiries? (You're on the wrong page.)

And Italian, poor Italian, running for a renaissance medal in the courtesy relay and overshooting as usual, deems it (except when it's in high heroic vein, when it reverts to an old Roman second-person-singularity) politest of all not to see you, single or double, head-on at all, but slides fawning up and, as if too awed to look you in the front-face, addresses you obliquely in the third person. The person is, what's more (for excellency or some such over-jewellery), feminine, a *she* which becomes *you* by being raised to the capital we reserve in Egolish for *I*. A provincial excess of would-be-good manners is displayed by a language that renders 'you (sing.) are' by 'she is' and 'you (plur.) are' by 'They are' — though you keep your native sex in the adjective.

And this Italian does, povero innocente, without a clue how camp it's being. Poveri inno-gents politely addressing one another as she. Is She satisfied, sir? (I've read that Mussolini banned the Lei form, but of course it came slipping, fawning, back afterwards.)

But among languages that slide on the rules of the numbers game, my heart goes out to Greek, whose nouns need not be in either the singular or the plural, but may be in the in-between, the numerically

42

hermaphroditic condition, the dual. (The Greek for *two* has – o blessed logic – *only* a dual.) Matching verb forms are available in every paradigm. The dual is for things that don't duel, that go in pairs not antagonistically but side by side: hands, eyes, feet; ?balls – the grammar books are mute; yoked horses; double yolks of egg; Helen and Clytemnestra, Leda-laid on our home farm this morning (?Hendiadys).

Do you call *that* 'intimate', French/German, to refine the you to a singular tu/du? In what way do I insinuate myself into intimacy with you by the mere act of perceiving there's only one of you (which I have in fact also perceived of a person I am not intimate with, but I am too polite – by your curious rules – to let it shew in my pronouns)?

But Greek: sweet honey Greek wooes by that dual, thinkable only of things thought of as a pair. Thus wooed the antique shepherd his (masc. and, at any one time anyway, sing.) love, thus Zeus Ganymede and Achilles Patroclus. Will you share my dual? Come pair with me, and we shall be inseparably paradigmed in the syntax of love.

11

I have not stepasided beyond the magazines but already my consciousness has slewed towards the books.

I doubt if there will be any aviation fiction here. Appropriate it would assuredly be, but perhaps also disquieting.

Yet I must have my shot of quietus. I'll settle for pornography, of which there's quite a lot, or thrillers, of which there are hundreds but even so I may have read them all.

The thriller is the cardinal twentieth-century form. All it, like the twentieth century, wants to know is: Who's Guilty?

I will even risk disquietus with a novel of ideas. I have my eye already on a fat French one whose broad red-paper cummerbund tells me the book concerns itself with twentieth-century man's search for an identity and has won the Prix Fixe.

I am not sure, bombarded to linguistic baldness by invisible fallout (my languages have the falling-out sickness; they have come to a polyglottal stop) whether I can still read French — though I suppose I have just read the cummerbund, which can scarcely have radiated its message, without intervention of either language or ideogram, directly into my mind. It is not even a phosphorescent red. French publicity is very un-uptodate.

But in any case I can feel no sympathy with supposed loss of identity. I can conceive of losing many things, of which my polyglottism is only the easiest shed. Memory, even, I can imagine blotted out — though if I had not forgotten the existence of Freud I trust I should start from the starting-point of remembering that one forgets only what one cannot bear. Identity, however, is unloseable. That which feels the loss, that which searches and doubts — that *is* your identity. I have doubted often what I am, but never who.

Please, Saint Anthony of Padua, I've mislaid my identity. Favours gratefully received. Replies, in confidence, to — but to *whom*?

I shall buy a thriller, epitome of the discontents of narrative. I shall chew out my needs, its little contents-ment of what the people say and think; but their only excuse for existing, and my only only interest in reading, is the story. In their own right thriller-people amount to nothing worth my while. I can love them only for the dangers the plot makes them undergo. Eternal war has been declared between content and this form. For he, the creator, will make his book less and less worth my while as he cramps and clamps his characters in order to cram them inside his narrow story lines. Yet it is those lines which will increasingly accelerate me through the book, lust-hunting-down the characters who are increasingly not there.

How did he lure me into his book to begin with? By promise of puzzle, by a rebus, a ship in a-bottle. He played, corrupter, on my infantile sexual curiosity. But I have long ago settled that puzzle. *I do not want to be told the sex of the murder weapon.* So why do I continue through the book? Because he scares me on: on through his dark wood. I dare not turn back now. Who could leave that wood unpenetrated? I tumesce; I bristle; I shiver. Only the closing orgasmic cadence can resolve me now. And now at the end the puzzle is accomplished: so what? The beads are slotted into the eyes

44

of the joker's face, which is no longer human nor even a scaring apparition at the window. I am left with myself, in the form of a popped blown-up paper bag, on my hands.

12

Flash magazine snap-polls the man in the street. (Who is Guilty?) This week's *Flash*point: Nunhunts. Is nunhunting cruel? Ought it to be stopped by law?

Vincent St Cape, 27, apprentice fixer: Well, somebody's got to. I mean: they're virgins, aren't they? You can't just let things like that go *on*.

Jock Strap, 59, parks superintendant: I don't like women who shave off all their hair. I think them unwomanly. I like a woman who grows it so long that I can sit on it.

Jasper Ware, 43, company prompter: What many people fail to realise on this controversial topic is the loss it would entail for businesses, large and small, throughout the country, were legislation introduced.

Mercy Dash, 43, voluntary worker: Anyone who has actually seen a nunhunt, as I frequently have, living where I do, would know from the expression on the nun's face that she enjoys every moment of it.

Terry Towel, 46, gymnast: There's too much interference from bureaucrats as it is. They'll be interfering with children next.

Pixie Hood, 14, housewife: I think they're spooky, nuns.

Expert opinion. A scientist writes:— It is obvious that, like it or not, nuns have to be culled. So far as this country is concerned, nuns are not at present in danger of extinction.

Not at all humane and progressive people agree. A spokesman said at headquarters today 'It would be perfectly simple to organise dragnunhunts instead'.

Note:— 'Dragnunhunt' is a technical term. One of the fraternity explained today: 'A dragnunhunt is a hunt where the victim is a monk dressed up as a nun.'

45

13

There are some miniature aeroplanes, of three to four inches in the wingspan, displayed on the counter.

They are set out in a charmed circle in the mushroom shade of a larger model, wingspan some twelve inches, which is perched like a recent bill at the tip of a thin spike and is evidently not for sale.

I select from the smaller planes a Caravelle. Grasping the crustacean sides of its fuselage between my thumb and forefinger I carry it, slowly writhing, to the shop assistant beside the till.

She takes it from me, miming that she mustn't drop and break it, and plops it into a thick shiny paper sack, satin-striped green and gold on the outside.

The woolly handles of this sack she extends towards me.

I extend my forefinger, stiff, parallel with the floor. She slips the sack's handles over my finger. It is like the wedding ceremony.

'Grates me', I say; 'the sum?'

'Pardon?' (French pron.)

'Parmesan.'

'Come?' (Ital. pron.) (Translate:– Come [again].)

'Grates, grazie.'

'Prego.'

'Pray go? Pas encore.'

'Parse *encore*? Interjection, surely, originally adverb, now employed as a noun or as a verb in the imperative.'

'O, you speak English.'

'Of course.'

'Dunque: quanto costa?'

14

I needed a flip.

So, after priming my magazines, I taxied out of the bookstall area. (Fly with me. But do not deCamp.)

Near the perimeter I noticed a tower I hadn't seen before. It was stacked with gramophone records.

As I approached, it flashed me green: 'Melodic Gems from Erin' (what could be the flip of *that*?), wearing its shamrocks on its laminated starboard sleeve.

And is it not, o my anarchic, my back-biting, my essentially *internecine* countrymen, a touch suspect that your island is called Erin and that *erin* is the accusative (at least in the Attic {form shape} − a very fair attitude) of the Greek work for *strife*?

What name shall we coin for the natives of Erin? Erinyes.

Do I loose strife? Quick then: check fuel, test ailerons, notice, out of the corner of my I, that recordings are on sale of several of my dearest operas: then UP (I will arise and go now, and go to duty-free) before the Furies can come a-buzz, at their most accusative, warring after me (who am a very strange − twice-born − god) to bite my back.

Safely away, I throttle un-bitten-back and cruise past the farmacia, going in low enough to see, on one of its glass shelves, an economy-size press-button dispenser of Cio-Cio-San, the toilet cleanser with the Butterfly touch.

I buzzed the cubic fishtank that sold clothes, seeing inside two fair, square women − assistants, probably, not customers, since I saw no handbags attached − with the cubic faces of Piero angels. ('Angelico?' *No*. Ann Jellicoe.')

I made a quick reconaissance dash in the direction of duty-free liquor. Caution: don't ditch your kite in the drink.

Then I headed back to base.

For fear of Erinyes, I came in from a different approach this time and saw, on a different facet of the records tower, a sleeve called 'Highlights from *Alitalia*'. This little known opera seria by Belpaesiello has not been performed since 17 . . . .

Please doctor I think I need an operation seria.

I made a perfect three-point touchdown (happy landings, as the bloke said as he toiled up the stairs), without even feathering my prop, and finished with my nose in a magazine.

15

Down Hillingdon High Street sweeps the hunt, with all its traditional excitement and colour.

The quarry, an Irish-born virgin of about 46, is black-avised and sturdy. She is tiring now, but there's sprint in her yet. Of course she's hampered by habit.

The men are gaining on her. A little while back, she thought up the ruse, the cunning little creature, of prising up a manhole cover and slipping down. But of course they were onto that one and dug her out, and I don't think her morale has quite recovered.

Can she pull it out of the bag?

Everything turns on whether she has lost the will to run.

The front-runner among the pursuers is almost on her heels.

Can she put on a spurt? The configuration of the High Street at this point — the main body of the pursuers are just rounding the Scotch Wool Shop — may tell in her favour.

Can she spurt?

Can she? YES. She's pulling away. She —

She's DOWN.

I think that was a femur I heard snap.

She's down; she can't find strength enough to even try to pull herself up and on.

She's subsiding like a black paper bag. The men have caught up now. How the wind does get up under these habits and swell them out, and how long it takes them to settle down again.

She's put her hands over her face but that leaves her breasts open to attack.

She's lowered one hand — rather feebly, I'd say — I'd say that was a very fatigued nun indeed — in a last attempt to protect her breasts, but the men are tearing the cloth away now —

There she goes. Topheavy these habits. Face sideways down in a puddle.

That leaves her throat exposed, of course. And the master of nunhunts has seen it, he's there, his teeth are into her neck, he's broken the skin . . . He's well away now.

48

Now they're all there, like a swarm of angry bees, elbowing each other aside to get their lips to the open wound. Well, bees will be bees. Good sucking, boys.

Can she spurt.

16

Public-address befriended me.

It didn't, after all, page me. ('Turn over the page', the Great Camp King gravely commanded.) ('I like to look on the flip side.')

It ceased even to loose on me chromatic scales of the speaking voice, and therefore ceased to practise on me its witchcraft of anxiety. Those do-not-panic-but-hurry voices, even when the flights they call are no concern of yours, even when your flight has, like mine, actually gone, are calculated to pull you each time an inch forward in the slope of your chair. It's no concern of yours: yet a little fear flows through the ducts, provoking instant muscular flexion: you brace to put away fear, to meet threat, to act – to deliver the goods (sc. you) promptly, invoice in hand to be shewn, sop to Cerberus, as you pass the gate, packaging tucked in (mackintosh folded, not slurping, over arm), *not* alarmed at the thought of take-off, cigarette extinguished. No smoking until the witchcraft is airborne. (I can fly any type of crate, including a broomstick.)

Instead, public-address put on a record.

('In my youth', reminisced the Great King, 'I was happy. But then he was, as well as pretty, rather talented at sex.')

I recognised, with the aplomb of an eighteenth-century poet enunciating a truism, that music does soothe.

Balm slithered onto my leprous affliction.

('Hautboy', urged the King, 'haut.')

How could I, in logic, have foreseen?

I am Irish and logical. Barbara, Celarent, Darii, pray for us.

(I am as logical as the child who obeys idiom to the point of conjugating *better* as a verb. 'I better do it', he says, 'bettern't I?')

49

Logically I could not have predicted that the next cut would he swifter, sharper and to the bone.

Unpredicting, I let myself be lapped and presently immersed in the deep sweet waters of the Symphony (fine pastoral symplycyty of that usage) that prefaces Act Two of *Alitalia*: —

> Breve; breve.
> Scratch-fiddle scratch-fiddle scratch-fiddle.
> Clarinets: declare, clarify, conclude.
> Moan oboe: squeak flute: oboe moan.
> Ti pom tiddle logical-closing-cadence pom.
> Draw two lines underneath.

New paragraph, opening in trumpets and timpani, debouching into: —

IL RE ARTASERSE	KING ARTAXERXES
(contralto)	(contralto)
Alla città giocosa (timp timp)	To the joyous city
torna la dolce calma,	sweet peace returns,
di guerra vittoriosa	to the victor's vict-
ha il vincitor la palma (trump trump).	orious brow the palm.

And by that trumpet my forces are recruited. Music now has me drummed up, drilled and thrilled. I think it must be the very existence of key which, before harmonic pattern or even melody discloses itself, utters a summons to the constituent assembly of the human constitution.

CORO DI CITTADINI	CHORUS OF CITIZENS
Alla città, ecc.	To the joyous, etc.

How does key summon? (Key? Enigma, rather.) Perhaps it enunciates the hope there may yet be order in the universe. The phenomenon of the octave declares that logic is not mocked.

goes the oboe, and we all (including us non-playing members, audience) t{ ^u_o }ne up.

Not that it's unfairplay to play on our expectation of key and, instead of playing in key, dispense with it. The object is to unstring us: one of the psycho-tortures self-inflicted, by way of pleasure, in masophisticated societies.

BRUTO	BRUTUS
(mezzo-soprano)	(mezzo-soprano)
(*recitat.*) Giusto ciel!	(*recitat.*) Just heaven!

All the same, such masophistications should be reserved to humanity and not imposed on the brute beasts, whose sense of pitch is acute but inelastic and whose appreciation of harmony is elementary to the verge of the hymnological. I've known dogs that could tolerate nothing later than late Beethoven, including one in particular who had it pointedly in for Brahms and at the first bar of Brahms on the record-player would sigh, by bar three would rise and before the end of the first page (supposing you to be following with a miniature score) would be asking to be let out of the room.

BRUTO	BRUTUS
(aria)	(aria)
Vanto vano!	Vain vaunt! The
L'empio tiranno	impious tyrant cannot
non pùo fuggirmi.	flee me. He shall
Morirà, sí,	die, yes, etc.
morirà il tiranno, sí, ecc.	

And with that my banners are truly flaring in the forum. (Come strut with me', invites Brutus, and how shall my egalitarianism not be stirred. I'm coming, you trouser-rôle tunic-kneed strumpet. Wait for me, hussy tyrranicide. Wait only till I buckle on my baroque chest. Quick page (is your name Eros?), unsex me here and strap me into my torso-moulded breastplate whose breasts are neither male nor female but undulate in the papier-mâché landscaped contours of a more-than-Teiresianly-heroic heroic-convention. Quick now (I rage

51

to engage): my helmet. Ah so: good: now, tyrant, now, where is the plume of your taunt?

And yet even as the last plume shakes on that angered *a* of *tiranno*, I am re-sexed and unstrapped, undone, by a flight of pretty-winged amoretti (are your names Eros?), who have flown with my armour and hung it up votive on a statue of Venus. For love is coming out, like the sun, in the orchestra.

PATROCLO (soprano) ed ACHILLE (soprano) (*duetto*) Mio bene, idol mio, davanti a questo rio (orchestral ripples) che nel suo mormorio parla del nostro amor, (pastoral piping in orchestra) fedeltà giuro anch'io qual pecora al pastor.	PATROCLUS (soprano) and ACHILLES (soprano) (*duet*) My well-being, my idol, in front of this rivul- et whose murmur speaks of our love, I swear fidelity like sheep to the shepherd.

O sun-smiling soprano voices. First you exchange phrases like lovers' face-to-face looks, sunlight chasing momentary shadow; and then you are rapt, Greek lovers, into the true dual, the duet of a long-drawn, warblingbreath-commingling kiss.

Have you exchanged, now, senses? Or lost sense of sense-proprietorship? Can you no longer tell whose tongue wags (and runs and glides and trills) in whose head?

IPPODAMIA (contralto) (moglie d'Achille, ora, vestita da uomo, paggio al gran Re)	HIPPODAMIA (contralto) (wife of Achilles, at present, dressed as a man, page to the Great King)
(*recitat.*) Che cosa sento? Ohimè!	(*recitat.*) What do I hear? Woe is me!

SAFFO (baritono) SAPPO (baritone)
(*recitat.*) (*recitat.*)
Agli accenti di quel ragazzo, At the sound of that boy's voice,
tremo! I tremble!

(Thunderclap in orchestra, succeeded by gales and rain, until:—)

(*aria*) (*aria*)
Grazia femminile, (viola) Feminine grace,
aspetto virile, (trumpet) virile appearance,
viso ermafrodito: (strings hermaphroditic face:
pizzicato)

soave conflitto! smooth conflict!
cor mio, coraggio! (french horn) Courage, my heart!
adoro il paggio! I adore the page!

What bandits in a landscape they all are, these dramatis personae, every last man-woman among them muffled in a cloak and hiding behind the nearest tree and peeping round its trunk to spy. Serve them right that they're all riven by what the lightning flash discloses.

And you, opera, yourself, you matter for monumental statues, you are entirely seen by lightning flash. You extravagance, you illusionarily airborne massiveness, you assemblage of prancing baroque monsters, how apt it is to you that your personages, whose beauty is buckskin deep (and now Jonson's learned wind-soc flies on the airstrip outside), should be so many (and no doubt man-made) man-maids . . .

But soft, my lord interlocutor, here's yet another hider behind a tree.

L'IMPERATORE THE EMPEROR
ALESSANDRO ALEXANDER
(contralto) (contralto)
(*recitat.*) Di Saffo son amoroso. (*recitat.*) With
Sappho I am in love.

(Urgency chords)
Ma silenzio.   But silence.
(Muffling chords)
Non si deve udire il pianto   The plaint of my secret love
del mio amor segreto.   must not be heard.

(Squaring up to aria chords)
(*aria*)(B flat minor)   (*aria*)
Perché, perché queste pene?   Why, why these pains? Why
(cello with sordino)   am I constricted by chains?
perché son stretto da catene?   Why dost thou palpitate, my
perché palpiti, mio seno?   breast? Where is, where is
dov'è, dov'è il cor sereno?   the serene heart?

(Orchestra finishes off lengthily on the bassoon, that lugubriously gay old fagotto.)

Sweet monster opera, I am in your whirlpool kiss. You have sucked me deep into your contralto throat, drawn me down into identification with your characters by your sheer liquid expressiveness of their emotions.

I am free of self, delivered from what seems the sinfulness but not from the delights of selfishness.

There is nothing so recuperative to the personality as that it should for a space impersonate someone else.

(Link up the patient's bloodstream to Alexander's bloodvessels for a while, nurse.

Doctor, this patient is asking to be linked up twice daily.

Hm. A grave case of fiction addiction.)

And do I take it that, while I am inhabiting the soul of a wildfowl or whatever else the librettists of this furthest-fetched of all forms of fiction may have chosen to include in the cast, my own propria persona is enjoying a rest?

I do not. To begin with, inhabiting Alexander is no rest-cure, those being my emotions he is bouncing up and down the alto register.

And for a further thing: I am present in my own person, commenting and being moved to compassion, throughout the performance.

54

The emotion *Alitalia* puts me to is simultaneously altruism and self-pity.

Listening to it is at once idealistic and hedonistic. I am as shut-up in my own self-seeking sensations as if I were doing invisible masturbation. And yet my enjoyment is a social act.

Such is the twin genius of art.

And the twin hero, the Cast-list and Paradox, of the arts that have characters is that I both am and observe them.

Those arts include, besides the obvious, some oblique cases: portraiture, of course (catch a narcissist in front of the Mona Lisa and watch them exchange smirks), and also history painting. Surely, *surely* you, too, have been the monkey on the parapet in *The Family of Darius Before Alexander*?

And now I am myself before Alexander, whence I accuse opera of being, of all fictions, the monster.

I am even prepared to name specifically *which* monster: the Amphisbaena (trans. colloqu. the push-and-pull or the have-it-both-ways).

For if opera exerts on us the audience the intensest whirlpull, it also gives us the coldest push.

O opera, opera, you seduce me into your kiss, yet at the same time you put me through the most rigorous schooling in etiquette. Well-bred persons, you frigidly imply, do not so much as touch hands. From the stage your characters make me a lordly bow. And I, rolled back by your repelling rollers to the tide-line of the stalls, where I huddle emotionally wrecked and castaway (irretrievably away, that is, from the cast) may, if I have the strength left, touch my own hands together to — conventionally, merely ideogramatic-ally — applaud.

You are forever framing yourself and bridling, opera, in the proscenium arch of the formality of your conventions.

You hold me alien from you by the simplest of devices. You have set between me and you an unwrinkling sheet of plate-time.

For drama moves at the speed of speech (or of light, by which one sees action) and novels at the speed you read: all of which are speeds high enough to pass for representations of the speed of thought, so that you, reader-interlocutor, monkey-on-the-parapet,

55

may voluntarily undertake the illusion of inhabiting a character's (as it may be, my) train of consciousness.

But opera moves at no speed: only at the tempo of the music.

Of course I foresee how that cor sereno cadence will end. But it can't be hurried. I'd protest if it were.

By the next lightning I suspect I shall glimpse Amphisbaena itself, bulking monstrously from wing to wing and dinosauring to the flies. For in the next section, I know, Orestes appears. And though we are all Greek heroes, we Irish — O'Dysseus (whom Joyce disguised under the vocative form You-Lysses), O'Edipus, and most cogently of all, with not a syllable displaced, O'Rion — yet for me it is always, through the particularity of his circumstances, O'Restes who speaks most natively with my voice.

For listen

O R E S T E (mezzo-soprano)

(*recitat.*) O numi! O destin implacabile! Son orfano.

O R E S T E S (mezzo-soprano)

(*recitat.*) O super-natural powers! O implacable destiny! I am an orphan.

I *am* you, you she-hero and he-soprano. It's me you orphan for the third time as you step forth and, already stabbed to the heart by your bereavement, but stabbed, of course, off-scene, for the Decencies' sake (those Decencies who, with the Unities, are the counter-Furies that brood over classic drama), you take your three haut but faltering steps along the platform where you are raised in the sight of all. *Son*, you go (syllable direly ironic against you if you read in English instead of Italian): *or*, you proceed, yet more reluctantly: *fa-*

And here, on the very edge of your platform, you p{ $^{oi}_{au}$ }se, temporarily weighted down just enough to hold you back by the length of an extra almost imperceptible pause, the dot beside the note (What I have *rit.*, said the composer, I have *rit.*)

And on that retarding dot my identifying rush halts. I am stopped like traffic by the continuoist's raised striking arm. I am impaled on the lifted, arrested point of the conductor's baton—

— which whirls me over the top of his head back to my proper

56

side of the proscenium, after quite vulgarly bidding me, like a burp into the silence of that pause, WAIT FOR IT.

Behold me then skedaddling to re-install or re-box myself in, and thence confessing that it is not I but you, you unapproachably beautiful hybrid, Orestes, who now pitch headlong down the entire scale and from the bottom moan out your completing syllable, your dead negative -no.

A tear, perhaps of pure weakness like an invalid's, seeps from me.

(Nurse, this may be the onset of fiction withdrawal symptoms.)

And yet your -no is taken up as a statement in its own right and in another sense by that gently whispering, multiple-downy-wing-stirring, ministering chorus.

CORO	CHORUS
No!	No!
ORESTE	ORESTES
Sí!	Yes!
CORO	CHORUS
No, no! Siamo tutti la tua famiglia!	No, no! We are all thy family!
ORESTE	ORESTES
Ne sono contentissimo.	I am extremely happy about it.

(Orchestral preparations for the sun to come definitively out.)

I mourn your bereavement, Orestes, but I am also extremely happy about it because you are bereaved in tune.

Is (enquires the Curator of Pedantiquities) the orphanhood of Orestes rendered the less moving to the audience by virtue of the idiosyncratic circumstances in which it came about? (Scilicet, lap one, his mama does his papa in; lap two, Orestes himself completes the process by doing his mama in.)

(This type of tale, we might remark, belongs to the genre ancient-world thriller. Characteristically, this genre sets two trains-of-thought on a collision course. It then asks the perennial thriller-question, Who is Guilty? but the answer it demands is Both. For the sheer physical fright of the modern variety, the ancient thriller substitutes moral fright, insinuating down the back of the audience's necks the delicious suggestion that morally you can't win.)

The answer to our enquirer is No. To elaborate:— since all human beings have at some time orphaned themselves in fantasy on (roughly) the Orestes model, we incline to think the circumstances make his plight all the more deeply and universally moving.

And indeed, now I think of it, that's no doubt why the chorus describe themselves as all akin to Orestes — a point they are now on the point of reiterating in a chorus which, besides being

  (i) a metaphor of the social nature of the act of art, and
  (ii) a metaphor of the social nature of an operatic performance and the hybrid structure of opera as an artistic form (opera=coopera)

is

  (iii) an epitomised though no doubt (Belpaesiello being too Italian to think it worth remarking) unconscious account of the socio-texture of Italian life:—

TUTTI	ALL
Germani	Brothers (general
genitori	sense), parents (masc.
gemelli	plur. including in
zie	sense whereby masc.
cugini	sing.+fem.sing. =
nonne	masc. plur.), twins
cognati	masc. plur.), aunts,
nonni	cousins (masc. plur.)
suoceri	grandmothers, brothers-
fratellastri	in-law, grandfathers,
sorelle	fathers-in-law, half-
suore	brothers, sisters,
padri	Sisters (monastic
fratelli, ecc. ecc. ecc.	sense), fathers,
	brothers, etc. etc. etc.

SEXSHUNTWO
THE CASE OF THE MISSING (RE)MEMBER
Andante

1

I was a fine one to have declared myself out of sympathy with lost identities. Before a cock or a contralto could reasonably have crowed thrice, and while my system still pulsed to the informally fugal effect of that splendid closing chorus from *Alitalia*

> (cugi – gnati
> spo – selle
> geni – telli),

there went missing in my own mind not, indeed, my sense of my identity (on which I retained a clear, firm clasp throughout the lamentable incident which I am now going, in a manner as straightforward and circumstantial as I can muster, to narrate) but a piece of information which, though less individual to me than my identity, was in certain immediate respects even more vital.

I sat on for a little while in the after-throb of the music.

A gentle euphoria was swelling inside me which turned out, on examination, to be chiefly social. True to my theorisings about the socialness of art, I was emerging from the opera considerably better disposed than I'd gone in towards other people.

That was timely. There were now considerably more of other people to be seen.

My senses were being softly and agreeably buffetted by carnival streamers – which I presently recognised to be strands of coffee smell freshly unwound from the bar.

I lifted my head to sniff these skeins and discovered, by the same operation, that while I'd been plunged in listening the spaces round me had silently silted up with people.

My sitting knees were in some danger of being stepped back onto by circumambient vertical knees.

In place, however, of my usual social emotion, which is alarm, I experienced a warm access of human brotherhood.

By what crass infantile egoism, I thought, do we habitually speak of 'other people', a term that lumps them all together by no common characteristic except that they are other than holy Me.

(Hell is other people only by the polarity that puts Me in heaven.)

Once I had recognised that other people are not in reality a single body unified in conspiracy against Me, I found my compassion infiltrating the body of bodies presented to me and isolating a group here as my cugini and there as my (positively) fratelli. I was replying to the entire throng on behalf of my compatriot and alter ego O'Restes, to the effect that they were all my family, too. (Siete tutti, my thoughts thought towards them, della mia famiglia – for if we truly were akin, we could all dispense with that clumsy Loro sono form.)

The apéritif value of coffee smell was working on me strongly.

Emboldened by my social euphoria, I rose and bodily followed out the route my compassion had pioneered. Mouthing a clearly lip-readable 'permesso' to the group directly in front of me, I bent my way (while a cugino stole swiftly into the seat I was leaving vacant) round their backs and insinuated myself on to the group of fratelli, to whom I lip-spoke 'pardon'. By such means I slowly ravelled the coffee strands back to source and circuitously grinned and pardoned myself through to the bar.

There most of all, of course, there were now more people.

All the stalk stools in front of the counter were flowering with occupants. Between them was a running border of competitors for the barmen's attention.

With not a trace of my accustomed contradictory squeamishness (they're not fit) and diffidence (no no, it's I who am not fit) about coming to touching quarters with unknown human beings, I inserted myself briefcase first into a barely perceptible opportunity and prepared to wait.

But I wasn't required to. No sooner had I briefcased my way in than one of the two barmen moved deliberately downstream and stopped opposite me with his face turned directly on me.

My euphoria was set back on its heels. (I should no doubt have taken warning. But I was euphoric.)

The music of *Alitalia* having restored my mood, I'd been unthinkingly counting on its libretto to have restored me some command of language.

Apart from mouthing my passage through the throng, I hadn't spoken aloud since the crisis of my linguistic leprosy.

I looked to the barman for a prompt.

Instead, he kept turned on me a mere mute face of interrogation.

Instantaneously I reconstructed what must have happened. The airport authorities had issued a directive that language be replaced by ideograms. The barman was due to be supplied with a stack of cards (possibly printed '?', but more probably, since western punctuation would be non-significant to orientals, with a stylised face shewing interrogative raised eybrows) which he would flash at customers. Naturally, however, there hadn't yet been time to distribute the cards, and he was meanwhile making obediently do by ideogramming his own facial expressions.

By good luck, this dismaying fantasy was shattered as soon as shaped. A man four elbows along from me asked my barman something while his arc-lamp face was still trained on me, and my barman, his look undeviating from me, side-answered either 'Nine' or 'Nein'.

The fact he had answered, plus the fact that I'd understood the answer whichever language it was in, gave me enough boldness of mind to perceive that the true signal the barman's mute face was flashing to me was friendliness. He had recognised me from my previous coffee.

If, however, we were in the beaten way of friendship, that was all the more reason why I shouldn't keep him waiting with his lamp look on.

Yet I now knew I was still linguistically shaky.

I rapidly decided I'd do best to stick, for the time being, to comestibles with international names.

In the friendly flurry which had replaced my fright, I could think of only two. I asked the barman for a cappuccino and a brioche.

He turned and sped upstream.

I realised that neither of the things I'd asked for was nearly nourishing enough to fill the hunger which, I now became aware, was harrowing a painful channel across my diaphragm.

My barman reached for the glass dome which, like a shape abstracted from a roast turkey, was roosting on the counter and spanning the brioches. In mid-reach my barman's sleeve was detained by the other barman, who drew mine into consultation and calculation about, so far as I could tell across the distance and through the chatter, a bill someone wanted to pay in a far-fetched currency. And I, though far too hungry to please, had to wait till the conversion of the shekels.

Interlude

I've muttered you, my dear Reader, several asides on the
subject of the technique of fiction, including some about
alienation effects — one of which I am indeed practising on
you now, though this (at last openly) Open-Letter to you also
serves the representational purpose of signifying by ideogram,
while sparing you the sensuous experience of, the hiatus
I had to live through while I waited for my anyway
underweight snack to be delivered to me.

I have no wish to play god or conjurer; I refuse to simply
practise on you de haut en bas. I want, though I may fail to win,
your sympathy for me as narrator as well as for me as
character — if, indeed, the two are separable.

Constantly, therefore, I have invited you to inspect and
(I hope) concur in the machinery of my narration. And now I want
to urge your attention towards one particular and cardinal cog.
Has it occured to you there may be a specific determining reason
why this narrative should be in the first person?

After all, if I am after your sympathy, am I not risking
much by being an I? Suppose I'm right in thinking that when you
jump on the vehicle of my consciousness you shed some of the (of
course subjective) sinful sensation of egoism. Were I presented
to you in an objective frame, you might, in lending me your
sympathy, congratulate yourself on your altruism, and that might
conciliate you into lending me yet more; whereas, by persisting in

64

being an I, I very likely put you on your guard against identifying yourself with me, lest you thereby incur the disagreeable sensation of self-pity.

Would I, do you suppose, take such risks if I had any alternative?

Yours to the end of alienation,

(p.p. B.B.)

E.H. (P.) O'R.

P.S. So much for the strategy of this narration. With respect to the tactics, you will find that my prose falls into its proper cadences and yields up its tone of emotional voice if you read it in your head with the trace (rising to a quite marked intonation in passages of exitement) of an Irish accent, which is how I myself speak.

P.P.S. Pray you, Reader, read on.

Whiteness entered my frame of vision: the wax white of starch over the enlarged pores of linen. My barman's arm was advancing my order, like chess pieces, towards me across the counter.

I paid (in a banal currency and a human-brotherly grin) and turned to cast a look at the café area.

That had filled up, too.

I inserted my briefcase between my left arm and my left side, manoeuvred cup and saucer from the counter into one hand and plate and brioche into the other, and trekked into the hinterland.

I highstepped (over human legs protruding as in some bizarre sexual conjunction from between table legs) halfway down an aisle, and then paused to let my vision sweep the café like a radar scanner.

I could see nowhere to sit.

I became uneasy about my briefcase. My arm had furrowed the books inside (those books I had bought on themes pointedly other than loss of identity) into two weights, which now sagged fore and aft of me.

I spotted a brace of chairs one of which was gratefully unoccupied. They accompanied a small table beside the left wall.

Reduced, now I knew I was on the last lap, to clenching indiscriminately with virtually all the muscles in my body capable of clenching, I held my burdens and my limbs somehow together and shuffled towards the empty chair, knowing I could be easily outstripped by someone with no briefcase and, say, only one snack to carry.

From nearer to it, I saw that the left wall of the café was in fact not a wall but a length of glass-and-wood screening. It was actually on wheels, which gave my sense of insecurity a moment's further impulsion, though I then saw, to my reassurance, that it must be in at least semi-permanent situ, since a line of dwarf indoor shrubs in dwarf lead coffins had been funereally planted along its base.

I arrived, just outdoing a (so I conjectured) Finnish furniture designer who, on being foiled of this place, ricocheted swiftly off to the far side of the café.

Lowering myself from the knees, I fork-lift-trucked my crockery off my hands onto the table surface, to the relief of my briefcase.

I then saw that neither was the table in fact a table. A triangular slither of three-ply plastic, of which the under-plies were fake wood and the top ply bright yellow, it was a mere flap hinged down from one of the (genuinely) wooden stanchions in the screen at my left.

The apex of this triable was crowned by a glass that had been emptied of everything except an internal spiral staircase of lager foam.

From the glass my observation worked back to its putative emptier, my table- or flap-companion.

As he was sitting un-newspapered, politeness granted me only a brief inspection on the strength of which I surmised him to be a 37-year-old toy exporter who, while he travelled on business, had left his two children, who were good at mathematics, music and ice-skating, at home, home being probably Münster or just possibly, for a fallback guess, Bern.

He had a rimless face and wore one of those flimsy mackintoshes that would have been transparent had it not, seemingly, been smoked in case he should want to observe an eclipse through it.

I moved to take my chair.

My companion, however, had overspilled his possessions onto its seat — to the inexplicable extent, it appeared (again, to a brief look), of two further mackintoshes of the same smoky-cat tint.

66

I gave him the international Pardon and a nod of allusion towards my chair.

He returned me the Pardon, pushed with his right forefinger at the bridge of his rimless (and, I now had time to notice, octagonally-lensed) spectacles (I interpreted his gesture as a signal of non-aggression, since muscularly it much resembled tipping a hat), and lurched beneath the flap-table towards the seat of my chair, whence he pulled his extra mackintoshes onto his lap.

I sat down and set my briefcase on its side across my lap.

It at once began to slide.

I became linguistically anxious again, this time on the question whether I more naturally though of it as a briefcase (but it didn't, I was prompted to object by sitting face-to-face with a presumed German-speaker, contain letters) or an attaché case. (But it was becoming swiftly détaché.)

The case (the compromise I decided on – at the same time resolving that, should it tumble and my companion enquire 'Is this yours?', I would reply 'That is the case') was too heavy to be retained by friction with the corduroy tracks that ran down my thighs.

Neither could I sho{ ^r_v }e it up against the underside of the table. Only to my left, where the triangle-base met the wall, was that exiguous flap wide enough to roof a lap at all. The rest of it ran away from me as I sat, leaving a gulf over which I foresaw I should have difficulty in getting my coffee safely to my mouth.

Before it could finally drop, I took my case in hand and reached to the floor, feeling for the table leg to prop it against.

Of course there was no leg, the table being a flap.

Hanging at bloodheat head down, I pushed my case to the left and managed to shake its contents into such a shape that it would lean against the flower boxes.

As I came up, my vision was startled by the entrance into it of my companion, also coming up from floor-level and, thanks to the tininess of the table, embarrassingly in close-up to me.

Presumably he'd had the same difficulty in retaining his mackintoshes on his lap as I'd had with my case – indeed, worse, since his already mackintoshed lap must have been slippery; he must have been obliged to stow his burden, too, on the floor.

67

My social euphoria, I noticed, was already giving way to my more accustomed social sensation, embarrassment.

Slightly, however, I excused myself. This absurd table, which I supposed was not meant for use except in the emergency of the café's being full, insisted on cramming a pair of strangers into a proximity that flesh and blood could not be expected to bear without embarrassment. Only quite exceptionally uninhibited and social flesh and blood would have felt unconstrained face to face with a total stranger, with a distance of only some eighteen inches between face and face.

In order to disrupt this static-electrical situation, I pulled the left legs of my chair sharply in towards the table (they came with a startling noise, like the clearing of a mechanical throat) and slewed my own legs to the right, so that I sat profile-on to the table.

When I was a third of the way through the manoeuvre, a similar sound came startlingly, from very close, to my left ear.

With an oblique glance I saw that by ill luck my companion was engaged in the exact counterpart to my own manoeuvre and that he had begun on his too soon after me to be able, without ostentation, to halt when he saw that I was in train of doing the same.

We were now sitting profile to profile, my left to his right, with scarcely twelve inches between profile and profile.

Neither of us could, with any resemblance to naturalness, put a shielding hand to cheek, because neither elbow could reach across the gulf to rest on the tiny spit of table.

And if we had tried, we would have risked — since we seemed to have a musical-comedy-like fatality for moving in concert-colliding elbows.

I decided to pretend to attend to my food, which at least my companion, having finished his beer, which was all he had had on the table, could not plausibly do.

So obliquely was I now placed to the table that to address my food required of me a twist that gave some discomfort to my ribs. That recalled me to my quite unfeigned hunger. Reaching across the gulf to my cup, I tested its outside with my forefinger, found it still a little too hot for me, and moved my hand on to my brioche.

I remembered, as I hadn't at the flurried moment of ordering,

68

that the secret vein of yellowed marbling that runs through the heart of most brioches is made of almond paste, which I dislike.

I returned my hand to my coffee, took the teaspooon and began chasing the foam (some two thirds of which had, however, already exploded spontaneously) over the surface.

It was during the scudding of the back of the spoon across the opaque liquid that I realised I could no longer remember which sex I was.

2

Interludibrium

Open memo

Yes, dear clever as cartloads of monkeys on parapets Reader, that's indeed why. I who snort and fret under the cumbersomeness of Loro sono could hardly (could I?) commit myself to a main character at whose every appearance in my narrative I would be obliged to write he/she, his/her, etc.
For which reason
    I *have*,
        dear Sir/Madam,
            to remain
                your
                    I
P.S. You'll notice that I've, even so, sleighted you out of hand — that is to say, trickered you off with mirror effects. For instance, if I were not an I, it could not be I who would be committed to a he/she. And am I not surreptitiously shunting the time telescope? From what time-standpoint I am writing is unknown. But it is clear that at the period of the thoughts and events recounted in Section One I could perfectly recollect which sex I belonged to, though, knowing that obvious fact so well, I had no particular need to mention it. Am I therefore trying to produce an *effect* of verisimilitude by

the non-realistic method of pretending that I cannot now remember remembering what, it is admitted by internal evidence, I did at that time remember quite clearly?

The *ludibrium,* by the way, on which I've punned in the sub-title of this interlude means (allow me, who have recently looked it up, to spare you the trouble of the Latin dictionary) 'Lit. *a mockery, derision, wantonness'* – from which you might conclude I'm playing games, like a painter who includes in his picture a mirror in which he shews himself standing outside the picture painting it. An alienation effect may be a fiction within fiction, purporting to thrust the spectator back into the real world outside the frame but in practice drawing him deeper into the fictitious perspective. A stuccoist may appear to open up arches in the wall you know stands next to the garden, but it may be a frescoed sky and garden he shews you between them. Perhaps these interludes are holes I have torn in my canvas through which you see the veritable wall on which my picture hangs. Or perhaps I have simulated on my canvas both torn canvas and the wall you see through to.

Do not, however, please, assume I am making a monkey of you. *Ludibrium* had also a *meton.* meaning, which is given as *'an object of mockery, laughing-stock, butt, jest, sport'* – and that, in the entirely ludicrous fix I have described myself finding myself in, can refer only to myself.

Remember above all, if you please will, that the relations between us are by no means so straighforward as they often pass for being because writers and readers have grown so used to the conventions as not to notice them. Suppose for the sake of argument that I am a fictitious character or at least one who appears so to you. I have invited from you a certain temporary identification. I am prepared to be taken over, possessed, by you. In your own eyes, I don't doubt, you are a very real part of the real world. But please remember that, to me it is you who are the fictitious – the, indeed, entirely notional – character. To be engulfed by you into an identification must be like being nibbled at, ticklingly, by

70

a void. I have to summon my weightiest resources of gravity to take you seriously. I don't even know, for example, what sex you are.

3

Such gross forgetfulness was, of course, preposterous.

My gaze, twisted across the gulf between me and the thin delta of table, continued to rest though no longer to focus on my coffee. My hand continued to hold the spoon, emptily. Meanwhile I felt my intellect moving like a computer into routines quite inadequate to my problem.

I promised myself that it was impossible for an adult human to forget what sex he/she belonged to – and then added, in an effort to undo the strangulation of panic which set about me, that it was doubly impossible for an adult human in public.

If, I went on to parley with myself, the thing, though impossible, had happened, it could have happened only for a moment. It was a moment's mental slipped disk, like being unable to recapture a familiar word; at the present moment plus one, I should be released from my absurd situation by an internal click like the click behind the jaw which relieves your ears' congestion after high flying.

No click came.

I edged closer to the spit of table and lowered my head in a bout of faintness, as though I expected that the knowledge of which sex I belonged to could be brought back to my brain by gravitation.

No such knowledge arrived.

Instead, I was seized ungovernably by the ludicrousness of my plight.

Now I kept my head down, feigning that I was gazing into the in fact impenetrably opaque depths of my cappuccino, for fear that that shaven-and-graven German-speaking head opposite me should get wind or tremor of my being on the verge of a splutter of giggles.

I'd been, thanks to such mental maladroitnesses of mine as my compulsion to pun and my liability to become geographically disorientated (which latter I attribute to the geographical transplantings of my early years), in funny fixes before, but in this one I had excelled my – what I had excelled, I completed the thought more soberly than I'd begun it, was chiefly my powers of getting myself out.

I plunged the spoon into my coffee and stirred it to storm. (It was now lukewarm, but my stomach had turned angry.) I lashed it in lieu of myself, whom I now bitterly blamed for the wantonness with which I'd played that game of Topping and Tailing Happy Families without heed to Consequences.

Obviously my mind had set its own confusion it train as it went around setting masc. plur. endings on fem. stems and, in my fatuous euphoria, saluting groups of the crowd here as my fratelle and there as my sorelli – that crowd under whose unified and conspiratorially contemptuous cold eye I might at any moment, in the ignorance I had reduced myself to, make a blundering fool of myself.

Hooligan, I accused myself, o hooligan O'Hooligan: *you*'re the hooligan who by night crept into the hall of sculpture (glided into the gliptotek, you did, hooligan) and vandalised the exhibits by chopping 'em all in two across the waistline, after which you hooligamused yourself by re-assorting the demi-torsos and putting the from-the-waist-up of the Venus de Milo on top of the from-the-waist-down of the Hermes of Praxiteles.

A grand old mutilation of the sperms, *that* was. Welll'llbeciades.

Anyhow, you are paid for't now, you praxitical joker you. You're paid out by your own confooligan, me brave boyo/colleen. You glipt up, my friend, and got tekted.

I even blamed opera, which I Irished and reproached as O'Pera, O'Pera.

For O'Pera it was that had introduced this confusion in the very first place – by its habit of so perversely running counter to the tenor of the secondary sex characteristics and ${send \atop cast}$}ing up camp castrati to a contraltitude

      (cugini
      cognati
      castrati) . . .

Was *I*, perhaps, castrato/a? Was the truth behind my oblivion that
I *had* no sex?

4

The question could not have so panicked me had the answer been
Yes.

By that consideration I was steadied.

I looked up from the cold tempest of my coffee

> (cugini
> castrati
> cappuccini).

All over the café chatter was proceeding. My opposite numGerman
was looking rigidly and rimlessly not-at me, trying, I thought I
detected, to not-react to my having looked at him.

And all those people knew not only what sex *they* (severally,
themselves and one another) were but also, presumably, by casual,
look-and-pass-on-inspection, what sex I was.

I oed for a thoughts-radar screen on which I might pick up just
one casual bleep that would signify m. or f.

Suppose, it came to me, I were to ask my companion?

Lean forward: clear throat: Pardon (international pron.), would
you please tell me what sex I am?

My fantasy feinted it in.

All I learned from the exercise was that one does not mention sex
to strangers (Clause One of the Social [Non-Aggression] Contract).

No grace would be granted me to explain I was mentioning it
only in its categorising or old-fashioned sense. What misunderstand-
ing would befall an eighteenth-century revenant who spoke of 'the
sex' meaning women, not a part of the body. And if you want to
state (the major premiss of my present anxiety) that human beings
are beings either male or female, you must beware of putting it that

they 'have sex'. We shall soon reach a point where the questionnaire item

sex | |

gets filled in

sex | yes, thrice weekly | .

My own question, had I indeed leaned forward and asked it of my oppositeMünster/oppositenumBern, would have been received as a verbal rape. He'd have assumed I was (but heterosexually or homosexually?, I pressingly wondered) soliciting him.

I was re-sealed into my predicament.

Yet, now that I'd admitted it was likely to last more than a moment, I found myself less supine in relation to it.

It was impossible: it had nevertheless happened: now the impossibility was that I shouldn't, since I remained in possession of such cunning as I'd ever had and all my memories except that single grotesque fugitive, work my way out.

How? scrabbled my mind – and then saw the obvious method and flung its embrace wide to it: empirical enquiry be my guide.

Going, in a matter that was, after all, elemental, straight to the point. I looked down my sitting body to the point where my legs met.

I was wearing trousers.

They were of black corduroy (the thick, broad-ribbed kind). They opened down the front by a zip, a few of whose metallic railway sleepers I could see at the top of the track but the rest of which was concealed by fly.

At the region round and below the base of the fly I peered closely down.

I was sure that direct enquiry, now that I'd at last come up with the coolness to call on it, would have me out of my fix in a trice.

At least, I congratulated myself (at the same time reminding myself that a conspicuous absence of bulges would be as conclusive as a bulge), I was no child. For I assumed that the last time I could have had recourse to a scrutiny of this sort must have been in childhood, though, as it happened, if such an incident had taken

74

place I'd suppressed the memory of it. Now, it seemed to me, I enjoyed two great adult advantages: an adult physiological development, plus an adult knowledge, of what (or its absence) I was looking for.

To my surprise, deduction was not easy. What baffled me seemed to be that mine were not close-fitting trousers. A second scrutiny shewed that up as inexact. It was rather that they closely followed their, not my, configuration.

So far from presenting a significant lack of bulges, the region made a whole rolling landscape of bulges. The difficulty was to know which, if any, were significant.

Corduroy seemed a material contradictorily both soft and stiff. It draped softly, but it created airpockets of its own to be draped over. It was virtually erectile tissue in its own right. Indeed, I was now doubly glad of my adult knowledge of anatomical possibility. If I'd had to go on the evidence of my trousers alone, I would have been obliged to believe that an exceptionally long penis took its rise halfway down the inside of my left thigh and presently curled like coral over the front of my leg towards my knee.

Obviously, corduroy would not disclose to sight alone when it was rolling over flesh and blood and when it was rolling over a ridge of air.

I opened my right hand and placed it, palm down, on top of the junction of my legs.

Gently, I pressed.

My palm reported a perceptible thickening. I pressed harder and realised that all I had discovered was the double thickness where that unyielding material had been formed into the fly.

I edged my fingertips (which I now realised would be more sensitive than my palm) towards the seam and, pressing harder, let my fingers begin to curl into a grasping position.

Suddenly conscious of the non-concealment afforded by that narrow triangle of table, I flicked a look up at my companion.

He was staring directly at my hand.

Aware my vision had flicked up, he turned his own sharply away, in a manner in which I read that he intended to look back the moment he should judge me off guard.

75

I considered taking a book out of my case and seeking shelter beneath it.

But I realised I would be sheerly incapable of, in a public place, opening a book, humping it v-upside-down over my crutch and reaching a hand beneath it to feel myself.

Impatiently I calculated that my problem would be solved in three seconds if only I could have the privacy in which to rip open that zip and — no matter how cursorily, provided wholesalely — *look*.

I realised that, of course, I *could*. This genteel amateurish probing was the act of an idiot, when the wholesale solution to my problem lay within a minute's walk and a descent of shallow steps.

I was actually flexing my thighs to rise and extending my hand towards the floor to gather up my case, when I counter-realised that, no, I couldn't.

In social reality, which is every bit as tough as material reality, I could not go to the lavatories so long as I did not know whether to go to the men's or the women's.

The realisation disappointed me. Its corollary hit me as a second and graver shock wave. If I could not go to the lavatory, I should presently, if I were not to add flagrant infantile disgrace to what no doubt already seemed to my table-companion furtive infantile fumblings, be squeezed out of my quest for happiness in transit by sheer bodily discomfort.

And I'd have to solve pretty quickly en my route, I added, that lesser problem of how to get out of a Transit Lounge otherwise than by plane. I now regretted having so cavalierly $\left\{ \begin{array}{l} \text{let go by the board} \\ \text{passed up the validity of} \end{array} \right\}$ my boardingpass. On that plane which had now long since taken off without me, I yearningly thought, the lavatories would have been undifferentiated for the sexes, freeforall including even those who had suffered the unaccountable, unbelievable mishap of sexual amnesia.

The subject was such, I decided, that I couldn't afford to let my thoughts contemplate it with too vivid a kinaesthetic imagery. Even at the cautioning inhibition, half a dozen images started into my mind of accidents that might casually undo me: at the bar, a soda siphon might squirt or a bottle of wine be innards-liquefyingly poured; even, it was not inconceivable there was a fountain

76

somewhere in transit which someone might suddenly pushbutton into play . . .

With less conviction than attempt at auto-suggestion, I assured myself that my last visit to the lavatory would last me out a goodish time further — easily until I should have solved the really not very difficult puzzle my ludicrous oblivion had posed to my empiricism.

To that puzzle I re-applied myself more resolutely, both because it gave my thoughts a needed change of subject and because I'd been (though I didn't want my thoughts to dwell on my being) impressed by its urgency.

I looked down myself again, though this time less far down.

I had only a small hope of direct physiological disclosure. On its way down to the obstinate corduroy of my trousers, my vision had already taken in that the upper part of my body was wearing a material which, though unribbed, resembled corduroy in consistency and unyieldingness.

All the same, I looked. There was always the chance I was a woman with such large breasts that they would, from underneath, dent even this material unmistakably.

My look told me at once I was not *such* a woman. Annoyingly, however, I couldn't be sure I wasn't *a* woman, with merely average-sized or small breasts.

The landscape that descended from beneath my tucked-in chin to just beyond the waistband of my trousers ran away in all directions beneath my gaze into fold mountains and rift valleys of its own. But whether the crucial cleft valley definitely and definingly was or was not there I could not discern.

I declined to feel cast down. There were still a hundred clues I hadn't tried. I could afford to enjoy meeting the challenge to my ingenuity.

My clothes might not permit me to read through them, but they were quite likely to be sex-indicating plumage in themselves.

I raised my hand to my throat and set it to roam and grope, uninhibited now it found itself in a neutral area. (*Let* my table-companion look — as, indeed, a quick look on my part shewed me he was doing. He was welcome to suppose I itched.)

I triumphed. I was quite certainly not wearing a tie.

77

I might have continued to think that fact conclusive, had I not gone on to make surer still by probing left and right lest a tie had gone askew.

Reluctantly I admitted that my fingertips were informing me that the quasi-corduroy (which by an irony felt agreeably feline to their touch) was folded back, all round my neck, into a deep roll collar.

I tried but soon failed to resist the inference: even if I were a man, I couldn't have worn a tie. Its absence was nonindicative.

On a quick but not a strongly hopeful thought, I ran my fingers round to the back of my neck and tested the length of my hair.

It came, as I had feared it would, just about to the roll of that angering roll collar. It was a perfectly plausible length, this decade, for a man — and equally plausible, this half-century, for a woman.

I returned my attention to my upper garment and realised it was a construction of perfected, foolproof ambiguity. Neither shirt (masc.) nor blouse (fem.) nor yet jumper (which, though of common sex, could have been expected to lie close enough to me to shew unambiguously whether or not I had [fem.] breasts), it was sheerly, ambiguousexedly a *top*.

I began to sense that my ingenuity, which a moment or two before I'd felt so bouncy about, was coming at every vital point into engagement with something as delicate, intricate and toughly-wrought as itself, namely the sexual ambiguity of modern clothes.

And I, of course, egalito-libertarian I, had always defended and even applauded that ambiguity. It released people, I was given to arguing, from rôles into individuality. Society has no right, I had thought, to treat you differently according to whether you are a man or a woman, and so society has no right to require you to wear a livery that will help it to classify you at sight. My imagination had not, of course, thought to allow for the predicament of a person who might want to deduce his/her own sex from his/her livery.

Raising my eyes, and dodging those of my companion which were still set firm on me, I passed a sampling gaze over the café and counted the persons I could easily examine (I picked standing ones) who were wearing trousers. Ten of them were men, three women.

I was irritated in passing (though, since I wanted to know, my irritation was perverse) that I had no difficulty in discerning the sex

78

of any of my examples. All those who were in fact men wore trousers thin and tight enough to disclose the fact unmistakeably. My three women (Three Ladies, I corrected myself — in homage to Mozart, not in a gallantry that might have come amiss from me who might be a miss myself) all wore tops which, though as ambiguous as mine in design, had been made in materials that $\{^{sh}_{dr}\}$aped themselves to breast or brassière cup.

Having counted, I simplified the sum I was setting myself by pretending not to have seen the last man on my list, and then worked out that the fact I was wearing trousers gave me a three to one likelihood of being a man.

I was pleased with this definite-sounding result until I saw it did not advance me a pace. There was no limiting factor, no stop at the end of the curtain-rail, which prevented the anyway not very exceptional exception, a woman, from being *me*.

If I forced my thinking to an application, the only one it could have was to reduce me to a non-existent, like that notional one-third of a child whom statistics inclines to locate in every family like the unmentioned idiot brother among Jane Austen's siblings, by requiring me to believe myself three-quarters man and a quarter woman.

My sampling had issued in frustration. That, I was after a moment aware, turned into a sort of crossness about, unaccountably, my trousers.

Had I been panicked into irrationality, I wondered — a question which itself panicked me a touch: and then I saw the perception behind my anger. The ambiguity of trousers is unilateral.

If only (I now saw I meant) I had been wearing a skirt, I could have been (provided it wasn't a kilt, Celtic or Balkan — or, of course, any sort of soutane) absolutely sure I was a woman.

For the matter of that, if only I had been wearing these trousers ten years earlier, I could have been all but absolutely sure, from the fact they opened down the front, I was a man.

I had an illumination of hope: surely the intellect so apprised of the change fashion had recently made in where women's trousers fastened must be the intellect of a woman? An instant later I recognised that unfamiliarity might make a man pay the greater attention to that. In the end I admitted that where and how trousers do up is something which, thanks to the persistence of the habits of infantile curiosity, everyone notices.

The airport authorities, I remarked from memory, had not yet caught up with the ambiguity of trousers, since the multilingual inscriptions which allotted the lavatory doors to the sexes were reinforced by ideograms in the silhouetted shapes of a skirted and a trousered figure. But the authorities did not mean, I knew with a twinge, that anyone wearing trousers might enter by the trousers door.

I am no fool: I of course tried, at that point in my train of reminiscence, to trap my memory into relaxedly visualising my last visit to the lavatories so that I might pounce and notice which door I had pushed. But I could remember only that I of course pushed, in the too taken-for-granted knowledge I then possessed, the one that was appropriate.

Being no fool was, I began without pleasure to see, half my trouble. The ambiguity of my clothing was the result not only of my high egalito-libertarian convictions but of a quality in me I found it harder to think of romantically, sheer practical good sense. I felt towards my good sense, which had caged me into my clothing and thus into my problem, the admiration I might accord to the plotting of an enemy who had perfectly framed me for a crime.

Even the unyielding materials that bounced my scrutiny unavailing back at me had been chosen by good sense to defy crushing and changes of temperature.

For my stay in air-conditioned transit was impromptu. I was a person who, at the end of a modestly rough-living, mildly openairish sort of holiday, was expecting to spend several hours, without changing clothes, waiting for, boarding and sitting in aeroplanes that would shift me rapidly from climate to climate.

Suppose I was a man: would I not, in commonsense, discard shirt (liable to grubby, limp cuffs) and tie (so easily flapped by an airpocket into a pocket of one's airdinner tray) in favour of this practical, ambiguous top?

Yet suppose I was a woman — one who knew she must walk out across windy tarmacs and mount gusty boarding-steps: would I not, in commonsense, prefer trousers to a skirt?

80

Perceiving that my costume constituted, through cogent causes, an impregnable enigma, I saw I should have to encroach on my second line of reserves: the secondary sex characteristics.

Reluctantly (because if this failed me I did not see what I should try next), I brought my hand up to my face, spread my palm against my cheek and began to feel my jowls.

I was not bearded.

I extended my forefinger along my upper lip. I was not moustached, either.

I came back, with a greater delicacy of touch, to the exploration of my jaw. Certainly I felt on it some roughness. It was not quite a raspingness. It might be stubble, but minimal recently-shaven stubble. Or it might be the roughness of a female skin that had recently been on holiday.

My touch could not quite come to determining point because some creaminess on my skin made my fingers glide.

Make-up, I identified – qualifying that, a second later, with: Or after-shave or talcum.

I dredged the side of my forefinger, digging with an impetus of fury, along my cheek.

I brought my finger down to be scrutinised. Along its edge there stood a fine line of liquid beads. They were colourless. Not makeup, I deduced, and raised my finger to my nose expecting a smell of after-shave. But there was no smell.

Suspicious, I pouted my lips forward as if in baby's greed and sucked at the side of my finger. The liquid on it was undoubtedly my own recently exuded (whence its lack of smell) sweat.

I guessed I had sweated in panic. I raised my eyes in that sudden help-seeking way that probably makes a rolling display of their whites and certainly pains one's eyeballs, and saw my table-companion fixedly watching me taste the side of my finger.

As a refuge from embarrassement, I lunged down for my briefcase. When it was on my knee, I had, for plausibility's sake, to unfasten it.

Done without purpose, the action put purpose into my head: I would consult documentary evidence.

I reached into the case and hurriedly sifted till I found my passport. I had half-drawn it out when my haste jammed it, like a paper-knife, between the pages of one of the bigger books. Too hurried to disengage it, I peered inside the case for what I wanted — and simultaneously saw and remembered I was bound to see that little blemish on the name-space which, leaping from my earlier cappuccino of the day, had dissolved for ever the record of whether I was Mr, Mrs or Miss O'Rooley.

It gave me no compensation at all to realise that, had my splurged-away title been Dr or Prof (which it was not), it wouldn't have revealed my sex in any case.

Disgusted, I jammed the document away. I knew there was no help to be had from its contents. Every passport contains a space for the holder's wife, but the fact they've drawn a line through it signifies only that your wife is not travelling on your passport (as who but a tyrannous skinflint would want her to do anyway, since it means the poor thing can't travel abroad save in your company?), not that you have no wife — and still less that you're not of the sex that *could* have a wife.

No more would it avail me to look at the record of my first names. To begin with, my memory being in all but this single absurdity unimpaired, I could remember them perfectly well without prompting. In the second place, they are Evelyn Hilary.

As it happens, I am not addressed as either Evelyn or Hilary. Mine is one of those cases of random para-nomenclature which I suspect occur particularly in the British Isles (geogr. sense, inclusive of Eire). On the continent, people seem on the whole to be called by what their names actually are. In the United States, tribal goodfellowship submits them to the humiliating puberty rite (no American grows *beyond* puberty, of course) of instant diminutivisation, every Robert becoming a Bob and every Katharine a Kathy within two dialogue-lines of the introductions. (Of course, many British Roberts are Bobs, too; but you have to find out if they are; it is an issue of fact.) Only in the British Isles does a sizeable piece of the population go by names bearing no discernible kinship to their given names. (A British Bob is almost as likely to be an Arthur or indeed a Katharine as a Robert.) I exemplify that randomness. I am always called Pat.

It would be plausible if Pat had been hung on me, a botanical tag of my Irish origin, at the time of my transplantation. However, I can't remember a time when I wasn't Pat. So i assume it dates from before I was transplanted; and I can attribute it only to a waywardness whereby my first parents, having thought one thing at the font, thought better of it on their way out though the porch.

Obviously it was no use setting my memory to hunt down whether I was Pat short for Patrick or for Patricia, because in my case the Pat was not short for anything at all.

I was by now, I had to admit, rather reduced.

Interlugubre

And what of me as narrator? What indeed of me as character? Am I to remain forever a spawned but not yet hatched, not yet freeswimming personality?

For I am imprisoned inside this I like the tadpole-pupil inside the jelly eye.

I understand now that it is often self-disgust which causes suicide.

I am hateful to myself through claustrophobia. It is not a personality, this jellysac I can't break out of; it is a mere agglutination of personal characteristics. And must I forever shew you everything, including myself, though this not quite transparent, this yellowed, wobbly and probably distorting gelatinous envelope, myself?

I am weary of the limited permutations on predictable refractions which it imposes on every light I pass through it.

And now I discover that suicidalness is a social emotion. It is you I am afraid of disgusting with my smeary self. Left to that self, I could wear my personality as unthinkingly, and move inside it as (b)lithely, as an animal in its pelt.

It is for your sake I am seeking to arrange my suicide, batting about almost frantically in my race against excretion (my dear time's waste matter) to locate the predestined masc. or fem. murderer who shall destroy, by gobbling up, this I.

For I cannot shew you anything of myself in its entirety — no not the simplest action on my part, not the extending of my arm.

83

I have to shew you the internal sensation of my muscles flexing, the breaking-into my frame of vision by a segment of arm I intellectually know to be my own.

And that is, I know, not very appealing. It's like shewing you a constant dissection, with a square of skin cut, folded back and pinned down in order to display the sinews.

Am I never to present to you a whole, a completed arc of movement? Shall I never offer you an entire outside of skin, that might tactilely attract you? Why should I not appear to you as a free-moving figure in costume?

My pelt, could it move away from you, might by its narcissistic unconcern with what it provoked in you, by the mystery of its self-movingness, excite you into admiring pursuit. Free-standing, my plumage might curl into crests and cartouches and thus cut a dash on the retina of your imagination.

I am weary of being unattractive to you.

I fear I shall lose whatever little I have of your affection to one — to *any* one — of the far from interesting bystanders and bysitters in the café, simply because I can shew you, uninspiriting though the exhibit is, the back of their, as I can't of my own, shoulders.

Yet don't leave me.

P.

I WOULD NOT capitulate to so silly a beleaguerment.

I gathered myself, mentally growling. I was a leonine wave, preparing, with a little sucked-back silt and a rattle of pebbles, to mieux sauter.

My chosen (and, I had thought, the obvious) method of enquiry had failed me — or I it; I was by now too short of bounce to bandy recriminations. So: I must (rather rapidly) pick and try another.

I had in reality no choice about *which* other, there being only one I had any acquaintance with.

I kept meanwhile experiencing, like subcutaneous itches, intimations that I hadn't exhausted my previous method. It, however, had exhausted me. I remained willing to try any definite-shaped idea when it should present itself, but not myself to pursue that enquiry

84

systematically. I could not emotionally afford to risk further defeats.

So I addressed my thoughts to a subject whose title had long rung in my ears as resoundingly as, and a great deal more plausibly than, Holy Catholic and Apostolic Church: namely, the Traditional Formal Logic.

My thoughts had, after all, been boasting, not so long before, of my innate Irish logicalness. Let me, therefore apply it.

The weakness in my plan, I knew before beginning it, was that Logic does not profess to deliver goods so flat and material as facts. The utmost it undertakes is to criticize and permute your reasoning.

That, I had now to hope, might be exactly all I needed. From the factual information I already possessed there might well be some obvious inference to be drawn which I'd so far been too flurried to draw.

Logic is a machine — whose disadvantage to me was that, factually, it is only as good as the information you feed it and whose advantage was, precisely, that you do feed it.

A machine that gives you something to do gives you, by the same token, a possibly quite spurious feeling of doing something.

With logic you can, for example, take a syllogism couched in one of the other three figures and (by exploring the immediate inferences of its constituent propositions) 'reduce' it to the first figure. This activity (which it had quite likely come into my mind to do because I was feeling reduced myself) gives you the satisfaction of doing sums but requires of you no mathematics.

A passage of my nineteenth year, consisting of two terms I spent at London University, had been almost wholly occupied by my dazed fascination with Formal Logic, a subject I not so much studied as played. I found Logic less arbitrary than crossword puzzles (though I'm quite prepared to believe it stands to thinking in the same specious relation as filling in letters in a crossword does to writing literature) and at the same time less disturbing than chess.

That passage of my life I have come to see as an (architectural sense) passage. I look back into a low-ceilinged, darkish, superficially chilling and austere hall, like an air-raid shelter. Immediately, no doubt, it represents an amusement arcade or the children's annexe to a science museum: beyond that, it probably images (why else did I call it a shelter? why else should I call it a children's annexe?) the womb. (Sirens wail ai-ee, and wombs fall.) Inside, my tunnelled footsteps echo excitingly from mood to mood of the eternal Logic machine, as it casts on me its child-binding spell of buttons to push to produce lights — which dazzle, if they don't illuminate.

I now needed, since Logic gave me something to do, pen and paper.

I felt my way into the flap pocket I'd noticed, during my inspection of my obstinate upper garment, just above my waist, and found a ballpoint pen rolling in the unspecifiable crumbs and fluff of pocket-interiors that might have been a material deposit left by the act of remembering childhood.

Into the gape of my briefcase, which had been aproned across my knees ever since my disappointment with my passport, I inserted the flat of my hand, as if I were fishing back a too precipitately posted letter from a pillar box, and edged out the first book I met.

A remote sense brushed at me that I hadn't exploited books. But I put it down as absurd. The information I sought had certainly not been published in a book. Instead, as the book I had pulled out had come conveniently upside down, I opened it the wrong way about and at once encountered a rear page that was blank.

On that, pressing through it to my briefcase, which I thereby pinned to my knees, I set to work to write out the valid moods of the syllogism.

There is, of course, a mnemonic for them. And I had, of course, forgotten it, as I always do mnemonics.

(I must explain, in case my Reader had wiser things to do at nineteen than play Logic, that each valid mood of the syllogism has its own name, which is in effect a code: the consonants are in many cases significant of how you go about reducing the thing; and the three vowels in each name indicate the types — A,E,I, or O — of the three propositions that make up the syllogism.)

The syllogism mnemonic, if you forget some of it, happily gives you a second chance. It is composed in (Latin, medieval) hexameters, so scansion may help you to fill in the blanks.

By jig-saw-puzzling over   and ⌣ syllables, I managed to

86

reconstruct and (after I'd wiped the furriness off my ballpoint on the edge of my blank page) to write out the first line entire:

BARBARA, CELARENT, DARII, FERIOque prioris.

That left four lines to go. For, although there are only four figures of syllogism, some figures contain more valid moods than others, and the total mnemonic runs, with the inclusion of some shameless and therefore unmemorable metrical fill-in, into which I saw my memory might pitfall, to five lines of hexameters.

I made an attempt on the second line but was at once held up. Did it begin CESARE, CAMESTRES or CAMESTRES, CESARE? If I jangled the order at the outset, metre might refuse to help me out with the conclusion.

Now that I'd paused on the word, I found myself noticing for the first time that CESARE isn't Latin but Italian.

The medieval scholastic who'd devised that one must have been already tainted with the vernacular. Considered as Latin, CESARE's an aBorgiation.

Then I was diverted into a yet wider loop from my route by remarking the curiously Persian look of CAMESTRES.

Surely CAMESTRES would pass for a descendant of one of the later, obscurer dynasties of Dariuses. (My imagination set the family of CAMESTRES before an all-conquering CESARE — and ran back to wriggle-in, with a quick scratchy brush, onto the parapet, a very wrinkled, very heavily jewelled, very sad monkey.)

And in general they have very attractive — very, I was now finding, diverting — names, these moods of the syllogism. Even BARBARA, so banalised nowadays, begins to glitter and clang again with her of-right barbaric majesty when you consider her as the queen-pin of the whole machine, the first mood of the first figure (to which all the others are reducible).

Somewhere in the second figure came (I wrote it in, feint, at the edge of my page, to wait till I possessed enough information to fit it in to the metre) the magnificent BAROCO.

(And indeed *was* it from formal Logic, stashed away as Logic had been in a spiced treasure chest in a highly but not frequently thought of corner, that that name had seeped out and into art-history?)

By the side of where I planned to assemble the third figure, I perched, to wait in feint until it might swoop down into its place on my hexametrical clothes-line, FELAPTON, a mood I was fond of because its name suggested some interesting medieval felony that was also, no doubt, a breach, probably sexual, of canon law. (Brush up my better gaiters, Mrs Godlibody, as I am expecting Canon Law for tea today.)

Into the fourth figure I knew I must insert the exotic BRAMAN-TIP (and what dome-breasted, nipple-pinnacled architectural manner might *that* denote, what Taj Mahal baroque, what pavilioned-in-splendour Brightonrockoco?) and also CAMENES, so obviously easily confusable with CAMESTRES of the second figure and for that reason never thus confused; for whereas CAMESTRES rang Persian, CAMENES looked to me Greek, but lateish Greek, the surname perhaps of one of those eastern emperors who came, exactly, *so* late as to *have* surnames.

Suddenly I saw I'd started at the wrong place. I ought to have begun with the types of proposition.

In a rush of excitement, I perceived that I'd in fact misunderstood my own point. Those $^-$ and $^\smile$ symbols, which I'd been deploying in their metrical sense to try to body out the mnemonic hexameters, are used in Logic to shorthand whether the Terms of a proposition are distributed ($^-$) or undistributed ($\smile$).

The distinction has to do with whether the Term wholly or only partly overlaps with the class or society it is brought into relation with.

What I had been getting at, though I'd refused to let myself see it, was the notion that it was through my own involvement with society (my, if I thought of myself as a Logical Term, distribution) that I should be able to discover my sex. (And might there be, I ardently hoped, no Mutilation of the Terms.)

If, therefore, the key was to be found in my social relations and reactions, I must first tabulate their possible forms.

Hastily I scribbled, so that I might have it before me, the paradigm of the types of proposition, with an example beside each:

$$\bar{S} \quad a \quad \breve{P} \qquad \text{All men are amnesiacs}$$
$$\bar{S} \quad e \quad \bar{P} \qquad \text{No men are amnesiacs}$$

| S̆ i P̆ | Some men are amnesiacs |
| S̆ o P̄ | Some men are not amnesiacs. |

Using that as guide and analogy, I then wrote out what my thoughts had been working towards in despite of myself, the paradigm of the possible truths of my own situation:

I am a man
I am a woman
I am a homosexual man
I am a homosexual woman.

I noticed I had unconsciously compared being a woman to negativeness and being homosexual to partialness. (Would the comparison have been more logical the other way round?)

I had also, I noticed, left 'heterosexual' to be understood in the first two propositions — but I easily saw that that did not necessarily mean I was heterosexual myself but only that I'd observed, as who could fail to?, the heterosexual bias of society.

I now possessed an exhaustive tabulation of the sexual ways in which I could, and in one of which I must, be related to my fellow beings.

Only: I did not immediately quite see how it advanced me. For I didn't see how I proposed to crack it and make it reveal which of the four propositions applied to me.

As I sat looking down at it, I became aware that one of my fellow beings was also looking down at it, from above and behind my shoulder.

I raised my head. A trolley made chiefly of rigid wire had been stationed, in the aisle, alongside our table.

Paused behind the trolley, one nanny-hand on its pramesque push rail, stood a blue uniform overall — whose free hand now explained itself by reaching out to and hovering above my unsipped coffee and unbitten brioche.

Pleased by my coolness under scrutiny, I neatly tore out the page I had been writing on, folded it and enflapped it (don't flap), along with my pen, in my pocket.

The hesitating hand decided against my snack and reached on to snatch away my companion's emptied beer glass.

I passed my companion a quick look, hoping he might feel hinted into departure.

He was of course looking at me. But he was giving not a sign of intention to go.

The trolley trundled away past our now unjustly, I felt, shared table. The glass that was being carried off had been my companion's only stake in the territory.

Watching the retreat of the blue overall, I had no difficulty in being sure that its occupant was a woman, though I would not have predicted quite the breadth of shoulder that trolley-pushing had, in the evident reality, developed.

As she distanced herself from me, I noticed she was wearing (blue, serge, presumably also uniform) trousers.

I reflected that the airport authorities rather contradicted themselves by employing that archaic trousered silhouette to differentiate the men's lavatory from the women's and yet issuing the women on their café staff with trousers as an item of uniform.

The uptodateness of that consideration drew me out of my hermit's-cell refuge in medieval scholasticism. As I emerged, my mind was set on by two simultaneous trains of idea.

(i) edged me again towards the books I'd bought. Perhaps I had not exhausted documentary evidence when I had discovered the uselessness of my passport.

However, (i) was coming to me out of the weaker speaker.

Technology errs, I contrived to think just before fadeout supervened, in propping up our bifocalism: wasteful to direct the two speakers of a stereophonic system, or the two lenses of a pair of spectacles, to helping two sense organs to focus on a single object.

The true advance of civilisa-

(ii), meanwhile, put it interestingly to me that there was a secondary sex characteristic which I had so far completely ignored.

It was, moreover, the very one you would have expected to jump first to my mind, given my passion for opera and my even having received, somewhere in my child-hinter-hood, the elements of a vocal-musical education.

At that point I set my mark on a theme (ii)(a) to be resumed later, if need be.

In some hope that, as a result,

90

tion will come when science enables a human being to see two Veroneses, one out of each eye, at once or to lend each of his ears to a different opera at the same time.

My own intellectual stereophony was, however, so little perfected that at that point (i) was, for the time being, drowned out by (ii).

need would not be, I rushed on to (ii)'s main burden.

Idiot, negligent idiot, I had not tested the pitch of my voice.

The speaking voice I discounted, that mere internal turning over of a gravelly mechanism, pitchless, claimed not by the external ear as notes but by inner, prior knowledge as, simply, *mine*.

I meant (*of course* operatic I meant) the singing voice, which you loose onto and can retrieve from the surrounding air, and which you can then examine as though you were hearing it objectively and notice in which register you have naturally pitched it.

Come, fragments still humming in my head's repertory from *Alitalia;* come, any of you well-shaped phrases — soft-curving parabola (though bitten off by my defective memory like a broken pediment) (I suffer from a song-impediment) to which Belpaesiello set 'dov'è il cor sereno' or stutter of brass-lipped breath and percussed rhythms with which he celebrated that 'fronte vittoriosa': any of you will do: the shortest snatch of you will do: I have only to open my mouth and loose you . . .

I glanced round at the

(i) again pushed my attention towards the book I was still limply holding.

crammed café and across at my so close, so stolid, so staring companion.

That small act which was all I needed to do in order to discover my sex was an utter (social) impossibility.

But I preferred, though I had been shamed by my eager stupidity, to trudge back and retrieve (ii)(a), which had occurred and been marked down apropos of my education.

Could I, I now saw I'd been getting at, trap my memory into a stumble on that long strip of (remarkably bumpy) waste ground?

There had been so many enthusiastically started-on and scheduled schemes, into whose ambience of enthusiasm I had myself thoroughly entered, drawing up syllabuses and laying down timetables for myself — and all the schemes had, quite suddenly and briefly, like short-winded watches, run down.

My sawn-off two terms of Logic at London set the type for all my educadventures before and after.

(Could that misadventure conceivably, I now wondered, have been contrived by me as an unconscious rebus? For a Logical proposition *can* have only two Terms.)

I nodded now in cursory remembrance at plans to work up my natural polyglottism to a proficiency where I should always be able (if other enthusiastic plans failed) to work as an interpreter; plans to prepare me for the stage (including fencing lessons, good in general in the deportment department even if never needed for stage fights — I got through five of a course of twelve lessons); half-semesters here, abbreviated sessions there, dissipated seminars everywhere; stretches meant to combine educating me with some service on my part to some never quite defined community; and the early, melodramatically cut-off (I set accidental fire to the chapel) attempt to train me up as a singer by sending me to a choirschool.

No, that deceptive last item held no true clue. I was born into an age when the supply of boy voices had already run so thin that choirschools schooled girls as well.

And yes, though I remembered plainly that it was the treble part I sang in our choruses, that, too, was non-significant. The chorister bit of my schooling took place between when I was nine-and-three-quarters and when I was ten-and-a-half.

Three of my choirschool-fellows, who in this case *had* to be boys, were chosen —

(POUNCE: Why was I not chosen? Was I, then, not a boy?

Release that savage-hold, Rover. I was disqualified before ever sex came in question, by being neither sweet nor strong enough in voice, nor yet advanced nor diligent enough in musical theory)

— chosen, I was remembering, to sing the Three Genii in somebody's (professional) production of the *Zauberflöte*.

It was, at least until I fired the chapel, *the* choirschool sensation.

One of the three, an exceptionally pretty boy,

(a clue?, I demanded under the heading of (i), but quickly saw that, if it was, it could be read both ways)

who had an every-ten-seconds mannerism of hitching up his grey flannel shorts by wriggling the insides of his elbows against his waist, took it into his pretty, serious-looking head to learn also (having, I suppose, heard it at rehearsal) the music for the Queen of the Night.

A bizarre image has beset my memory ever since. He stands, in those snake-belted and much-hitched grey trousers, his grey shirt open at his innocent throat (overall he looked, now that I think of it, not unlike a Wimbledon ballboy), upright with that effortless verticality of the back of the neck attainable only ɔy pre-pubescents; pursing and un-pursing the pink o c f his mouth, he lets fly the acid-drop-shower of notes, the seething morally-evil syllables, of Der Hölle Rache kocht in meinem Herzen, with the most complete musical purity and precision and not the tiniest inflexion of emotional understanding.

The book in my hands was paper-bound in a way that suggested it was French, though the writing on the back of the cover seemed English.

My educational resumé had delivered disappointment. Through all the vicissitudes of my career as a pupil, tne one vital item remained constant: I had been co-educated.

The writing on the back was upside-down to me — but, I re-called with a faint anxiety I couldn't immediately place, the right way up for my close companion opposite.

A last, despairing recall of the final reaches of my higher education recovered only the

I turned the book round, which would put it out of bounds to my companion unless he had (which from the look of him he well might) the sinister knack of reading upside down, and skimmed through the plaudits patting it on the back cover:

'exploration of the I-thou relationship in the context of the post-Herzen dialectic' — *George Steiner*

'like Stendhal' — *Stephen Vizinczey.*

blank-faced fact that at London I had attended King's (co-educational, non-residential) College.

Another bizarre image stood stark on my memory. One turret of the castellated Victorian grange occupied by the choir-school was known as 'the Headmasters' Wing'. The headmasters were a pair of by then crumbling bass baritones, one with a flop of dyed auburn hair, one with a moustache we naturally believed spirit-gummed on. Both wore suede shoes. Both had in their time sung (or so ardently aspired to sing that they had by now fantasised they they did sing) Don Giovanni. Up in the Headmasters' turret, they must have had (it was forbidden territory to us, of course) two bathrooms side by side — or, conceivably and yet more bizarrely, two baths side by side in a single bathroom. Often at night, after lights-out, about 10.30., we would hear the slooshing of four taps, then splashing in canon: and then, neither quite syncopated nor quite concerted, but in the sort of uncertain rivalry in which you try to shew confidence by pretending you have not noticed your rival's existence, two equally but at different moments breathy renderings of the Champagne Aria would come resonantly rolling, winding and tumbling about one another down the spiral turret stairs.

Goodness knows why, apart from its own inherent vulgarity, theatrical tradition assumes the 'vino' Don Giovanni is singing about must be champagne.

If our two headmasters did drink in their baths, it was probably (inducing, perhaps, in conjunction with the hot water, a sort of vocal abortion) gin.

ID

97

on "discipline" and the "lessons" administered to the heroine, should make it a must for
school libraries' — *Gillian Free-
man*

'an account of the subjection
and humiliation of the student'
— *Tariq Ali*

I turned the book the right
way up.
Parisian it indeed was by
provenance, but it was an English translation.
I opened it at the title-page,
where I read:-

L'HISTOIRE DE LA LANGUE D'OC
(THE STORY OF OC'S TONGUE)

All Gaul is divided into three
tarts?, commented my thoughts
in fatigue. I went on reading.

by S.X.Y.

with an introduction by A. M. Smith, M.A. Venusmount Press: Paris
and San Francisco: 1953

I was relieved, after suffering my consciousness to be tossed from
side to side, and to no advantage either way, in my defective
stereo-thinking apparatus, to feel it concentrate it its entirety on a
single object.

I considered I needed a respite from my enquiry. It was an absurd
enquiry, but that didn't make it less wearying.

I decided, however, to skip the introduction and, indeed, the
opening of the story. I couldn't afford much time for my respite.

And in any case I have found that even when books are deficient in read-on, you can make them interesting by applying to recon-struct-back. The neo-surrealist gimmick of writing a coherent narrative and then re-shuffling the pages to render it incoherent is wasted on readers like me, who usually do-it-ourselves anyway. The device works particularly well, I've noticed, with pornography, probably because you fill in the book's past with material from your own fantasy and thereby bend everything you read to your own kinks.

INTERLEWD

I shall of course be at pains to give you too, dear Reader,
the utmost opportunity to employ that device.

Taking a random hunk of pages in hand, I turned them over, with the result that the book opened to me about four-fifths of the way through, and read:

the blindfold. A moment later, the leading-chain was snapped
onto the metal ring embedded in the deep, close-fitting
rubber bracelet she had worn on her left wrist since her second
lesson.
A twitch on her leading-chain told Oc her guardians were
leading her forward.
Without speaking, they conducted her down the stone
corridors. At the point she had learnt to expect, their course
veered aside.
Oc found herself mounting the three steps that led to the
great salon where her previous lessons had taken place.
The heavy, studded door swung open, and her guardians ushered
her in.
The salon was silent. But Oc could tell. from the almost
unbearably sweet trembling that fell on

I turned the page and noticed, almost as soon as I resumed reading overleaf, that my consciousness was no longer undivided.
I seemed, perhaps in sardonic mimickry of my recent and futile expedition into academic scholasticism, to be annotating the text as

99

I went with a pseudo-scholarly commentary, my thoughts writing-in an intermittent grumbly obbligato that might have been being propounded on a double-bass.

and possessed her whole body, that "He" was present.

Meekly, Oc waited, standing between her guardians, who had allowed the leading-chain to fall slack.

Blindfolded as she was, her gaze, in natural modesty, sought the floor.

From the far end of the great salon came a sharp swishing sound.

This was followed by booted footsteps.

Then, to Oc's joy, "He" spoke. "His" deep, grave tones were presumably addressed to the guardians of one of the other pupils. "Very well. You may take this one away now. But keep her in readiness, in case I require her again later this evening."

The booted footfalls then approached Oc.

She trembled again, in joy mingled with dread.

"He" was standing directly before her, contemplating the absolute submission of the slight yet full figure as it stood, naked, awaiting "His" will and pleasure, the thighs held slightly and invitingly apart by the rubber rings that had been immovably placed high up on them, like garters, at the completion of the fifth lesson.

Almost overwhelmed by the sweetness of being at "His" service, Oc waited for

The double quotes round *He* may be a mistake, on the part of a typesetter working in a language not native to him, for the emphasis of italics. Alternatively, it may be conjectured, but in the absence of knowledge of the earlier part of the text cannot be verified, that the double inverted commas (note the possible play on the word *inverted*) should be read as implying that the *He* in question is in some way not a genuine he.

We may make legitimate surmises as to the nature of the expected readership from the fact that a sophisticated reader would scarcely succumb to 'deep, grave tones' or gazes which 'seek the floor'.

Note the cardinal rôle taken in pornography by ritual:cf. the anxiety-allaying role of ritual in obsessional

100

the signal that "He" was ready to begin.

It came. The leathern loop of "His" riding-crop flicked round her left nipple, pulled sharply upward and brushed away again. It was the quick gesture, decisive, casual yet caressing, with which "He" always signified taking possesion of her being.

Yet "He" remained silent.

Oc was overcome with dread. Perhaps he did not find her wordy to proceed.

"He" had, however, only been lost in contemplation of the charming effect "His" riding-crop had made.

"He" spoke, gravely and courteously as was his wont.

"Good-day, Oc."

She blushed, which lent an extra prettiness to the tempting form.

"He" spoke again. "Is your tongue prepared, Oc, to be taught the seventh lesson?"

In relief and delight, she could only stammer out, "Master, yes."

Instantly the riding-crop leapt and cut cruelly into the flesh of her right buttock.

"Master!", she sobbed.

The descent of "His" raised hand was stayed.

The deep voice now spoke in accents of reproach. "Oc, Oc have you forgotten the first rule of the first lesson, the first rule of all language lessons?"

Too ashamed to speak, Oc sobbed.

The deep voice broke in on her weeping "Oc, Oc", she heard "Him" ask, "tell me: what is the first rule of the first lesson?"

neurotic acts, including communal ' (e.g. religious) ones.

It must be assumed that the rings round Oc's thighs were, in contrast to the bands on her wrists, of some thickness. They probably resembled deckquoits, though the author would think it undignified to say so.

One must of course emend *wordy* to *worthy*, meanwhile querying whether the high incidence of misprints in pornography and thrillers results from (i) printing in a foreign country or (ii) the fact that when the story is exploded it's exploded, with the result that no one can bear to read it through twice.

There — toll, toll — goes ritual again: a positive litany: indeed, a linguistilitany.

We may note the curiously illiterate effect made by those inverted commas round the *He*'s and *Him*'s. But then the whole work is on a level where a

101

She controlled her sobs sufficiently to breathe to "Him" the answer: "The first rule of the first lesson, Master, is that I am always to express my answers as a whole sentence."

"Very well, Oc", the courteous, grave voice said. "You will of course be punished for your forgetfulness later. For the present — "

"He" turned to Oc's guardians. "Is the apparatus to hand? Then prepare her tongue."

literate reader would scarcely —

Or am I simply defending myself against it?

I suddenly understood why I had all along urged myself — my idiot, idiot self — towards books, towards, most particularly, *this* book.

Of course. I reared my head from the page. I must test. How was I reacting? What was this Oc to me: self-subject-identified or submissively, supinely subjected object?

The answer was, for the first time since I had entered my maze of queries, totally clear. While I read, I *was* (except when my grumbling intellectual accompaniment held me off, which it did in rather the same bumpty, fending way as those ludicrous but slightly imagination-catching quasi-deck-quoits must have held off Oc's thighs one from the other) Oc.

Unhappily, a contradictory answer was no less clear. While I read, I also *saw* Oc — from the outside.

Suspicious, I forced myself to consult the text again (which was indeed, as I'd predicted at a time when I had no thought of undertaking the ordeal, almost unendurable the second time through).

I saw that I'd been the victim of a narrative method whose eye must by its nature be bifocal, peering sometimes through the subject, sometimes through the object.

What my grand test had tested was the nature of pornography, not of me.

Ironically, I rounded off my scholarly commentary by noting

102

that it's only to be expected that porno-narrative should be of that nature, since pornography is literary masturbation, and in masturbation one-and-the-same-person is both love-maker and love-object.

And that would be a high old shaming disastrous climax to my cold war with my graven companion, I reflected, if the *Histoire de la Langue d'Oc* were now to put me, imprisoned as I was in public, under a compulsion to masturbate.

I stowed the book back into my case.

Well, let me go on, I dared myself, my irony now sitting full on me like grotesque regalia: *did* it set any such impulse in train?

I briefly shut my eyes and listened to the sensations of my body.

I am not so ignorant of Freud as to deny that the two have a common psycho-genetic ancestor, but for immediate purposes what I felt was reciprocally exclusive with, if not actively antithetical to *any* type of erotic act (as, indeed, Freud himself pointed out in that brilliant paper of 1932, *The Acquisition of Power over Fire*). As I hearkened to my own sensations, I could not doubt that what reading the *Histoire de la Langue d'Oc* had in fact made me want, all but compulsively, to do was pee.

I gave it a moment, but the sensation did not go away. So I must.

I felt deeply inglorious: that my quest for happiness should be foiled by a bladder.

I hastily buckled my case, meanwhile looking round to locate the nearest of those entrances to the Transit Lounge one of which I must unorthodoxly, and quickly, use as an exit.

Fore-framing the blarney I should have to fountain forth to get myself through against the grain of the traffic, and then the despatch with which I must get myself to, and registered in, the airport hotel, on whose upper floors, at least, I could surely count on unsex-differentiated lavatories (but heaven send that on the registration card I should have to complete before I might ascend to those floors there be no space ogling me to fill in Mr/Mrs/Miss), I rose and began to walk, with a brisk step but a terribly failed feeling, out of the café area.

A voice from behind recalled me. 'Pardon.'

I half turned, paused.

My table-companion was looking graven interrogation at me.

Even at that late, forlorn moment I ironically noticed that he might, without cost or effort to himself, have solved my immediate enigma, prolonged my stay in transit and thus eventually have perhaps secured my life's happiness, if only he had thought to add two more syllables and call out 'Pardon, monsieur' or 'Pardon, madame'.

Had he been a French-speaker, he could hardly have prevented himself.

As it was, after uttering that one wantonly useless word, he seemed strangled about being an *any*thing-speaker.

He gestured with his head. He was indicating to me that I had not eaten my brioche or drunk my cappuccino.

I gave a great, sighing shrug. I forced myself to add a grin that mimed (truthfully – I was to that degree despondent) that I bore him no ill will. I hurried sadly away.

5

There was such a great bathtap whoosh (though that was a metaphor I quickly cautioned my mind to drop) of people coming into the Transit Lounge through the strait between desks (kindly hold your boardingpass in readiness to shew to either Scylla or Charybdis) that I fell back before it and took up a stance to one side, where I planned to wait it out while remaining well placed to nimble through as soon as it should slacken.

My station was just beneath a television set (closed-circuit, its purpose being, as I'd earlier noticed, to shew in clapper-board-style chalking which flights were due when and where, though for the present it was displaying only a muddy-eyed blank) which hung or, to be exact, protruded awkwardly downwards on stiff rods from somewhere in the unsearchably high ceiling.

Tantalisingly, from where I stood I had a direct, un-crowd-impeded vista to the top of the staircase which plunged down to the lavatories.

I turned away from that, of course.

104

For camouflage (for I now began to fear that this most urgent if least important of my wishes must be discernible by inspection), I pretended to scrutinise the throng that was weaving seemingly unmotivated molecular chains and skeins through the Lounge, though a deeper concentration in that neighbourhood gave evidence of its tendency to settle out towards the bar.

I tried to make (on anyone who might be noticing) the perhaps over-subtle impression of knowing I had a high chance of meeting, but no definite appointment with, a friend scheduled to pass through this Transit Lounge at the same time as myself.

And evidently some person behind me, perhaps one of the incoming whoosh, was indeed about to engage, by chance or design, in some such meeting. For a middle-aged man had shaken himself free of his fellow particles and was coming, straight-pathed as an electron, towards the strait, giving off an airedale grin that signalled incipient meeting and his pleasure in it.

He was transgressing, I crossly observed, a minor but crucial social rule, because I was directly in his line of grin and yet he had not given me a switching-off sign. A person less urgently preoccupied than I then was might easily have been browbeaten into believing in an acquaintanceship and might even have set about preparing to pretend to remember him.

He was obviously English, his tweed suit woven from (apparently) airedale wool.

I was convinced (though perhaps only because recent trains of my own thought were seeking their terminus) that he was a Don — academic, however, not (thought in itself grotesque) Giovannesque.

Socially, he was without doubt a lout.

My imagination visualised his magnum opus: an edition (apparatus criticus, glozes on glozes, conjectures about scholiasts' conjectures) of some commentary on a commentary (probably a late-Alexandrian critique of a mid-Alexandrian grammarian). Anxiously he would write to fellow scholars enquiring 'Have you read me on Ossa on Pelion?'

No, I was letting my own Greek speak.

Would his text be Latin, then? Perhaps that post-Ovidian, silvery imaginary epistle, *Hyperion to a Satyr*?

105

I was still over-Classifying. He must in reality be not merely English but English-school. And as a matter of fact surely that suit was made of Old-English-Thorn-Proof tweed?

'You don't know me. But I know you', he said.

Not merely lout but hobbledehoy, I thought, pitying whoever it was that had unsuspectingly entered the Transit Lounge to be met by him.

His airedale grin broke like a Japanese wave into droplets of airedale bark-laugh. 'Haw; haw; haw.'

He had hawlted slap in front of me. I was close enough to remark Old-English-Ash down his tweed front.

'Hilary Evelyn O'Rooley', he said. 'Haw; haw. Don't deny it. Haw.'

'Evelyn Hilary, actually', I corrected, at the same time correcting the focus of my eyes now that his stopping in front of me turned out not to be a blunder. (And my speaking voice sounded, in my own ears, a noise without single determinable pitch — which drifted on to be drowned in the chatter around before I could pluck it out of the air to hear objectively.)

'But in any case Pat. Haw. Non e vero? Sí, è vero. Haw; haw. I knew you from photographs.'

Was I, then, famous?

I was not. What's more, I well knew I was not. I was interested to notice that I had momentarily extended my specific amnesia into an entirely fake general amnesia in my own mind, depositing a smoke screen whose only purpose could only be to let protrude for a second through it that fantasy of fame, which in the ordinary egalitarian way I wouldn't admit as a conscious wish.

And in any case I suspect (o subtlety of English idiom) that, if he'd meant he's seen photographs of me in the newspapers and so forth, he'd have had to say 'I knew you from your photographs', whereas by saying 'I knew you from photographs' he rendered the photographs in question specific, private and probably adhesive-corn- ered-in to a deckle-edged photograph album.

But *whose* photograph album? , I wondered in a bewilderment that must have shewn, since he went on to semi-explain himself. 'Name's Donaghue. Not that that'll mean anything. Haw haw. Except, haw,

106

how we Irish-extractions do stick together, eh? , haw. Makes you sound like a tooth, doesn't it? , "of Irish extraction", haw. No, it's my wife who's your pal. *Was* your pal. Time etcetera, haw; haw. But she still has all the photographs. Marvellous collection. Well, you can tell how clear they are from the fact I recognised you. Haw, haw; haw. My wife Betty. Now are you with me? '

I squinted, to indicate the pain of thoughtfulness.

'No, how could you be? , haw', he resumed. 'Her married name won't mean a thing to you. She's Betty Bouncer, as was, as they say, haw.'

Bouncer, Bounder, Bowyer?, my ear queried. Which had he said? I'd let it go too long past, now, to ask him to repeat it. I didn't even much want to know.

I wanted only to look over my shoulder and, if the whoosh was by now stayed, escape.

But I couldn't be so rude as to look at this very moment.

'Don't say you don't remember', he airedale-panted.

'Indeed I do. Of course I do.'

It was true, too. The devil of it was, though, I remembered so imprecisely.

I couldn't even get the name right for sure. But those syllables, Betty Bow-something (Wow would have been the most appropriate, but I knew it wasn't that), were bouncing up and down in some trampolined recess of my memory.

I thought they probably belonged to the later reaches of my education.

That would fit. The photographs dated from some time back, yet I must have already borne in them my adult appearance or I shouldn't have been recognisable.

Had, then, Betty Boundy and I been drama students together? It offered a plausible account of her cult of her photograph album.

Or had (I suspected my escape route was now infuriatingly cleared at this moment when I couldn't take it) Betty Boundary and I belonged to one of those groups of 'young people' engaged on doing the community some such service as potato picking?

Had, in fact, Betty Boughbreak been the hostel's wit, whom I remembered as a chattery, small-statured (four foot eleven) teenager

107

who got herself carelessly pregnant and told us all she wanted to be known as the smallest womb in the house?

Could I ask the airedale husband if it was that one who was now his wife?

I snatched a glance overshoulder. Only two people were now coming through the strait, both shewing their documents to Scylla, which left Charybdis free for me.

I started edging, by little dance-steps, away from the airedale. My throat was already uttering breaking-off whimpers.

Could I imply I had a flight to catch? (Not if I then instantly left and was seen to leave the airport.) Could I frankly explain I urgently had to pee – or, as I'd better put it in case the airedale and I were of different sexes, which imposes, heaven knows why, circumlocutions, that I wanted to go to the loo? (No, because he'd simply wave me down that flight of steps and I could never explain the insolubility of the dilemma that waited to confront me at the bottom.)

'What a fantastic chance my running into you is, when you think of it, haw haw haw', he said. '*Won't* Betty be bucked when I tell her?'

I gave him a grin and prepared to break away. Suddenly we both staggered under a noisy flux of people. I realised with despair that a further whoosh was coming through, and blocking my hope of, the strait. 'Hey, let's move out of this, haw haw', he said, touching his hand to my feline-pelted elbow and nudging me further to the side. 'Whew; haw. I can't wait to see Betty's face.'

I have a point of sensitivity through knowing how easily I can seem to have forgotten the friends of my youth through callousness or snootiness. What the friends concerned seldom make allowance for is that, thanks to the vicissitudes of my education, there are simply *more* friends of my youth to hold in memory than there are of the average person's.

'Give Betty my love', I said.

'I certainly will.'

I was wasting, I suddenly perceived, the most promising opportunity I'd yet been given. To hell with all this probing to discover who Betty was. The airedale could be made to disclose what I was. I couldn't, anyway, leave the Lounge for a minute or two: I had only to employ those minutes to delicate advantage, and I might not need to.

'What am I *wearing* in Betty's photographs?' I demanded.

A flush of newcomers shouted their way past us. 'What did you say?'

'In Betty's photographs: what am I wearing?' (Why does one always re-arrange a sentence one has to repeat?)

'Clothes', he said. 'Haw; haw; haw. Don't worry, we're not going to use the pictures to blackmail you.'

Well, I hadn't lost ground by it, I consoled myself. It might easily have been the potato field Betty and I had shared, in which case we'd all have been in dungarees, and I'd have ended up back in ambiguity anyway, where I was now.

But I had in fact lost a little, for I hadn't foreseen the counterattack. 'Why', he shouted as another wave of chatter rose between us, 'do you want to know?'

'General historical interest', I shrugged. 'Progress of fashion.'

'That's a good one. Haw. Haw. Haw. You obviously remember the pictures perfectly. Betty'll be so glad.'

They must be in fancy dress, then?, I internally queried.

'Noisy place this. Haw. Haw.'

Whore, whore, my thoughts commented. I was turning against Betty.

'Amazing when you think of it', batty Betty's husband was saying. 'I just looked round and saw you. Knew you instantly.'

He was a man who, if I had a drink with him and if in fact I, too, was a man, would be almost certain to address me as 'old boy' or even (was I not by a good six or seven years the younger) as 'dear boy'.

I weighed the scheme. At the worst I'd be stuck with another of those non-significant negatives I'd grown familiar with. For I saw that, from an absence of 'old boy', I couldn't with certainty deduce that I *wasn't* a man.

It was worth trying, however, on the chance I might cleverly elicit a positive, perhaps even 'old man' itself.

I hesitated only because this was not the moment to be pouring liquid into my system on a mere off-chance. Would I even survive the pouring (for he'd surely opt for beer?) into a glass?

109

But, as a further bump against our shoulders reminded me, I couldn't leave at this moment anyway.

I prepared the airedale for a move to the bar by saying 'Yes, we seem to have gotten ourselves into the most uncomfortable corner of the whole place.'

He gave me look of airedale encouragement.

I am Irish and about to make you a Logical proposition, I thought; can we come to Terms?

But I came, instead, up against a difficulty. The way a woman would invite a middle-aged tweedy man to take a drink is, by the social rules, quite different from the way a man would.

My cunning in full flight, I neutrally said 'Don't you think we might shift from this corner and drink to Betty?'

He shot back his tweed cuff, glanced at a vast knobbly wrist-watch he had strapped there and gulped 'Can't. Would have loved to. But I must – haw; haw – fly.' (O.K., airedale, I thought, get airborne.) He wheeled and pointed up at the closed circuit television. 'Look. My flight's called. I must off.'

True enough, the details of a flight to London had been chalked up and were being transmitted.

'It's been nice – ', I began, despairingly.

'Splendid. Amazing chance. I'll tell Betty.'

He was tumbled away like a clout in a washing machine, absorbed, without time to leave a haw behind him in the slip-stream, into the latest gush of arrivals and carried from me towards departure gate eight.

Against reason, I felt deserted.

Even my personal past, in which Betty Bouncer had played I did not know what rôle but, I now felt, some warm and vivid one, had become indistinct to me and was being carried away.

Perhaps I shewed the cratering of my soul in my face. For suddenly the airedale lurched briefly back at me, almost bumping me. 'Betty often speaks of you', he flung. 'She says – haw; haw – you were her first date.'

I was still shaping my face to a social reaction when he was gone.

I turned. The spurt through the strait was easing, an opportunity of exit beginning to be presented.

110

First date, had he said?, my ear queried; or first mate?

I suddenly, joyously saw it didn't matter which. For I saw what he'd given me.

I could hardly dare to let myself believe, after so many single clues which had turned out to point to two-headed conclusions, that here at last was a bifurcated clue both of whose prongs converged on a single, unequivocal piece of information.

For Betty Bouncer, Betty Bouncer, I happily apostrophised, you are obviously heterosexual to at least the conventional extent of remaining married to the airedale, with whom you obviously observe the heterosexual conventions of speech: whether, therefore, I was your first date or whether we went further and I was indeed your first mate (and I will gladly concede you may have been also punning on some nautical pastime or get-up, possibly the fancy dress of those photographs which you have so sagely cherished; indeed, I will convince myself memory now brings you back in festoons of blonde hair jauntily but insecurely tucked up under a yachting cap, while you play cap'n or bo's'n or any other apostrophe'd rôle you please, on the fo'castle if it will give you any pleasure, and you may 'list or 'press me any day, in my sheer gratitude, as your bo's'n's mate, ma'am) — whichever word your husband said, beloved Betty Bouncer, and whichever way you care to read the evidence, I quite clearly am, must be and can only be A MAN.

I walked not towards the exit-strait, though it was now empty, but, firmly and quickly, to the stairs.

6

INTERLOO

And in hurling myself from top to bottom of them I shall be destroyed. For, triumph, triumph!, I have attained (or had handed to me on a chatter-platter) my suicide; and this, which I, being at the time in my bright mind, address to my Reader-coroner, is my suicide note.

Yours In Quest,

P. (Sir)(Knight Errant)

7

Shoulders effortlessly squared, back vertical, O'Rooley ran lithely down the steps: a man at ease in, and with, his own body.

His hands were in his pockets. His briefcase, its weight no burden, was held secure by the crook of his left arm.

He was softly whistling a martial air from Belpaesiello's *Alitalia* – or what he meant to pass for such: he didn't know it himself, but O'Rooley couldn't whistle in tune.

From the foot of the stairs he took a couple of firm but not particularly hurried strides across the corridor and pushed open the swing door marked $\left\{ \begin{matrix} \text{Messieurs} \\ \text{Herren} \end{matrix} \right\}$.

As it pushed, the palm of his hand deposited a sort of passing dog's pat on the little painted silhouette of a figure in trousers which reinforced the legend on the door. It might have been a gesture of amusement at the perversity of a world whose conventions made the bifurcated garment the emblem and indeed, until recently, the prerogative not, as would have been sensible, of the bifurcated but of the quasi-quinquefurcated sex.

Inside, there was a row of washbasins and, next to them, a tall stool. On that perched an attendant scarcely bigger than a dwarf, who must have had to climb to attain his seat. His white jacket, designed as half-length, reached on him to vestment point.

He was hunched over a paperback book whose spent pages he

112

That is inexact. Something — flesh briefly veiled by under-clothes — was there, but not in the expected form.

Half-fainting, Patricia staggered against the wall and dully heard that she had knocked her briefcase thumping to the floor.

8

Her first collected sensation was one she judged irrational: relief that, thanks to the modernity of the airport (and possibly a touch also to the fact that newly landed gentry might need, in addition, to be sick), at least the lavatory was of the decent, civilised, two ways two-way kind and not one of those men-only stand-up-and-get-automatically-flushed contraptions which Victorianly or perhaps Prince Consortly paternalistic municipalities donated to society on the presumable principle that the lower orders ought not to s(h)it in the presen(ts)ce of their betters.

Her relief seemed irrational because she did not see how the nature of the gadget made her plight one whit easier. Civilised the place might be but only relatively. It was not a civilised setting to spend the rest of the day or of one's days in. And Patricia did not see how the hell she was to, undetected for what she was, get out.

Then she saw that her thoughts were inviting her, now that she chanced or mischanced to be there, to make use of the gadget.

But shock had driven off the wish and probably the ability.

She picked up her briefcase. Suppose the attendant had heard it thump and surmised that she (or, as the attendant must think, he) had in truth fainted?

Would he come morse-tapping-out his concern on the outside of the door?

Or would he come peeping under the partition wall, which did not even reach the floor, from the next-door cubicle — in which case at least Patricia's standing trousered legs would look both plausibly masculine and reassuringly unswooned.

She put her ear against the door. She seemed to hear footsteps but couldn't tell their direction. It might be another customer (the

115

word?) newly entered. But no door slammed, no hiss of piss succeeded. It could be that a customer had looked in for some less primary purpose, though it was unlikely that that attendant was very conversable.

Could she count on the attendant, indeed, to remain sepulchred in that tomb-tome he was so keen on while she, face averted as by a crick in the neck, fled at her fastest past him and out? Or was he *so* keen on his book that he'd have by now finished it? Might he repent of his taciturnity and make a point, on the emergence of that customer who (in idiot, idiot euphoria) had sung him out that cheery Ciao, of returning the courtesy by engaging the customer in dialogue, whereupon the customer would be rumbled for an imposter at the first face-to-face look or the first female-piched note of her speaking voice?

Suppose she counted on speed to get away with it even if the attendant *had* turned talkative? Yes; and suppose she unbolted, stepped double-quick out and plumb into the next, possibly already unzipping customer?

Immobilised by panic, she simply stood, with her briefcase clutched like a child, in the middle of the non-room.

How *could* the mistake have come about? In what way had beastly Betty Bouncer, the smallest non-womb in the house, slipped up in the provision of seemingly foolproof evidence?

Patricia reconstructed the airedale's bounce-back at her out of the crowd. Surely the implication was clear, whether he'd said 'first date' or 'first mate'?

Well: *why*, then, had he come back to say it, whichever it was, at all? Sheer fatuity? He was capable. But no: he'd delivered it pointed, as if it were a joke.

He had in fact delivered the words with a sort of indrawn silence round them. His voice had employed inverted commas for emphasis. The words had been spoken exactly as that illiterate porno-narrative punctuated ' "He" ' – and *that* had provoked her to suspicion.

A hundred plausibilities could explain it. It could very easily be that Patricia and Betty Bouncer had taken part in some charade, theatrical romp, tableau, fancy dress parade or party where one or both of them was in naughtical drag, whence it appeared that

116

Patricia O'Rooley had played escort or partner (in a hornpipe?) to Betty Bouncer and had come to be jokily described in inverted commas as Betty Bouncer's first mate or date.

Fantasy was not wanting to fill in the gaps of any of twenty plausible surmises. Yet explanation, no matter how plausible, did not of itself release Patricia from the lavatory.

She took out her pen. She was thinking of adding, to the commonplace book of the walls,

O DEAR WHAT CAN THE MATTER BE?
THERE'S A LADY LOCKED IN THE
GENTLEMEN'S LAVATORY.

But on a better thought she tip-toed up to the inscription she'd earlier dedicated to Betty.

It seemed she had a longer stretch to reach it than before. She could not, she argued, have physically shrunk from shock? It must be the stunting effect of knowing herself a woman and of intellectually knowing that women are on the average shorter than men. Or it might be that in the light of her new self-knowledge she had become aware of missing her high heels (for with trousers she was naturally — and, whence all that puzzlement, ambiguously — wearing flat soles).

It was worth the stretch. With vituperative pleasure, Patricia scribbled out the word BLESS and then made the inscription as a whole read

BUGGER YOU, BETTY BOUNCER.

Thus was an emended Betty Bouncer set to strut eternally along the quays of a garish, shabby waterfront, her body no longer that of a bawd but flat and hard as a board. For this was the new crew-cut, button-breasted Betty Bouncer, who wore bellbottom trousers but whose torso swelled into neither bells nor bottoms, whose outline was straight up and down but whose temperament was deeply kinky. For she passed herself off as a sailor boy: not because she was queer: not she: but in order to get herself picked up by some tanked-up hunk off a tanker or by some boozed and in any case dimly-perceptioned stoker whom she could count on to poke her without

117

noticing she wasn't a boy: and this because she liked, and liked only, being buggered.

Suddenly Patricia noticed that the square of frosted glass above the lavatory was a window. A triangular protrusion of steel on each side suggested it was what stage directions (*was* it, then, at drama school that she'd been co-educated with Betty Bouncer?) called practical (*scilicet*, annotated the scholiast, *it can be opened*).

Hastily she pulled down the lid on the lavatory (giving again thanks that it was practical, scilicet civilised, enough to have one), stepped up onto it and opened the window (which was luckily modern enough not to creak).

Outside, there seemed to be a narrow, dim-lit (as she would have expected from its being beneath ground-level *and*, evidently, not for the use of the public) corridor, which for the present looked and sounded safely empty.

The window was one of those tilting across the middle affairs which, if tilted to dead horizontal, would leave the lower half just negotiable to Patricia (who was now as glad as she had been, during her self-scrutiny, sorry that she was not one of those women with very large breasts), provided she dropped her briefcase through in advance of her.

She dropped it. It thudded. She waited to hear if the thud would provoke enquiry from either side, attendant or corridor.

But the silence continued. Patricia prepared to continue, too, but was held up by the thought of leaving the cubicle bolted on the inside. Eventually, no matter how deep the attendant was for the time being in his book, to leave the door locked must provoke enquiry, leading no doubt to forcible entry and perhaps, via the clue of the opened window, to detective work and pursuit of her trail. But she dared not unlock the door before departing, because it looked secured only by the bolt. It might swing open and expose her in mid-clamber to the attendant, who could ignore much but scarcely a customer leaving by way of the window.

She might have done better to leave in the orthodox way and rely on speed for disguise.

But she had committed herself irretrievably by pre-dropping her case.

118

She placed her hands on the far left of the window-frame and by jumping and wriggling got her right leg across the far right of the window-frame — whose steel edge, she thought as she pulled herself into a position astride it, if she *had* been a man in the first place, would surely by now have castrated her (him). She could not, of course, ride upright but had to keep her head hunched low for fear of bumping the horizontal square of glass. However, by stretching her neck out parallel with the floor, so that she overhung the lavatory like a tortoise seeking to be sick, she contrived to make room enough for her left leg to wriggle through the space and join her right leg, so that the two of them might protrude parallel with the floor of the corridor. Then it was only necessary to keep her head always slewed out of the window's way and meanwhile corkscrew down on the far side.

Her feet touched down on her briefcase. She scrambled off it, then stooped and gathered it into her arms.

She glanced left and right along the corridor. So far as the eye could see in the dimness, it led nowhere in both directions.

She had an intimation of how easily a wanderer, once strayed from the areas signposted for the information of the public, might become lost in what must be the huge administrative and quasi-logistical infra-structure of an airport.

By good luck there was, however, in the facing wall of the corridor and only a step or two to the left of where Patricia stood, a low-set, oblong trap-flap of much the size and design that a considerate suburbanite might have had inset in the back door for the convenience of a biggish dog.

Where it led Patricia had no way of guessing, but she judged it safer than the amphisbaenically interminable corridor. Getting through it would be child's or dog's play after the lavatory window.

She pushed the flap, which hinged at the top and swung inwards, and began to scrunch herself through. As she squatted, a seeming gash in her clothes flashed at her through the dimness the information that panic and haste had made her culpably careless. Retreating momentarily from the flap, she stood up straight, if a touch furtive, face to the wall. Admonishing herself that neither the unorthodoxy of her leaving nor, indeed, the fact that she was no

119

gentleman dispensed her from the obligation laid on gentlemen before leaving, she belatedly adjusted her dress.

9

Patricia did not know it: but the lavatory attendant was deaf. While she was making her emergency exit, he continued to sit hunched over his paperback, which was a translation into Dutch. That was still the only language the attendant read with facility, though he had left his birthplace, the Dutch East Indies, at the age of fourteen as an apprentice in the galley of a cargo boat and had never gone back. During several decades of a widely wandering working life, in the course of which he worked his way up to an under-stewardship on a liner making Caribbean cruises, he put himself to some trouble and expense, whenever he was in port, in order to procure a supply sufficient for his next voyage of the only sort of books he read with pleasure in, which is not in all parts of the world the easiest language to come by, Dutch. The onset of his deafness, by making him inaccessible to oral communication, made him the more dependent on reading. At the same time it forced him to quit his career at sea. He could no longer hear the bell which passengers rang to summon him. (And in an emergency, which did not happen during his career, though the nightmare of it decided him to quit before it had the chance to, he might not have heard even the noisy alarm signalling Take to the Boats.) Carefully he weighed where his best advantage ashore should lie, and he fixed on, applied for and got a job as lavatory attendant at an international airport, reckoning that his seagoing experience would serve him for qualifications (for he was used to vomiting world travellers), that he would have plenty of time for reading and that, at the airport bookstalls, he would find a pool of international literature large and varied enough to include works suited to both his minority language and his minority tastes. The one he was reading at present was the *Histoire de la Langue d'Oc.*

What the attendant did not know was that the Dutch translation was extensively expurgated.

120

10

She crept through the gap and stood upright — only to rein herself instantly in by squatting down again, because she had a sharp sense of a drop directly in front of her.

Until her eyes should grow used to the even dimmer light on this side of the flap, she couldn't see beyond her immediate surroundings.

Evidently she was on a ledge, some two foot wide and made of stone or rough-cast cement. It gave off a smell or, more exactly, an atmosphere of dry, crumbled, dusty dankness.

Immediately in advance of her, there was a gleam. Exploring with her hand, she discovered that if she *had* stepped straight forward after emerging from under the flap, she wouldn't have gone sheer off the ledge. There was a broadish metal chute pointing, from her feet, downwards.

What it led down into Patricia could for the moment make out only as wide, deep, rather cold space.

At the bottom of the space there was a continuous subsound of human and mechanical traffic.

Out of it there rose, startling Patricia as if she had been drenched by a sudden errant jet from a fountain, a forceful, urgent whisper: 'A member is missing'.

You're, Patricia ironically thought as she squatted tighter on the ledge, telling me.

SECTION THREE
DE REBUS
Scherzo and Fugue

1

Most of the mechanical noise was caused by a moving articulated belt.

Raised a couple of foot above the floor on a permanent way which at places arched itself into a hump, the belt flowed round the perimeter of the area like a noisy metal river. The noise came from its metal slats, which rendered it flexible but at the price that it clanked like chain-mail.

There was an inner circle, too. When the outer circle was flowing clockwise, the inner circle undulated anti-clockwise. It encircled a great-girthed concrete pillar at the centre, which seemed to support the whole building like a huge mushroom stalk.

The two circuits were connected by various loop and hump lines.

Every third or fourth minute, the system would give a particularly pronounced rattle and then halt. After an always brief but precise-length-unpredictable pause, it would rattle and start up again, sometimes in the same direction as before, sometimes in reverse.

Beneath the clangour there was a stratum of duller sounds: thuds: mufflings and suckings: mutters.

The least human of those thicker sounds came, Patricia presently deduced as she peered down into the deepness and the blank smell of undergroundness, from a blunt-nosed bus with a trailer attached, which hurried on abrupt, short journeys, many of them in reverse, all over the free space between the belting. Every time the bus stopped it sucked on its airbrakes. Even so, it was often too late and thumped into some obstacle, which it hit with a front muffled in rubber and further reinforced by rope and rags.

Other thuds came from crêpe soles.

Most thuds, however, Patricia eventually made out, came from luggage. Suitcases, hat boxes, carpet bags, grips, holdalls, haversacks and more suitcases, many of them belted up for double security with leather straps: they were lifted onto and off the moving conveyor, heaved onto and off the trailer, dragged into convenient nests and then, strapped together and slung from a shoulder, carried to a loopline onto which they were released. At every point in every transaction they made a thud.

In other words the place, which on imperfect acquaintance had seemed so sinister, was simply a depot or clearing house for passengers' luggage. The flap Patricia had used for her entrance was a hatch leading to a chute leading to the conveyor belt.

For the first time since the shock of discovering it she got fun out of her femininity. She crept forward across her ledge, arranged herself legs first, briefcase on knees, at the top of the chute and, with a sense of recapturing a childhood skill (surely she had used to do this very early on, conceivably even before leaving Ireland?), let herself go, putting it to herself as she went that perhaps she *was* a bit of a baggage.

She took aim at a tartan travelling rug, which she had spotted coming along from the right on the belting and reckoned would make for a soft landfall. Unpractised, however, she miscalculated. The rug had just passed when she arrived, next to it, directly onto an antelope-hide wardrobe-case with something bumpy inside it.

With automatic caution Patricia judged it would be better if the porters did not know she had joined them in their underworld. Possibly, though she hoped not probably, they might have been already alerted against a delinquent female who climbed out of men's lavatories. She slipped quietly off the moving belt onto the floor, dragging with her the tartan rug she had failed to hit. This she now pulled completely over herself and her briefcase as she sat squashed up, inconspicuously she trusted, feeling the rough narrow ruts of the concrete floor like a second series of ribbing under her corduroyed buttocks.

She was, however, safe only until one of the porters should, approaching her as a fallen travelling rug, try to lift her and sling her somewhere.

She raised one of the multicoloured, Red Indian fringes of the rug and spied out. Disturbingly, two pairs of blue serge legs were standing almost immediately beside her.

126

From under the muffling of the rug, which she recoiled into, Patricia heard a secretive whisper, which she almost certainly identified, though whispering voices are not fully characterised, as the same one that had accosted her when she had just come through the flap.

It whispered something about 'organisation'.

An Italian-intonated voice, which was difficult to keep down, whispered a reply about 'la cosa' or just possibly 'la coda'.

Belatedly Patricia realised she'd had another and better reason for wanting to remain unseen. All this luggage must have passed through the Customs and be now under seal or in bond or whatever the technical term might be. No reunion was meant to take place between a passenger in transit and his luggage until both reached their ultimate destination. This part of the airport must be strictly forbidden to unauthorised persons.

And few persons, Patricia's train of thought added, could be less authorised than herself whose boardingpass was by hours invalid and whose own luggage had been carried away in a plane she wilfully did not board.

She caught a sound of crêpe sole. She peered out again. The two pairs of serge legs were separating, creep-soling apart, with a slight furtiveness, as if trying to give the impression their two owners had never been in conversation.

Hearing no further human sounds close to, Patricia raised a whole corner of the rug and looked round.

To her relief, she saw that one of the branch lines of the conveyor belt defied gravity by flowing upwards at an incline like a ladder. A few pieces of luggage were even now, rather wobblingly, being carried by it somewhere towards ceiling height.

There the belt passed through a flap like the one Patricia had already used but opening outwards.

She watched while a canvas grip teetered to the top. It shouldered into the flap, which it flattened upwards, and then disappeared. The flap flopped closed again, having given Patricia a glimpse of the light not, perhaps, of day but at least of ground-level.

She knelt up, though still with the rug drawn over her head like a praying shawl, to work out the belting's route. She calculated that if she remounted the stretch she had quit and then, on reaching the first junction, rolled to the left, she would find herself on her way up and out.

She looked round to see if she was under observation. The whole area thudded with heavy manual and muscular labour, none of it, however, immediately near her.

The porters heaved and lumped for the most part without speaking.

That in itself signalled to Patricia some tension in the social group. She felt confirmed in her surmise when she witnessed, this time from a distance, another of those encounters and exchanges of information that were not meant to look as if they were any such thing.

Obviously some secret activity (trade-union activity?, Patricia queried) was being conducted beneath the surface of the muscular activity.

The porters' blue serge trousers, which put her in mind of those worn by the trolley-pusher in the café, were obviously uniform. In the porters' case, there was a uniform (blue, serge, battledress-pattern) jacket, too.

Patricia realised that all the porters were women.

She had no hesitation in recognising that what she had chuted into was the lesbian underworld.

Rough-trade union activity, then?, her thoughts emended.

Indeed, some of these muscular porters, she discerned now that she looked more sharply, had their doxies in attendance, their little Betty Bouncers bouncing after, with whom at the end of the day's sweaty work they intended to sweat again in the sweeter labour of making the beast with four breasts. Alongside the bulking serge form, as it strapped and hurled, would trot a flounce, a flutter or a flirt of frill: attendances that made the group look like a herd of buffalo in which some of the cows had calf at heel.

An image beset Patricia of their schoolage. (Could it, then, be that the bond depot or whatever it was properly called resembled a huge, chill gymnasium or some unwanted covered waste-space that passed for a playground?) She imagined the echo rising inside the concrete of a perpetual prattle about crushes and pashes which had

128

been to everyone else, as everyone pointedly pointed out at the time, merely a phase or a stage, a convention of schooldom like the unfelt conventions of a formal love poetry, but for *them* had been, ironically, real.

Patricia slipped onto the conveyor belt. It immediately stopped.

She arranged herself as comfortably as might be, the briefcase on her lap and the travelling rug over all.

There was a clank. The belt wriggled beneath her into movement and she felt herself being tugged away.

At the correct moment, she rolled sideways, like a landing parachutist.

Evidently she had shunted herself successfully. After a moment she felt her journey begin to move slowly and slightly uphill.

Just beside and a touch beneath her, a female voice whispered 'O.K.' or possibly 'O, Kay'.

Patricia was hollowed by a second's panic. But no large tough hand reached up to disturb the tartan rug. Her journey jolted on.

She was travelling facing forwards, both because she was liable, on trains and planes, to nausea if she travelled backwards and thought the same might be true on the conveyor belt and because she did not want to be slugged on the occiput by the flap that must be opened by her arrival at the top.

As she trundled upwards towards that, Patricia was visited by a new hypothesis about the origin of the expression 'O.K.', to account for which the dictionaries preferred only very far fetched surmises. After that long-ago divergence between the langue d'oïl and the langue d'oc, between the language whose word for 'yes' was 'oïl' and that Southern language whose word for 'yes' was 'oc', it looked as if *oïl* was the outright winner, taking to itself, in its modernised form of *oui*, the yea-saying function in the vocabulary of all French-speakers. Might it not, however, be that the stream which seemed to have dried up had gone underground and had now emerged to sweep victoriously not merely through all French dialects but through virtually all languages? Might not, in other words, 'O.K.' be simply a spelt-out and variantly-spelt old Provençal 'oc'?

It was clear to Patricia that her hypothesis was bred of the whispered 'O.K.' (which, even if it *had* signified 'O, Kay', *sounded* as

129

'O.K.') she had overheard, together with a classic of picaresque-utopian pornography which her fantasy had conjured into a moment's being and which was called the *Histoire de la Langue d'Occiput*.

Sensing that she was near the top of the route, she turned back the tartan rug like a visor and looked ahead.

Wall was approaching closely.

She could now see, chalked on the concrete in vast letters, two inscriptions, one on each side of the flap she was headed for.

The left flank read

WOMEN OF THE WORLD UNITE.
YOU HAVE NOTHING TO LOSE
BUT YOUR LABOUR PAINS.

The right complemented the doctrine with

WOMEN OF THE WORLD UNITE.
YOU HAVE EVERYTHING TO
GAIN — IN PARTICULAR,
YOUR DAISY CHAINS.

Patricia drew down the rug again, and her forehead struck the flap with a bang muffled, as she had designed, by the rug.

Even through the rug she was dazzled by the sudden light.

The conveyor belt straightened out in its course. Patricia felt with a foot over the side. She touched smooth, level floor, onto which she stood upright, letting the tartan rug lapse into a stole's position, secured at one side on her briefcase.

Eyes scrunched against the glare, Patricia heard and deciphered from the air currents that a man was rushing towards her and breathing delight.

'Ah!', he cried, reaching her and pulling at her shawled arm, 'just in time! The missing member!'

2

'... four

    three

    two', counted-down (with the gestures and in the costume [white shirt sleeves] of a boxing referee counting-out) the man who, via his ear-muff headphones, was in constant Saint Joanly communication with voices inaudible to everyone else,

'one...'

At zero, he bent double and ducked away at a Groucho Marx run across the flex-infested floor.

The man at the centre of the great bank of desk, which resembled those from behind which airtickets were sold, set his face in motion, creasing it into the warm, fleshy-petalled grin of a tropical succulent in flower.

'Welcome to the Seamus Shaughnessy Show and another edition of our panel-game, WHAT'S MY KINK? The rules of the game are quite simple. Everyone knows that a straight line is the shortest distance between two points. Well, a kink is a straight line that's got bent. Our challenger has come forward to sit in our witness box and bear witness to his kink. Our panel has the job of eliciting, by skilful questioning, bullying, harrying, grilling or third-degreeing, what his kink is.'

Seated in the extreme right chair of the five behind the desk, Patricia frowned at her scratchpad and pencil, both because the lights were so bright as to pain her eyes if she raised them and because she wanted to avoid the notice of whichever might at the moment be operative of the cameras she could see dimly nosing their ponderous way about the floor with the same type of sucking mobility as the bus in the luggage depot.

'And now let me introduce our panel. First, that attractive young lady, Miss Emerald Isle. Next, the well-known Irish-German writer, Thomas Mahon.'

A square of paper appeared before Patricia's frown. On it her next-chair neighbour had scribbled 'You're on camera. Look at the monitor'.

Patricia scrumpled the message up. (This term's form monitor, her memory said, is Betty Bouncer.)

She bent lower over the desk.

She who had lately entertained a fleeting fantasy of fame was now camera-shy: as who wouldn't be, she put it to herself, with an escapade-escape and a flit through the out-of-bounds underground in her immediate past and a tartan bit of stolen goods even now folded, swelteringly, on her lap?

Too dazed and dazzled to do otherwise than stumble after her guide (being on television was much like making a journey by air: you were inert and had to be nannied wherever you went), suffering herself to be led through a lath-and-plaster forest into this clearing where the tropical light struck with an intensity almost lethal and snakes squirmed across the oily-surfaced floor (which was chalk-marked passim), Patricia had none the less preserved enough caution of mind to decline, as her guide leaned over her thrusting his clip-board towards her chest and an unpredicted arm shot out from nowhere and daubed a giant powderpuff into her nose, to yield up her name.

'I confess I hadn't read any of Tom Mahon's books before today, but I'll certainly make a point of it from now on, Tom. And next to me on the other side we have Dr Don Donovan, the Don who specialises in John Donne. And, fourthly but not lastly, we come to our mystery panellist who, when invited onto the panel, wouldn't even tell us his name.'

His?, Patricia's thoughts mimicked ridiculingly. She'd have taken Seamus Shaughnessy for too experienced a tele-man (o music, o eighteenth century, ached her thoughts) to fall into slips of the tongue.

Unless, she queried, panicking, it was no slip of the tongue but a factual error? *Could* she have been mistaken for a man? Granted her travel costume was ambiguous. Granted she'd no doubt come out from under the tartan a bit dishevelled. (But dishevelled was not necessarily the same thing as male. Seamus Shaughnessy himself, for one, was quite kempt. The long arm had powdered his nose, too.) The utmost pretext for error Patricia could be giving would be to be looking, today, a touch butch. Perhaps she'd even taken on by

132

contagion a dash of the butch in her dash through the lesbian underworld.

'However, let me assure him, anonymous or no, he's equally welcome.'

No slip of the tongue, then, Patricia thought.

Or was it, Patrick thought in horror, he (Patrick) who'd made the error?

Squirming in his hot seat under the tele-heat, Patrick remembered that after all he'd not, when he had the chance, made the direct and wholesale inspection he'd earlier promised himself. And why not? Because he'd been convinced, on the evidence provided by proxy by poxy Betty Bouncer, that he knew the answer already. He'd been content with merely feeling. And on not feeling what, with such certainty, he'd expected, he'd panicked to the wrong conclusion.

But how how how could such a thing, *such* a thing, be mislaid?

Easily: lamentably easily. During all that wriggling about he'd self-exploringly done in the café, he'd rearranged himself in relation to the sit of his clothes. And then in the lavatory he had, quite simply, felt on the wrong side.

This perception, so cuttingly simple in itself, so reverberant with implications he needed leisure to fathom out, had come to Patrick at the least convenient of all conveivable moments.

Not now, his thoughts tried to pray off; not here and now; not under the publicity of these lights; not just as the camera finger prepares to point at me.

Seamus Shaughnessy's creamed Irish voice was enfolding him in a reference to him like batter round a spoon.

Patrick ought to look up graciously. But how could he, with so much to conceal, dare?

'A big big hullo, then, for our resident mystery.'

But is it, demanded Pat's thoughts, the shame of a public blush bowing his head like a blown red Irish rose into deeper still flight from the grilling interrogation of the light (*so* deep that he caught sight of the hot shameful layers of rug on his lap) – *is* it Mister Y? Or is it, still just, confusingly, conceivably, Miss Tery?

'And now: I see our challenger is ready in the witness box and straining at the leash. Who'll take first crack at him? Emerald?'

133

'O Seamus. I simply can't think.'

'Very well then. Thomas Mahon, then: what do *you* think our challenger's kink is?'

'Well this is a rather knotty problem, without too many clues to work on. I would say, on superficial inspection, our challenger has a rather stern look. Yes, I think I would definitely put him down as stern. Therefore I should say he comes somewhere under the broad heading of S.-M. Within that category — '

'I think I ought to — ', said Seamus Shaughnessy.

'I would place him — ', pursued Thomas Mahon.

'Can you just hold it a moment, Thomas?'

'Mm?'

'Hold it. I think I ought to just explain there, for the benefit of our less initiated viewers, what S.-M. stands for. S.-M. is short for sado-masochistic. Carry on, Thomas.'

'Within the category S.-M., I would incline to place the challenger somewhere in the bondage group. With, quite possibly, a seasoning of discipline. Mild discipline, I rather think. Or of course it is always possible he goes in for fladge.'

'That's four or five guesses you've had there, Thomas. Which one are you settling for?'

'Well, as I say, it's a knotty — '

'Go on. Fix on one. Be a devil.'

'Well if I have to be pinned down— '

'Crucifixion is it, then?'

Laughter.

'No, seriously, Thomas. What's your guess?'

'Well, fladge, then, Seamus. If I must.'

'Splendid. Thomas Mahon guesses fladge. Now then: Dr Don Donovan: what's your view, Don?'

With a panic that drowned out even the problem of his/her sex, Pat saw that the questionmasterly probe was inexorably getting round to him/her, Pat.

Time ponderously raced: a count-down of seconds passed at fever-speed and yet in the detail of slow-motion. This was an experience of time with enlarged pores.

When the moment came, would he/she be able to utter a syllable?

134

It was a clenching pressure of dread, in which a soul might crack: and be publicly exposed. (How could anyone, ever, have wanted to be famous?) A count-down of seconds, it was, until the very second when this individual, Pat, should have one second to make or mar: and if it was a second of shame, there was no revoking it, ever.

'Well, I must say I take an entirely different view', said Don (John Donne) Donovan. (No pity flowed in Pat for the others. For the others it was, for an indefinable reason, obviously easy.) 'I must say I incline to put him under fetishism.'

'Any particular fetish, would you care to opt for?'

'Silk? Feathers? Anything, provided it's shiny?'

'Now, now, Don. Multiple guessing is out. Which?'

'Oh, well. Let's say silk.'

'Fine. Now — '

Now. In which persona should Pat speak? His/her own. Don't deceive the public. But —

'One moment. May I come back on that?' Don Donovan enquired.

In the second of reprieve, Pat resolved to be Patrick.

'Right. Back to you, Don Donovan.'

'I'd like to change my guess. I now guess high heels.'

'High heels it is, then, for Don Donovan. Let's move on, then — '

Sweating at this apex of torture, soul splitting apart, Patrick for the first time raised his eyes and regarded the challenger in the box.

Two splurges of flame-coloured light dazzled back at him, like a sunset reflected in the windows of a house on the horizon.

' — to the mystery member of our panel. What's his guess?'

Patrick realised the splurges were being flung at him from octagonal rimless glasses.

'Plastic mackintoshes', he coolly and decisively said.

'Bang on first shot!' cried Seamus Shaughnessy, slapping the desk. The panellists spontaneously clapped. 'How *did* you know?', cried Emerald Isle. Donovan patted Patrick's back.

3

At the door marked 'Exit to Transit Lounge', the man with the clip-board patted the tartan travelling rug that was now folded over Patrick's left arm and said 'Splendid having you with us. Splendid performance. Himself would be here to thank you himself, only he's just rounding off the show with a spot of chat. Will you kindly accept this' – he handed Patrick a small leaflet – 'with our compliments, and' – he held out the clip-board, horizontal – 'sign here.'

'I performed anonymously.'

'Then make your mark.'

Patrick took the pencil, which was fixed to the top of the board by a long spring, and considered rendering his mark as 'seX' but decided instead, now he had more confidence in himself, on 'Mister Y'.

'Splendid. I hope you'll join us again. My name's Kevin Kelly, by the way.'

Patrick pushed the door and was back in transit – beneath, indeed, one of the protrusive closed-circuit television sets, on which the final roller captions were even now appearing.

'. . . with SEAMUS SHAUGHNESSY', he was just in time to read; 'programme devised by Brigid Brophy'.

Feeling suddenly sick, persecuted by persons with Irish names and destined to rehearse in retrospect, over and over, his moments of tele-terror, he went to the bar.

4

He queued second to nun.

Inside the leaflet that had been handed him he found a tear-off card that read

136

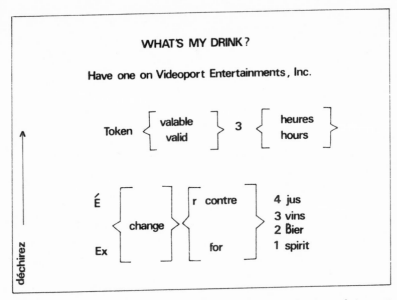

As he queued, he worried lest he had been immoral in not disclosing that he had seen the challenger before. Contradictorily, he also worried lest he had let his 'plastic mackintoshes' slip forth too tamely; perhaps he ought to have accumulated suspense by holding a pause before speaking.

Then he began compulsively to go over the words he had not said but should have done.

S. S. Well, if you won't tell us who you are, tell us what you do.

P. O'R. By all means. I'm a scholar.

S. S. And that's a grand thing to be being. In what line of country would you be after being it, now?

P. O'R. I am preparing an apparatus criticus for the text of the post-Ciceronian discourse, *De Rebus*.

S. S. Are you indeed? And what would that be about?

P. O'R. O, things.

And all the time he felt blanched and drained, like veal.
It was as if he had been talking for days, and all about himself.
He decided he was suffering the self-destructive self-reproach of

137

selfishness: the sheer egoistic conceit of him, Pat O'Rooley, putting himself on show in public, as if he had something to Sh $\{^e_a\}$ w.

With luck, the nun ahead of him at the bar would be Italian, in which case she'd quickly rap out her 'Strega' and be up on her broomstick and away, leaving the bar for Pat to claim the 1 spirit he'd decided on.

The barman turned the light of his countenance on the nun. But 'Have you a drop of John Jameson?' she enquired.

'Jammy sun? What is? Confiture, hein?'

They were jammed at cross purposes.

And all the (considerable) while that their jam continued, there was a bottle of the stuff blatant on the shelf behind the barman's head.

The nun's gilt-rimmed eyes were perhaps too feeble to see it. The barman was K.O.'d (o Ok, Ok have you gone bak on me?) by the native pronunciation. And you, Pat? You were too weak to speak.

You were not. You were too idolatrously set on contemplating yourself as a public image, sneaking half-wonders here and there whether some of the people standing about might not have recognised you from the screen.

You are the self-regarding eye, Patrick. You are the Evil I. You have made your own image an image of cult, you cheat. You are the original I-con-man.

Are you so morally degenerated now that you cannot even bring yourself to intervene to the aid of a poor ignorant Irish Sister that's bewildered abroad?

Ought it not to be you that would constantly demonstrate, when in the presence of the religious, that religion has no monopoly of human charity?

How low have you skunk?

You, you horsecoping whorespoking tinker, with your stolen goods worn brazen as a blazoned horseblanket over your arm?

The nun settled for Scotch.

O'Rooley moved forward, requested an armagnac and presented his token. (Perhaps when the barman sees *that* he'll put 2 and 2 together. If he liked my performance, he might even stretch it to 2 spirit. But)

138

'What is? Cheques we don't take.'

Chequemate.

'This is a token.'

'Token not taken.'

'Television token.'

'I find out.'

After removing the already poured brandy out of O'Rooley's reach to the far side of the bar channel, the barman carried the token away.

Behind O'Rooley two women arrived at the bar and met each other.

He'd come to expect them to be Irish. (*Why* was the place so full of Irish? Well didn't it only bear out his theory the Irish were the one truly international race?)

'Top of the morning to you', one of the women said.

It was 4.27 in the afternoon.

(Was this, O'Rooley tried to remember from infancy, Irish idiom? And if so was it the one that made Lady Bracknell arrive at an afternoon teaparty with the words 'Good afternoon' and quit it with the words 'Good morning'?)

'Top of the pops to *you*', the other woman replied.

'Top of the popes.'

'And which would *that* be?'

'Bias the Ninth.'

'Have you tried that rejuvenating jelly they have at the chemist's, Bio Nono?'

'Are you imputing the need?'

'If the imputation fits . . . '

'Shall you wipe that grin off your telefis or will I give you a poke in the jaw?'

(And will *I*, thought O'Rooley, this time intervene?)

'What a contentious pugnacious disputatious old Irish woman it is to be sure.'

'I am not Irish.'

'Are you not?'

'I am not. I'm international.'

'Is that a fact?'

'Do you doubt me? I am so, international.'

'So am I, international.'

'Are you indeed? Then what are we fighting for?'

'What indeed? Should we drink to international peace?'

'We should. Can I tempt you to a Holy Fly sherry?'

'You can.'

O'Rooley turned and took the opportunity to inspect them: tweeded, woolstockinged, virtually wellingtoned; broad and peasantly broad-faced; fair to Irish-reddish. One was a decade older and some inches broader than her barcountercompatriopart.

They were, O'Rooley recognised, the two solid P. della Francescesque angels who sold woven weeds in the glass tank within the glass Transit tank.

Raising their eyes and sherries, they pledged one another: Irish blue to blue Irish.

'Here's Kerry Blue in your eye.'

'And the Pig from Connaught to you.'

The first barman placed the token on the counter in front of O'Rooley and said 'No'.

Resigned, O'Rooley transferred the tartan rug to his other arm and felt in his pocket for (Norwegian) currency.

The barman gave him his brandy and his change in Greek coins.

The natural affinity of the Irish foreign-accent to the Greek language, O'Rooley thought as he drank, resided in the rough breathing: scilicet (explained scholiast) the Greek mark for an 'h' sound, which in Greek appeared not only in front of aspirated initial vowels but in front of all initial *r*'s. When Latin transliterated the aspirate before *r*, it tidied it into second place, and English copied Latin, with the result that Greek-derived words appeared in English as, for example, 'rhythm' and 'rheum'. In logic, however, those words ought to read 'hrythm' and hreum': and that was precisely how the Irish pronounced them.

O'Rooley put down his emptied glass and

      (I am, Sir,

            your iota subscript)

turned away.

The rug on his arm brushed against one of the Irishwomen.

140

'Hreally', she hremarked in protest.

'I hrepent', he cried quickly, knowing her to be contentious and pugnacious and himself not wanting a public scene in which his divers delinquencies might come to discovery.

'Look, darling', she said to her friend; 'if it isn't one of ourselves.'

Did she mean, Patrick questioned as he loped away to one of the sloping armchairs he saw vacant deep in the Lounge, just that he was one more of the internationalised Irish about the place?

Or did she mean, Patricia queasily queried as she sat down, that here was another contentious, pugnacious tough-breathing Irish butch just like herself?

5

Settle in; and settle it for once and for all. Fold the rug over the no-matter-which-sexed lap; snuggle under, snugger than a bugger in a scrum at rugger; and forward (all Gaul is divided into three tartans?) the story of the tongue of Oc.

The clue to it all, the editorial-I/editorial-oui is now assured, resides in disentangling that enigmatic inverted-comma'd He. I am (déchirez whichever does not apply) a he/a she/a "he"/ a "she".

There's, as the pages flick, a passage to arrest the scholarly eye. For didn't eye catch 'apparatus criticus' as the pages turned? Let us re-turn and find it.

And there's, on our re-turning way, a page that would take an apparatus criticus of its own to decipher: a regular fog-bog of printer's (or printers') errors, one vast squelchy black-sea literal.

(Miss Og, take a reproof to the proof-reader.)

Was this it; was this the red-sea passage read, seen in passing, the apparatpassage, the hospital corrida of tauromachiocracy?

(Doctor, will this opperatus prove criticus?)

(A puff or two of criticus dotted the kerry-blue sky.)

(I wonder why the critics puffed *Oc* to the sky? 'ShOCking! ErOCita! Sharper than OCcam!')

Here: was this the bit?

blindfold, and she could tell from the taste or sensation on her tongue only that her tongue was in contact with warm, responsive, delicate skin.

Oc could, of course, move only the very tip of her tongue, and that but a millimetre up or down, because it was clamped firmly into the apparatus.

Damn: not criticus at all; merely that old S.-Mapparatus, the masomachine applied, in the language laboratory, by the sado-mysterious "He".

Ritual CatemasOChism:-

Q. Who is Master?

A. I do nothing except on your sado.

Q. Where is Oc's tongue?

A. In her cheek.

Q. Where is ox tongue?

A. At the counter that has the OCcam's-razor-sharp bOCan-slicing apparatus.

Q. O.C., and while we're at the grOCer's, then, what does Oc look as if?

A. As if bugger wouldn't melt in her mouth.

Q. And WHERE is the passage that explains why that *He* has an initial capitaspirate and is placed between double-inverted (THERE's a kinky pun) commas?

In logic, the vital passage should come somewhere not too long after the start. Apply textual criticism. Apply constant contextual criticism.

This is admittedly not the wholesale exegesis we are seeking, but is it a clue? Or is it merely a further appearance on the part of the unacknowledged, unsung, unstrung heroine of our story, Miss Print?

Unfortunately, although the passage we are discussing does contain the word *his*, the word is not placed between inverted commas and therefore cannot be a reference to our mysterious "He"ro.

All the same, that's quite a revelatory slip you're shewing down there, Miss Print.

On second thoughts we exonerate the printer and assume the translator was a touch fatigued at this point. Obviously the
142

translator forgot to invert the absurd French habit of using the possessive adjective to inform the reader of the sex not of the possessor but of the object possessed; and the translator has thereby coined a character who (your editor promises to apply sexual criticism throughout), to an English-thinking mind, simply cannot exist: namely, 'his husband'.

(Did he have a space on his passport for his husband?)

And indeed, now that we think of it, a further exoneration may be due.

For we are not at all sure it was you, after all, o Irish O'Pera, who initially set this sexchange in train. It may quite well have been you, O.Fr. (= Old French [signed Scholiast One]), you sly old wench, with your already remarked habit of being coy about what's girl and what's boy and your vicious officious imparting of misinformation about the sex of objects possexed. For you are basically, you rude crude Old Provincial tongue, the tongue neither of *oc* nor of *oïl* but of murderously reiterated superfluent erroneous implied statements such as that tongues are female.

And now quickly yield up, you misprinted mistranslated overestimated sadomasturbatory pornofantasy-narrative (please send one copy on approval, by return of post, under plain cover to:- Master Bate, Saint Giovanni Choirschool) the information, as requested, about "He".

It should be, surely, in the neighbourhood of HERE. No; we've inverted too far; there's the very first entrance of the Master (the well-known flogging headmaster Bate). Turn on a page (your masojesty!) or two; it MUST be precisely HERE.

But the page on which sexegesis occurred had been the one bound up (o bondage) as opposite-number to the blank page at the back which Pat, having from memory reconstructed on it the Logic mnemonic, had torn out. (Déchirez→ . . .) Unsecured without its pendant, the exegetical page had drifted loose and gotten lost.

6

In charity, Patricia now felt, the public-address system might at this point have provided a musical interlude, as it earlier provided *Alitalia*. What about, say, a setting, by George Steiner, for Steinway of *Der Hölle Rache kocht in meinem post-Herzen*? Or couldn't the closed-circuit television televise George Steiner's talk on the decline of the post-*HerzOG* novel?

But neither machine was giving out anything except details of flights.

Unexpectedly it was *Oc*, whose pages Patricia was hopelessly turning, which provided (an item through which, she quickly saw, her thoughts would not need to supply a double-bass obbligato)

THE RECITAL

The audience was assembled and quietly expectant.

The brightly lit platform was bare apart from a high stool, against which was propped an outsize double-bass. The instrument stood face down, secured against the floor at the bottom by the pin, which was fully extended.

The curtains at the side of the platform parted, and the Maestro entered. "He" was wearing full evening dress with the green sash of a distinguished order across "His" shirt front. "He" bowed to the applause, unbuttoned and peeled off "His" white gloves and then, approaching the double-bass, lightly seized its curled top and twiddled the instrument on its pin so that it faced the audience.

Naked and at full length, Oc was bound to the instrument. Her crossed ankles were strapped to the pin. Her arms, pulled taut above her head, extended up the neck of the instrument and were tightly fastened, by the wrists, at the pegs at the top.

The Maestro climbed onto the high stool and arranged the double-bass with its neck resting against "His" shoulder.

"I will just tune the instrument", "He" told the audience.

With that, "He" twisted the pegs a turn or two tighter, which drew Oc into a yet more stretched position and one which thrust her breasts into yet more extreme prominence.

The Maestro slipped "His" arm round the neck of the instrument and cupped Oc's left breast. With a light vibrato- tremolo touch, as if stopping a string, "His" .finger played on her nipple.

A moan escaped her.

The audience applauded.

"Oc's music lesson will not be fully effective", "He" said, "unless we have recourse to the mute." Lightly pulling it from his pocket, "He" inserted the gag between her lips.

Then, taking up the bow which was leaning against the high stool, "He" began to draw it lightly to and fro across those pretty second lips on the lower half of Oc's body, which came just at the bridge of the instrument.

Applying the bow with "His" right hand, "He" continued to 'stop the strings' with "His" left.

Even through the 'mute', Oc gave a cry of delight, which was almost drowned by the thunder of the audience's applause.

Setting down the bow for a moment, the Maestro leaned forward and extended "His" bare hand towards the bridge of the instrument.

"Do you want", "He" asked Oc in courteous tones, "to learn to be played pizzicato?"

Well, slap my double-inverted-bass, Patricia's thoughts vulgarly commented; and she became aware that someone was standing, as if with intent to speak, beside her armchair.

She closed the book and looked up: up an entrench-coated military front to a commanding, self-controlled head held stiff-necked. The face displayed some of the withdrawn austerity of the skull beneath. The upper lip bore a curled tartar moustache, auburn. The temples bore a white, vertical duelling-scar.

A punctilious bow was inclined to her. The voice that addressed her was strong but soft; baritone; gently foreign in accent.

'It is an impertinence that I should speak to you at all. If I offend you, you have only to tell me to go away and I will go on the instant, without arguing or asking why. If you do not wish even to speak to me, a gesture of your hand will dismiss me for ever.'

Patricia's hands sought one another on top of the closed book,

145

which lay on the folded rug. They clasped with an intensity that blanched their knuckles.

'I have been watching you for a long time as you read. I knew from the delicacy of your hands on the pages the scholarly spirit in which you handled the book. You did not merely read, gluttonously. Fastidiously, you searched.

'I found myself possessed by the desire to approach you and speak to you. At the same time, I was seized with a trepidation I had never experienced before. I am no stranger to casual encounters in places of social resort or international exchange. I will not conceal from you that I have led the life of a Don Juan. So long as my heart is not fully engaged — and that means all my life until now — I am able to cut what is conventionally called a dashing figure. Now I find myself without dash. I have, am and can offer nothing but myself.

'As I watched you, my trepidation increased. So, however, did my sense of time running out: my time in this place, my — any-one's — time in this life; perhaps human time on this planet.

'I understood that the Don Juanism of my life hitherto had been my pursuit of such echoes and glimpses as I could catch of my true romantic ideal — that person whom one should perhaps call rather an icon than an ideal in one's life. I understand now that adoration is a gift as rare as talent: and when it does, all uniquely, come, only a coward retreats from it without taking up its challenge.'

7

And meanwhile, in the mythological dimension, in an ark-space beneath a jagged, gothic-fretted gable, Almighty God bestrode the thundercloud, his William Blake nightgown weeping out on the wind, and cried in his wrath: 'Who or what is there in the universe that I did not fabricate out of my own fantasy? Where is the sustenance that shall stay the pangs of *my* romantic love? Who is there for *me* to adore?'

146

8

'In four minutes', the self-confessed Don Juan resumed, 'the flight I am due to catch, if I am to take up my everyday life again, will depart. If you speak the word, I will never catch it. I will never return to that everyday life. Instead, you and I will go wherever you name, and I will be to you whatever you want me to be.'

He bowed to her again and stood, held tall, waiting.

Patricia's eyes sought his and found them intent on her.

She regarded him in naked silence.

Between his anguish and her appreciation of it there was a transparent barrier. He suffered set apart from her. He was like the weather outside an aeroplane she was in. He was rain weeping across the outside of the double-glazed cabin window.

She recognized not a coldness but an insulation in her feelings towards his whole sex.

She felt his pain indeed, but only because it had been her own in other relationships. Sympathy for him caused a second's stumble in the unremittingness of her conduct towards him; but it made no falter at all in her inner gait, the high proud lesbian-queen steps of the dedication she had vowed during her schoolage (and had maintained even through the double-glazed insulation of the other's marriage) to Elizabeth Donaghue (née Bouncer).

To the Don Juan she gently, gravely said: 'I will see you off on your flight.' He bowed.

As she arose, 'You permit?', he said and carried the tartan rug for her over his arm.

They walked in silence to the vast glass wall.

One of its panels was already slid open, the gap policed by a uniform. Inside the Lounge, a bunch of travellers made a balloon that was slowly deflating as they passed through the gap in the glass.

Beyond the glass, the upper air was already drained of sun, leaving the top of the sky a childish, Chiricoesque blue devoid of luminescence. Low on the horizon the late-afternoon sun still burned bronze, throwing balls of flame into the building to blind people who wore glasses, and casting, with one of its broad, low-angled

147

shafts, an autumn glow onto the Don Juan's already autumnal moustache, touching it into the sad colour of the cherished, fruitful wood of a stringed instrument.

The aeroplanes parked on the tarmac just beyond the glass wall were already dusky silhouettes, darkling into the ground, making shapes strange as moths.

The way out was almost clear. A last loud-hail for the flight was distributed by machine.

The Don Juan placed and arranged the tartan rug on Patricia's arm as solicitously as if it had been a lapdog.

Patricia had a sudden panicking premonition that she was seeing him off to his death, his plane being predestined to crash. (And *was* her quasi-coldness, then, a lethal iciness? *Had* she willed her parents' metal wings to − o Daedalus reversed − ice up?)

She reminded herself that, at the start of every flight, fear fantasised a premonition, yet most flew safe. Perhaps the flights whose take-off was accompanied by the largest number of unseen, winged, bat-squeaking, attendant premonitions were the very ones least liable to hazard − a thought as superstitious, she quickly perceived, as the original premonition.

The Don Juan took her hand. 'Goodbye.'

'Goodbye.'

Still his hand held hers. In the strange, painted-nursery brightness which the gleaming lower air had given to objects in the Lounge, the scar on his temples glowed colourless as a slither of moon.

'Kiss my hand', she said, letting fall the separate words like queen's pearls or tears.

'My dear', he said, letting the tones of a roué cynic curl the edges of his words like autumn-leaf mustachios tobacco-cured in an irony against himself, 'I know we are said now to live in a permissive society. But I would not risk exposing you to the comment and disapproval which, I very strongly suspect, would ensue were a middle-aged man to be seen, in so public a place as this, to kiss the hand, be it never so beautiful, of a boy.'

148

9

With the zeal of a recent pervert, Patrick made haste to put himself on view in the slave market.

On the broad strip of clear floor which ran, without interruption by armchair or bench, alongside the plate glass wall, like an interior tarmac, there promenaded, up and down, the pretty boys. Up, along the side far from the glass; round, by an apsidal route unmarked-out on the floor but long since conventionalised by pittering feet into an invisible Mincing Lane; down again, keeping close to the glass: they promenaded and often virtually pomaded (well, now you mention it, and now the darkness beyond is usefully turning the plate glass into a mirror, perhaps just a *touch*, just a quick crimp between the lengths of two fingers, to that wave – well, I say wave, but it's really almost more of a *bang*), they peacocked and peacocquetted, for the most part singly, occasionally in twos, very very occasionally in gaggles and giggling garlands, but always keeping to the current's pace and direction, as traffic-disciplined as the promenading interval-audience in a German provincial opera house.

The empty space down the middle of the two perpetui-circulating flower wreaths was the gauntlet destined to be run by the gentlemen: the stagedoorjohnnies, the overseers, the bidders at auction. (Would they slip an eyeglass into an eye cavity the better to eye their prey?)

Patrick opened out the tartan rug and slipped it round his shoulders stole-wise. (I stole it, he proudly thought.) He wished he had something to twist into a rimbaud for his hair – something to render him a bit more suitably-dressy for the fast-approaching cocteau hour.

He hipped his way into the circulating line. A soft suppurating susurration of malice greeted him from the others.

He knew himself at a disadvantage in comparison with them by virtue of the loose fit of his trousers. He remedied it so far as he could by driving his hands hard and deep into his trousers pockets and drawing the material taut to him.

Corduroy had, perhaps, certain compensations, too. Might not its bloom make of his buttocks an image of peach?

149

And he was positively glad of the wide legs of his trousers. For with the superfluous material he could — and did — swish. Even, as he bounced and flounced in his steps, he could froth and foam round the ankles, obeying his governing compulsion, which was perhaps archaically psychic, perhaps Jean-genetic, towards fur-belows.

When he was bid for, he planned, he would look demurely down and confess his name was Pat or 'to my intimate friends, Patricia'. (Perhaps the unknown Ray, whose gay name was evidently Miranda, was somewhere in the parade?)

"Patricia" titupped along, every moment expecting the exploratory touch of a prospective purchaser on "her" buttocks.

"She" would make sure of a good price: not for need or greed of money, but as a sexual refinement, the last and juiciest twist to the whole sexual extortion.

A signal soon sounded for "her". Somewhere in the central space, just behind "her", a mouth was sucked in with a lubricious-lipped wet slap of erotic admiration.

"She" paused, as if prettily poised on the modest verge of nymph flight, and, in "her" posing, contrived to steal a demure glance.

What had nosed along the space and was now halted behind "her" was one of those bus-trailers that carted luggage about the airport.

Its driver was no auburn-tartar-moustached aristocrat. All the same, "Patricia" well knew that manual workers fetched home good money these days; and they had probably always been rather more to be relied on than aristocrats for muscle.

Dimpling, "she" sidled up to the bus. Whimsically or perhaps to display "her" kind, if twee, feelings towards animals, "she" gave a pat to its flank and (perhaps in order to signal to "her" muscular, manual prospective lover that "she" was no off-puttingly intellectual snob but could make an ignoramus's pun on *De Rebus* as well as the next "girl") whisper-lisped to the quasi-creature 'Dear bus'.

Simultaneously, "she" dared a further and more direct glance up at its handler.

True, there were still no auburn antlers, but there was, winking down at "her", a brisk little vulgarian of a moustache, gothically fretted and Clark-gabled, which, engagingly scrubber-hard, made
150

"Patricia" thrill to "her" bottommost frill when "she" conceived of the coarseness, the sheer slap-and-prickle, it must betoken.

A huge, work-red hand reached forth. Was, then, "Patricia" to be flung across the crupper of a bus?

But the hand was reaching for and now hooted a klaxon.

With a release of air (had *that* been the sound that first sucked at "Patricia"'s attention?), the bus lurched forward.

"Patricia" cat-leaped aside, only just furling in "her" trouser-legs in time.

'Mind your backsides', the driver coarsely called.

"Patricia", looking sharply up in injury, saw, as the bus plunged on its forward start, something like a curved prow or figurehead plunge too. "She" looked harder. The black bristle of moustache was a piece of secondary decoration, the merest scratch of iron-work balcony clipped to an upper, servants'-bedroom storey. At the level of the piano nobile there was a whole huge curved bow front. What had plunged was the bosom of the woman bus-driver.

10

Off, drag. Fold, drape. Mincing, away.

(What we need now are our après-she clothes.)

The time is past for slackly or charitably assuming that valuable objects that cannot be found have been somehow (snort: *how?*) mislaid.

Quite obviously, the object has been STOLEN.

WHO (cardinal twentieth-century question) IS GUILTY?

11

Slim O'Rooley slammed straight back to the bar, his passport at the ready in his hand.

He secured the barkeep's attention and slapped the passport, open at the photograph, down on the counter under his nose. 'You seen this party?'

'Sure.'

'When?'

'I got amnesia.'

O'Rooley whammed a drachma onto the counter, slid it across but kept his finger on it.

The barkeep looked at the coin and then at O'Rooley. 'Few hours back. Ordered a cappuccino 'n' a brioche. Didn't touch neither. Some folks don't know which side their brioche is buttered.'

O'Rooley released the coin and the barkeep's soft hand flowed over it.

O'Rooley slid the passport back into its holster.

'You a shamus?' the barkeep asked.

'That's right, a shameless.'

'See your licence?'

O'Rooley gave him a flash of his no longer valid boarding-card.

'You after this gang of smugglers, then?'

'*What* smugg – – – .' O'Rooley stopped himself, converting his question into a contemptuous glance round the bar and the comment 'What a smug clientele you get in here.'

'You didn't know there *was* no smugglers, did you?' the barkeep said, glowering suspicion directly at O'Rooley low over the counter.

O'Rooley laughed a bark. 'Ever heard of the double-bass-bluff-double-inverted-indemnity-catch-as-fall-guy?' he asked.

'No', said the barkeep.

'O.K., barcreep', O. Rooley said. 'Get me a shot of Scotch.'

'Well, could be I will, mister', said the barkeep, 'but you have to pay for hard liquor in hard currency and that means not Greek.'

'O.K., O.K.', O'Rooley said wearily. 'What d'you want me to pay in? The crown jewels?'

'I don't want no hot rocks here, I'm no fence.'

'Just an offence', said O'Rooley and added waving his hand: 'Let it go. I didn't say a thing.'

He paid for the Scotch and took a slug of it.

He turned and rested the backs of his elbows on the bar, looking down and shuffling his shoes to and fro across the dusty floor.

152

Somewhere in the depths of the café area, a customer slipped a jeton into the juke box.

There was a tin-whistle wheeze, and the place was taken over by one of those unkillable dance numbers from the Thirties, the kind that get dug up out of retirement and re-paraded once every five years, like a military reserve.

He and Betty had come in on maybe the sixth revival of this one, and that was long enough back heaven knew. The thing must have been in and out of fashion half a dozen times since he'd last heard it. He could barely remember the words. Betty had always hummed them under her breath.

> I'll keep my heart ex-directory
> So that it can't be wrung . . .

He looked down at the scuffed toe of his shoe swinging in sad time to the music.

This was a fine way for it all to end. All that high hopeful 'quest for happiness', and what had he come to? Sobbing facile Irish tears into his Scotch, nostalgising over a tune from the days when 'sophistication' meant dressing for dinner, while he kicked, to its hrythm, an extra scuff onto his already scuffed shoes.

Pat (Slim) O'Rooley: dead-beat dick; weeper peeper; down-at-heel heel; no-account, never-amount, small-time, all but buddy-can-you-spare-a-dime, virtually peg-leg leg man, living on the edge of having his licence revoked and carrying a pocketful of currency even a ninth-rate barkeep didn't want.

Why did he have to be this way? Why couldn't he have done a deal with Sham Rocks on those stones that were ringers? Why hadn't he let little Tish Vecelli cut him in on that load of heisted gats? Who asked him to play hero, anyway?

That's what Betty had wanted to know, and she'd been right. She was right to quit, too. She'd had a premonition he'd never amount to more than scuffed shoes and drachmas.

Why him, anyway? Why did he have to be the only guy left who cared who was guilty? Why was his the only sense of justice left in this world?

You make me sick, O'Rooley. Why don't you tote your shabby

153

integrity back home to the holy island and painlessly drop it into Bantry Bay?

He turned back to the bar and whistled up the barkeep.

'You like to do me a favour, bud?'

'Like I'd like to climb up to the top of the control tower and walk out into the night.'

'Don't cause me to do my manhood an injury while I laugh at your wit.'

'You started the wisecracking, mister. Didn't I hear you say "favour"?'

'O.K., little human brother', O'Rooley said wearily, hauling another drachma out of his pocket.

The barkeep picked it up, spat on it, and put it down again. O'Rooley replaced it by an Irish threepence. The barkeep didn't even pick that up. Resigned, O'Rooley proferred a Swiss franc. It was accepted.

O'Rooley placed the tartan rug on the counter. 'Keep this for me till I call back for it', he said. 'If anyone asks, you never saw me.'

The barkeep put his hand on the rug, then paused. 'Is it hot?' he said.

'Sweltering.'

'I mean is it stolen goods? Is there an alert out for it?'

O'Rooley made a wide frank Irish countenance, and spread his hands, too, for good ideogrammatic measure. 'Brother. Don't you trust me?'

'Like I'd trust you if you was brother to Judas Iscariot. Which wouldn't surprise me.'

'Brother, can't you *see* my shabby integrity written all over my endearingly beat-up face?'

12

A man might sustain any loss except that of his honour.

O'Rooley wished now he'd thought to put a tail on that suspiciously aggressive Irish pair he'd overheard at the bar. But he hadn't understood the case so clearly then. Determined to recover

154

what, he now realised, had been filched from him, he had to pick up a cold trail. He admitted he was without a single lead, fazed. He would have to play it by ear and trust to the luck of the Irish.

Whatever type of organisation it was he was up against, clearly it operated in secret. So when he quit the bar he made for the nearest door he could see marked (in several languages) No Entry.

By good luck, it wasn't locked. O'Rooley went cautiously through and found himself in a corridor of closed doors, all of which were marked No Entry, too.

He turned the knob of the first, flung the door open and waited on the threshold.

No one jumped him.

No one, in fact, paid him the smallest attention.

The room inside was bisected by a waist-high conveyor belt. Behind it stood a row of jolly, rolled-sleeved wenches. Past them teetered on the belt a series of pink plastic trays, each of which was moulded, like an irregular palette (painter's – but there *was*, also, just a suspicion, coming probably from the colour and material, of false teeth), into several shallow depressions. Into the depressions the wenches were ladling foods (from kettledrum witchcauldrons): a dollop a trollop.

Meanwhile a superwench, standing to one side like the reader-aloud of works of piety to her Sisters in a refectory, recited from a clipboard the day's requirements, intoning a countdown of world religions:

'ten Mohammedan
nine Jewish
eight Catholic (is it Holyfishfryday?)
seven Hindu
six Diabetic . . . '

Unable to conceive that the thieves, whoever they might and despicable and desperate as they must be, were cannibals into the bargain, O'Rooley concluded there was no clue here and backed out, closing the door.

Caution unabated, he opened the next door in the same gingerly way.

155

Again, no one reacted.

Indeed, he thought at first the room was empty.

A swaying and humming, however, drew his eye upwards. It was merely that the room was unfurnished and unoccupied so far as ground level was concerned. At eye level, it was thickly slung – it was asway – with hammocks.

Again the impression was dominantly of pink: pink of a slightly slubbed shininess: the pink (and occasionally peach, with a still more occasional coffee here and there) of immaculately ironed petticoats reclining in the hammocks, their unwrinkled nylon legs, all of the regulation glamorous pattern and proportions, protruding in horizontal relaxation at one end. (A very few of the hammocks held two occupants.)

The slow, gentle pampas-grass swaying of the hammocks in unison proceeded undisturbed by O'Rooley's presence. So did the soft singing of massed voices, soprano slotted into alto part in a creamy conjunction like the union of milk and plain chocolate into elaborate hand-made fancies:

How I'll trounce her, how I'll trounce her,
When I get my hands on that false Betty Bouncer.

O'Rooley gently withdrew, silently closing the door after him. He noticed that, beneath its No Entry sign, it was labelled AIRHOST-RESTROOM. Down the corridor he was pursued by the gentle soprano voice which now took up, solo, the verse part of the old air-shanty, sad and slow as a mermaid's lament:

Betty Bouncer was a fair young lass
When she met that sailor bold
But her answer was 'Yes sir' (alas)
When he cried 'Come into my hold'.

And then the refrain returned, the voices massed again but softened, now, to a thick whisper as O'Rooley distanced himself down the corridor:

How I'll denounce her, o how I'll denounce her,
When I get my hands on that slut Betty Bouncer.

It was some way to the next door. A foxy, gingery little man with

156

the face of an honest weasel, eyes red-rimmed from the dust of many quests, he loped — he was a touch bandy — along the corridor.

It was like a chronic cough, his habit of thinking of himself as unlovable. Whenever he could, he went disguised. He believed that, unlike the big glamour boys, even though they were far less skilled, he could never engage and hold the affection of the spectators. He believed that the freckles which covered his face and neck — they were huge splodges, more like the mottling on a tortiose than like ordinary freckles — were emblems of some mottling of his soul. The ginger gooseberry hairs of his bowed, muscular legs gave him the creeps.

Because of his dislike of his own name, of his very self, (a dislike that might have impelled him to suicide long before, had that not been against the rules of chivalry) he would often enter the lists anonymously, or, if the tournament promotors insisted, he would invent some self-scorning soubriquet for himself like 'The Knight Errant, Most Grievously Errant' or 'The Chevalier O'Hooligan'. But whatever he called himself he was, from the moment he came into engagement, unmistakable. Howls of recognition would rise from the delighted crowd as he betrayed himself, perhaps by the very couch of his lance under his arm or by one of those seemingly impossible forehand half-volleys down the line or by the sheer agile effrontery with which he would wham an apparent ace straight back to the feet of the incoming server . . . It was as if he had worked and worked from boyhood up to achieve this dogged mastery (which he carried without panache, without sign of pleasure, even, almost as if it were a burden) because he had been convinced all his life that he would never be good at anything else and, above all, that he would never be loved. That people *had* loved him did not shift his conviction. He believed it was an aberration — or, just possibly, a kindly meant pretence — on their part. Giving a strong impression that he was apologising for the fact, he simply was the best knight in the world. Often he went through an entire tournament without dropping a set or being unhorsed, never losing his look of slightly inattentive apology.

He flung open the third door, still half-expecting a rod. But only a lather of steam ballooned out at him.

Through it he discerned a large woman standing at an ironing board. On the board was spread a pair of blue serge trousers which she was energetically pressing with a steaming rolling pin.

At least, unlike the other people he had looked in on, she acknowledged O'Rooley. She looked briefly up at him and then disappointedly remarked:

'O, you are not my boy. He promised to return the third day. Promises, promises, always promises.'

She blew into the steam and resumed her pressing while she continued:

'Hour after hour goes by and still he doesn't shew bread. I should worry? I am only his mother. Only I am up since dawn deepfatfrying the little schikaneders he likes so much to eat, and already I am running seventy-five times to the window to take a matzo whether he is on his way. Matzo-schmatzo. All the same, he is a good boy. Always he is a good boy since right from when he made his Bar-Cafeteria, and never a passover at the girls to this day . . . '

Sadly Sir Patrice withdrew and silently re-latched the door, convinced he was not worthy to see the Holy Grail though at the same time knowing perfectly well no such thing existed.

After he had closed the door, a few whisps of steam seeped from beneath it, lit now to rather ugly sunset colours by an unearthly Caspar David Friedrich glow.

Deep in sadness, Sir Patrice proceeded.

Presently he met an airhostess walking on brisk high heels in the opposite direction.

'I think the Holy Grill may be about to blow its top', he called out to her.

'Thanks. It often gets steamed up', she called back cheerfully as she passed. 'I'll alert the Seneschal.'

Patrice came to the fourth door and walked in without precaution. An unseen lurker behind it clunked him on the head with the butt of a Luger. Luger-schmluger.

158

13

While he was out cold, a maiden ran screaming, hair-and-garments-streaming, down the forest path. She was haunted by the Holy Ghost.

14

Feeling groggy and twenty years broader, Burleigh (= a touch Raymond Burrly across the back of the shoulders – Scholiast) O'Rooley made his way back down the corridor to the café, where he had given Patricia orders to meet him at 7.15.

As soon as he came in sight of the place, he spotted her, sitting at a table in the centre, dainty, feminine and punctual as always.

The burly lawyer slid into the chair facing her.

'You look all in, chief.'

'We could both do with a black coffee', he replied, and signalled to the captain.

Patricia, otherwise known as Bunny, had been O'Rooley's confidential secretary these three hundred cases now. He had no secrets from her. Rumour had often linked her name romantically with that of the famous lawyer but somehow O'Rooley always drew back before the prospect of making their working partnership into a marital one.

INTERLUDE

It must be left to the Reader to guess whether the
procrastination or hesitation, whichever it might be, was
caused by some inner doubt on the part of the famous lawyer – a
doubt ostensibly anomalous in so fine a figure of a man, who
yet was also, as Patricia knew, a man far more inward-feeling
than a spectator would ever guess from his somewhat flamboyant
performances in court – as to his virility.

The red-jacketed captain of waiters was leaning over their table. 'May I take your order? It is a pleasure to serve you, Mr O'Rooley. I recognised you from photographs at once, of course.'

O'Rooley nodded. 'Then perhaps you will kindly see that my confidential secretary and I get some privacy in which to discuss an important case.'

'Certainly, Mr O'Rooley. And your order?'

'Two black coffees. With' — O'Rooley looked up at Patricia — 'French fried, Bunny?' She nodded, smiling. The lawyer gave the order, and the captain withdrew.

'You look as if you could use some sleep right now, chief', Patricia solicitously said.

'Take out your notebook', O'Rooley replied. 'You know I never sleep when a case is commencing to break.'

'Chief, you don't mean you've cracked this one? But I thought you were completely fazed.'

'We're not out of the forest yet, Bunny, but I see a glimmer of light down the forest tracks. People are apt to mistrust circumstantial narration, but that is because they don't practise natural selection. It isn't the facts that are wrong, Bunny. Facts can't go wrong. It is the factition that may err. And it is easy to be led astray when asses make up alibis out of whole cloth ears.'

The captain placed their order before them. O'Rooley waited till he had withdrawn out of clothearshot, and then resumed:

'What people forget is that detection is ninety per cent deduction. I am frank to admit I don't yet know who. But I know exactly where and how.'

'Why, that's marvellous, chief. I just don't see how you did it.'

'Mostly by pure Logic, Bunny. Let us take *where* first. If you. were organising a ring for stealing valuable objects and smuggling them abroad, where would you choose to operate?'

'Why, chief, I guess I don't know.'

'At an airport', O'Rooley said.

'Why, chief, that's brilliant. I just don't know why I didn't see it.'

'Our friends have the simplicity of geniuses. And now, let us consider the *how* of the organisation. Remember, Bunny: it is a secret organisation, and therefore you will want to structure it
160

cryptogrammatically. Yet you will want it to preserve an inner lucidity. If you were structuring such an organisation, Bunny, what is the most Logical system you could think of to Predicate it on?'

'I guess I must be dazed for lack of sleep or something, chief, but I just can't think', said Bunny (Patricia).

'You shall have a night's sleep just as soon as you've done one or two small commissions for me', O'Rooley chivalrously said, covering her small hand as it lay on the table with his large one. 'Go to the airport hotel and book yourself a suite. Charge it to expenses.'

'Why, chief, that's swell of you. But what' – she blinked back a tear or two of gratitude and perhaps of something more– 'about the structure of the organisation? Go on telling me, chief.'

O'Rooley sometimes wished Bunny would vary her habitual 'chief' with, say, 'Master' or 'Maestro'. However, he uncomplainingly resumed:

'Well, Bunny, the most Logical structure for such an organisation would be to divide the members into four groups. To preserve secrecy, each member would operate under a code name. The code names in the first group or figure would be' – O'Rooley consulted a scrap of paper he drew from his pocket – 'BARBARA, CELARENT, DARII and FERIO. Etcetera, etcetera, etcetera. I won't worry you with the details.'

'I guess that's a superb exercise in Detective Logic, chief', Patricia sighed admiringly.

'The bulk of the work', O'Rooley admitted, 'is now completed. It remains only to locate the felons and round them up. In particular, we must concentrate on bringing in the sinister BARBARA.'

'You *will* take care of yourself, chief?'

'Don't worry.' He smiled reassuringly. 'And now just make a note of what I want you to do.'

Patricia smiled, pencil poised.

'First', O'Rooley listed while she listed and scribbled, 'I want you to go along to the lobby. Put through a call to the D.A's office and throw them off the scent.'

'I'll do that, chief', Patricia (Bunny) smiled.

It was a standing joke between them that in all cases involving the

161

identification of scents O'Rooley was in the habit of having recourse to his secretary's finer senses and feminine expertise.

'Then call Doctor Lancelot and have him go down the corridor to Door Four where he'll pick up a concussion case in need of attention.'

'You *will* be careful, chief?'

'I will be careful. Tell the Doc to keep it under his hat.'

(Doc Lancelot, specialist in boys' boils by no choice of his own but by dint of his thirty years' service as medical officer to the Sir Giovanni Choirschool, was a retired practitioner who, having reason to be grateful for the lawyer's discretion in the past, undertook all O'Rooley's medical work in cases where secrecy was of the essence.)

'Then I want you to type out a writ, take it down to the courtroom and get it sworn, and then serve it straight down the line before meeting me back here at 7.27. You got that?'

'Yes, chief.' (By *dint*, she'd got it.)

'You'd better make a shorthand note of the form the writ is to take. Mainly it follows the usual outline of the procès lingual. We stipulate that evidence may be entered subject to our right of re-redirect examination. We also object that any objection is incompetent, immaterial and not part of the Ray's jest I read on the men's locker room wall.'

'Gee, chief, that's a brilliant legal manoeuvre. That'll get the D.A. over a barrel.'

'I don't mean to let him get off the hook, Bunny. We are accepting an aged retainer in this case, and that means an attorney must always put the client's interests in a position of privileged communication. We must make sure our client obtains complete restitution of the stolen property when it is recovered.'

'We sure must, chief.'

'One final point, Bunny. Wherever, in a normal procès lingual, you would type the words "corpus delicti", please in this instance substitute the words "membrum virile".'

'O.K., chief', said Patricia, efficiently snapping her shorthand notebook to and rising. 'I'll be right back. Take care of yourself.'

'I will', he promised, as he rose and courteously drew back Patricia's chair, 'and I'll have a bourbon waiting on the rocks for

162

you. Meanwhile I'll take a drink myself and think some more about the case.'

'You work too hard, chief.'

'It's the only way to crack 'em, Bunny', he smiled. 'But I have every hope this one will turn out to be a brief case.' And so saying, he unbuckled in very truth his briefcase and, taking out the necessary papers, settled to work on the problem of *Who*?

Who, he realised it boiled down to, had a motive?

15

At 7.27 O'Rooley carried two bourbons on the rocks from the bar to the table where Bunny (Patricia) was to meet him. But she wasn't there. Suddenly he saw the criminal folly of his letting her go about unprotected when he was up against a gang of such declared desperation. Now the moment he had often, in the course of three hundred cases, foreseen in his nightmares had arrived — the moment of

Determined not to default on a record of punctuality maintained through three hundred cases, Patricia (Bunny) hurried into the café at exactly 7.27. She went swiftly to the rendezvous table. The chief had gone. Now it had actually happened, she recognised from her nightmares the result she had often dreaded would issue from his strenuous handling of his cases. This plainly was nothing else than

THE SNATCH

Disrupt the connexion. It is broken, this working relationship that may also be erotic and, if so, is probably incestuous. The long established interlocution stops. Each is left without the secret interlocutor to babble secrets or admiration to.

THE THRENODY. Pity Bunny, that doomed to wait through three hundred cases child bride.

16

Slamming back to the bar, O'Rooley slapped down Patricia's passport photograph. 'Seen this dame?'

'Nope', said the barkeep.

O'Rooley placed a drachma on the counter. The barkeep ignored it. 'Ain't seen nothing', the barkeep said. 'Don't know no one.'

O'Rooley guessed the guy was dummying up. He spoke like a man under orders. Someone had got to him first.

There wasn't much O'Rooley could do about it.

'O.K.', he said. 'I'll have my rug back.'

With ostentatious slowness, the barkeep went in back to fetch it.

Behind him, as he waited, O'Rooley heard the two Irishwomen.

'Well, just a last rose of summer, then, if you insist.'

He heard them clink glasses.

'More Tyrone Power to your elbow.'

'May your shadow never grow Connemara.'

Two glasses were heavily set down. Two pairs of heavy footsteps moved away.

O'Rooley turned and followed them eagerly with his eyes— which were all he was at present, thanks to the infuriating slowness of the barkeep, free to follow with.

He lost the two figures in the crowd. Then he picked them up again and saw them — he was pretty damn' sure he saw them — entering their shop.

'Don't you want it now I got it for you?' said the barkeep.

The figures had vanished. O'Rooley snatched up the tartan rug and (incipit FUGUE) set off.

Left alone, the heroine sings forlornly of her love for the vanished Patrick, a love she had never dared, she avers, to declare to his face.

The mood of the scena changes. Two brisk trumpet calls introduce a mood of resolution. In her famous D major cavatina ('Vestita da uomo'), she sings 'Find him will I at all costs . . . I will don male attire.'

(The conventions of the period forbade, of course, a change of costume on stage. Although the heroine sings of her *intention* to assume male dress, we know from old prints that, in the original production, she was already at this point *in* masculine clothes. So much for

165

the naturalism of early product-
ions — and the logic of aud-
iences!)

As the timpani tap out a
war-like rhythm, the heroine
draws her sword and sets off in
search of Patrick (Aspettami,
Patrizio').

O'Rooley knifed round three
sides of the cubic tank and came
to the gap in the glass which
must be the entrance to the
shop. Cautiously, O'Rooley
slithered through.

A blue rinse of neon light laid
everything stark to view.

The glass-topped counter was
illuminated by its own internal
floodlighting, which picked out
the contents of the sliding draw-
ers beneath. One drawer,
O'Rooley perceived, was piled
with pram quilts, labelled by a
display card 'Soft as County
Down'. In another, long-sleeved,
button-up, porridge-consistency
(under)vests were laid out like so
many large corpses. The display
card read 'Go Irish Navvy this
Autumn'.

The right flank of the shop
was occupied by a hanging rack
of striped, woven jackets. 'Gal-
way Blazers', said the notice at
the top. At the left flank hung a
row of slightly thinner and finer
garments: 'Kerry Blouses'.

166

And everywhere, in freestanding piles on the floor, in snow-drifts huddled up against the glass and crammed up behind rack and counter, were huge stocks of horseblankets.

O'Rooley looked about him, half-expecting a section somewhere, designed to tempt clients of the Betty Bouncer fancy, to be labelled Connaughtical Dress. There was none.

Neither was there any sign of human occupants.

And yet surely he had seen, or as near seen as made no matter, the two women stomp their way in?

Baffled, he paused beside a man-high revolving tie-rack that stood just inside the entrance.

Wait.

Did not his delicately attuned sleuth's sensory apparatus detect from somewhere a distinct, a regularly rasped in and out, a definitely Greco—Irish hrough breathing?

With an agility amazing in so muscularly built a man, O'Rooley rounded the tie-rack and took refuge behind it.

Having asked directions ('My friends, I rely on your simplicity') from the Three Geniuses (the rôles, originally written for bôys, are nowadays usually sung

167

O'Rooley realised that the hand with which he intended to steady himself in his concealment was in reality pushing the tie-rack round. Following its course automatically, he found himself

precipitated, as by a revolving door, into the middle of the shop again.

He cast a look about. There was still no one in sight.

Concluding that the rough-breathing he had heard was an auditory illusion or just possibly the result of some defect in the functioning of the neon light, he left the shop.

He turned sharply to his left, and, still exercising a sleuth's stealth, moved like a shadow along the North wall and then, turning left again, set off down the outside of the West wall

by wômen), the heroine arrives at the shop.

Just inside the entrance, she pauses, leaning her hand casually on a tie-rack that happens to be standing there. While she sings despairingly of the hopelessness of her search for the hero ('Patrizio, dove sei andato?'), she gradually turns the tie-rack and herself moves slowly behind it.

The heroine vanishes behind the revolving rack from the view of the audience.

168

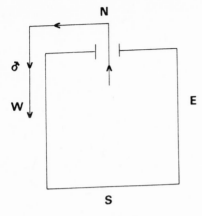

Having rounded the rack without finding the vanished Patrick, the heroine emerges again onto the centre of the stage. After a brief lament ('Luce, luce, ma tutt'è oscuro per me'), she leaves the shop and turns to her right and then right again.

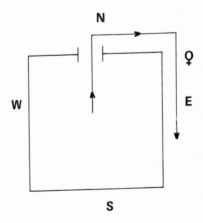

After travelling the length of the West wall, O'Rooley turned left again and set off along the South wall.

Urged on ('A destra, a destra' — a melody the composer had previously used, in the *Gloria* of his C minor Mass, Op.69, for his setting of 'Qui sedes ad dexteram Patris') by the Three Geniuses, the heroine sings of her resolve to turn right again, and thus walk alongside the South wall, so soon as she shall reach the end of the East wall, which, indeed, she is fast approaching.

At this moment the heroine turns the East-South corner.

Advanced perhaps a third of the way along the South wall, O'Rooley, realising he had missed the chance to tidy up one small corner of his business, swung rightabout and, starting up alongside the West wall again, retraced his route.

Halfway along the South wall, the heroine halts and invokes the Three Geniuses.

(Explicit Fugue.)

He crept into the shop. Again, he was convinced of hearing, though he could not locate, rough breathing.

Silently slipping the folded tartan off his forearm, he refolded it into a more accurate oblong and then placed it on top of

170

the nearest pile of horseblankets.

You can sell that to some customer, perhaps indeed its original owner come to seek a replacement, his thoughts remarked to the unseen Irish genii loci; and in the meantime, he added, get on with your rug breathing.

He'd given a goodbye pat to the pile and was on the point of creeping away when the Irish women spoke.

The sound murmured up to him from floor level, from somewhere down behind the counter, between, O'Rooley presumed, the counter and the stock of muffling hoarseblankets shored up against the wall.

The voices came hushed but flushed.

'I'm not sure this is working.'

'Toh, if your heart's not in it – '

'My heart is *so*, in it. Are you sure *you*'re really trying?'

'I am *so*, trying. But will you make allowance for the obstructions?'

'I *am* making allowance amn't I? Did I not say we were bound to be a touch inhibited since – '

'Hoh. Is there a whiff of the Irish puritan clinging about you still?'

'There is not. But since it is a

fact that we are aunt and
niece — '

'And isn't that a fact that
only makes the thing more glori-
ous? I would have understood
you, now, had you complained
of the publicity, and us living in
a glass house if you take my
drift.'

'Is it scared of a breath of
scandal you are now?'

'It is not. Will you wait till I
explain?'

'Where's the need? It's clear
as neon. You'd sooner go unful-
filled than infringe the bourgeois
conventions.'

'I would not. And anyway
not a soul can see us down here,
and us snug between the counter
and the County Cavan
cardigans.'

'And very confined for space
it is down here, too. Do you
suppose it might be the want of
space that's cramping your
style?'

'So you're out with it at last?
It's cramped you find my style?'

'Is it taking on you are now?'

'Do you imagine that was a
complimentary remark to make
in the circumstances?'

'If it's compliments you're
wanting — '

'And if it's style *you*'re wanting, there's places, you know,

172

there's organisations, I've heard, where you could no doubt pick yourself up an expert that'd – '

'Is it amateur you're accusing me of being?'

'Of all the tendentious – '

'For the matter of that, if it's equipment you're wanting, why don't you pick yourself up a MAN?'

An instant slap was followed by the muffled evidence of strugglings in a confined space, during which the breathing was suddenly much rougher.

The top layer of blankets behind the counter wobbled.

There was then a silence, after which the rough breathing began again but now in the form of a sigh.

'Heigho.'

'Mayo.'

'O, auntie.'

'O' – this with deep tristesse – 'my niece'.

'If we're forever after fighting, how can we *expect* to have a love affair?'

The case, O'Rooley suddenly perceived, was solved.

It had all fallen into place in his head.

He knew now who would have a motive. He knew now where he would have to go, would have to chute to, in order to retrieve his property.

'Will we have another shot at it?'

'We will. After all, it's not as if we were Irish.'

'It's not indeed. Contentious disputatious peasants that they are.'

'They are indeed. Though I *wish* it wasn't quite so public in this shop.'

'I wish it wasn't quite so narrow down here.'

As the Actress said to the Bishop (✠), O'Rooley thought, piously blessing himself across his chest as he hurried away. Outside, he noticed, though it was not of the smallest importance to him or to the clientele, that the facia of the shop bore the licensee's or concessionaire's (presumably, the aunt's) name: I.B. Ó Murchadha (pron. Murphy).

Warned by the Geniuses of the dangers she must undergo if she is to accomplish her quest, the heroine declares ('Agli infimi confini del inferno') her determination to descend, if need be, to the lowest circles of the underworld itself.

17

Beset by eerily invisible perils, the hero Oruleus (latinised as Ulrix and thence rather quaintly englished as Unruly) pressed, with the slight limp which he carried like the badge of his mysterious but high parentage and his heroic destiny, ever forward.

Protected by the nimbus of heroism, he waded unscathed across the river of metal and thus set foot in the dread realm of the Great Camp King.

The dimmed lights were as distant above him as stars. The ground beneath was hard, cold and gritty.

With every step he felt himself the prey of unseen seeing eyes. Behind every obstacle that bulked darkly on his route he thought he heard an unseen watcher's breath sharp caught and held till he should pass. Sometimes an inexplicable prickle of warmth just beneath his epidermis seemed to give notice of rays infra-red or radar, ascertaining by long-distance acupuncture his outline and the direction of his advance.

His advance, however, halted. Reflexions of the dull light had given him a glimpse of coils from which even his heroic heart must for an instant recoil.

Across his path moved a gleaming ooze.

The hero peered. He made it out. A monster was sliming past his heroic feet.

It was armoured. Unruly heard the rattle and saw the glitterings of its metallic joints as its self-moving undulations heaved up-and-downing before him.

He set his narrowed eyes to trace the course of its unconscionable length.

It was describing a perfect inner circle, cutting him off, as it flowed round and round, from the heart of the kingdom.

He wondered what treasure it might be guarding.

He raised his eyes and tried to pierce the darkness at the centre.

He discerned the huge, shadowed bulk of a massive central pillar. Against it, by the faint light, a paleness mooned.

With a pang of pity at the perception, Unruly recognised the paleness of a fair skin exposed. Naked, bound and gagged, the maiden Patricia stood chained, her arms stretched above her head, to an iron ring affixed to the central pillar.

Seized by a savage and righteous indignation, Unruly swirled his briefcase like an axe above his head and brought it down with a smashing blow on the monster's oozing bulk.

The monstrous length of muscle rose into a throe, gave a climactic rattle and relaxed into stillness.

Unruly scrambled over its body and began running towards Patricia.

A rattle warned him he had only stunned, not despatched the monster. He cast it a look, and saw its oozing start up again, this time in the opposite direction, which confirmed his suspicion that it was the two-way monster, the unique and notorious Amphisbaena itself, that had been set to guard this most priceless of treasures.

How, when he should have freed the maiden, he would circumvent the monster on the way back he would have to decide when the moment came. If experience had made it too wary to be stunned a second time, he might have to charm it with a snatch of magical opera or proffer an obol-drachma. But the first objective was to free the maiden.

He was already at her side, chivalrously trying not to press himself too obtrusively against her lovely and vulnerable nakedness. And indeed it seemed to him, even by the unreliable light, that a blush was rosing her face and bosom.

He tugged and tugged at her bonds, evidently paining her, since little cries were coming through her gag.

He hoped to desperation point that the Amphisbaena was prevented by its very length from circling any closer in.

He worked one string of the leathern thong loose but it ran instantly into a knot. The job had been done by an expert.

Thinking to give the poor girl the relief at least of speech, for no doubt she had bottled up in her the complex details of which king's daughter she was and in propitiation of what terror she had been demanded as hostage or sacrifice, Unruly decided to leave the bonds for the time being and tackle the gag.

That was easier. Indeed it came slipping out as readily as a boxer's gumshield into his second's hand, and with it the girl's spat words:

'What in hell do you think you're doing? I'm a bondage fanatic.'

'Oc', Unruly cried, staggering under the recognition.

'Foc Oc', the girl said; 'that is a trite, over-rated and amateurish little work. And what's it to you, anyway, you officious bastard?'

The gag slipped from Unruly's unnerved fingers. He stumbled away. The girl's voice pursued him through the dark, vicious, querulous:

'Kindly adjust my bonds before leaving . . . '

But unmanned Patricia reeled out of earshot.

18

She was jumped — jumped, rolled, pinned down — by the unseen watchers.

Concrete gritting into the back of her hair, she looked up into a sacra conversazione of the tough faces of her captors and interrogators.

'Who're you?'

She decided to give her butch name in the hope of sounding tougher. 'Bunny', she replied.

'And what're you doing down here?'

Bunny (Patricia) kept silence. (But suppose they decided to beat her up, these brawny blue-serged women?)

'Are you just snooping?' demanded one with very short, elegantly cut hair.

'Or spying?' demanded an elegantly cut chin.

'Or infiltrating?' said a thick knee on her stomach.

'Are you from the C.I.A.?'

'I am not', protested Bunny's libertarian indignation, rupturing her vow of silence. 'I am trying to recover my property, which your gang stole from me.'

'And do you suppose, then, that just because we're queer we must be crooked?'

Too her puzzlement, Patricia recognised the timbre of an indignation as sincere as her own.

177

Faltering. she asked: 'Do you mean to tell me your organisation is *not* devoted to the filching and smuggling of male sexual organs?'

'And what would we want with those?'

'Well — '. Insofar as her captive position allowed, Patricia shrugged.

'As if we couldn't do better than that.'

'But the secrecy of your organisation — '

'What do you know of our organisation?' they pounced.

Patricia let a pause fall, then blinked and said, throw-awayly: 'Everything.'

She could tell from their silence they were impressed.

'Yet you didn't even know we weren't criminals', countered the fat one, who was moustached.

'I was testing you', Patricia coolly said.

'And who're you to test us? You're just a privates-spy.'

'I am not. I will tell you precisely who I am, but not from flat on my back on this exceptionally hard floor.'

A whisper went round the conspiracy of heads.

'O.K.', said the fat one, cautiously lifting her knee.

Patricia struggled up and at once sat faintly down on a suitcase. Warily her captors squatted in a circle round her.

'Who *are* you, then?'

'I am one of you', Patricia said.

'A likely tale.'

'Do you deny', Patricia said, 'that you, too, have a member missing? You collectively, I mean.'

A whisper went from mouth to ear round the circle.

Appointed spokesbutch again, the fat one said:

'We neither deny nor confirm it. But this time *we*'ll test *you*. What's the password?'

Patricia snatched a panicking breath and then heard herself reply on a wing of inspiration:

'K.L.M. — Royal Butch Airlines.'

This time the whisper that went round was an open secret and it was of admiration.

Improving on the advantage she had won, Patricia said into the circle:

178

'If you insist on further proof of my identity — and as a matter of fact I am quite pleased to find you so security-conscious — I will give it by identifying each of you by your code names.'

She was encircled by a sussurration of scepticism.

Nevertheless the squatters hunkered-in closer, tense to hear the demonstration, and one or two standing stragglers outside the circle moved in to make an upper, outer ring.

Patricia looked, direct and commanding, at the fat woman. Inclining her an ironist's from-the-waist bow as she sat, Patricia said: 'You are KAY LARENT.'

She turned to the well-cut jaw: 'FAY LAPTON, I presume.'

Picking out a faunic, shy, beautiful, gentle, mid-oriental face, whose ears exotically tintinabulated with jewel-stuck pagodas and whose neck was gorgeously collared, under the harsh porter's uniform, in a gorget of gold, Patricia identified: 'BRAMANTIP'.

A wiry wisp of woman she recognised as 'FAIRY O'.

A legal-minded woman she distinguished as 'the D.A.RII'.

When she had named them all, they were hers.

On an awed breath, Fay Lapton enquired: 'And who are — you?'

'Who would I be', Patricia replied, rising, 'if not the organiser and queen-pin of you all? I am BARBARA.'

They stood in homage, silent, round her.

Only the legal mind of D.A.Rii dared frame and stammer out:

'N-no doubt there is some very s-simple explanation, b-but how *can* you be B-Barbara, when you are a m-man?'

Patrick gave only a second's b-blink. 'And do you suppose', he demanded, 'that just because I am a man I must be anti-lesbian?'

Discovering he enjoyed the thrall in which he now held them, he unthinkingly fell into a demagogic pose while he rhetoricised: 'Am I not an egali-libertarian? Name me two of the most grievously oppressed social groups in history. I will name them for you: Women; and Homosexuals. Tell me, then, in the sacred name of Logic, which is *the* most double-grievously oppressed social group in the entire history of the human race. I will tell you: Homosexual Women.'

His audience burst out into clapping.

'But now, my comrades', Patrick resumed, **'our scheming, our**
179

plotting, our organising, our secrecy are ripening to their culmination. Gather round, and I will divulge my Maestro-plan.'

Imperially beckoned, they found boldness enough to creep closer and peer at the leaflet Patrick had pulled out of his briefcase.

It was the leaflet he had been handed after his televisual performance. On the back, crudely mistranslated as 'guyed to the Airport', there was a groundplan, on which he quickly orientated himself (the main intercourse, leading to the castration complex . . .). Then he pointed out to his followers a mark on the diagram that resembled a coiled spring. 'The spiral staircase', he said.

'The spiral staircase?'

'The spiral staircase', he explained, 'leads, up the inside of a glass funnel, to the control tower. I need not tell you that the control tower is the nerve centre of the whole socio-architectural entity. Who gains that ganglion, who controls control, takes all. The plan, comrades, is simple. We shall take control of the controls.'

His boldness and simplicity had them for a moment stunned. Then they applauded like thunder.

Letting them release their nervous energies for a full minute, Patrick took the opportunity to slip the leaflet back into his briefcase and then to sheath his briefcase under his left arm. Then he raised his right hand to quench the clapping.

'Comrades, a great new movement stirs in the underworld. The days of oppression are past. Let the world note a new phenomenon: Lesbian Power.'

They cheered.

'The Microcosm shall rise and overwhelm the Macrocosm.'

They cheered again.

'The Lesbian Takeover is on. Barbara leads. Follow me.'

So crying, Patrick leapt onto the conveyor-belt, standing imposingly, though a touch wobblingly, on the branch line which he knew would presently conduct him upwards.

Inspired, the porters blue-serged towards the belt and one by one leapt on after their leader. Lumbering, wiry, wire-haired, scrubbymoustached, black and comely (BAROCO), Grecian-featured (CAMENES), thin, intense and cropped, sonsy and genial: severally,

180

but all muscular, all tough, they flung themselves forward as onto the barricades.

And already, in the lead, Patrick was high above ground level, the conveyor so steeply inclined that he could scarcely keep his footing and had from moment to moment to re-strike his heroic posture.

With a faint mechanical wobble he rose like an eighteenth-century masqued deity in a operatic machine; rose like the sun in his chariot; rose like a show-girl in a Thirties musical, like a show-man, like the drag demimondain demigod he was, like Myra Breckinridge, like scythe-wheeled Boadicea, like the glittering sequinny BARBARA, the Great Camp Queen-Pin herself.

'Don't forget to duck when you reach the trap-door', he remembered to call down to his followers. Then, turning a touch teeteringly about, he himself ducked, just in time, and fronted the flap with his forehead as, blessing himself across his folded chest, he murmured:

'Into your hands I commend this adventure. Pray for us, Saint Sappho.'

19

Piercingly top-lit, enfolded, as by a brandysnap, in gleaming, dark-outside glass, the black spiral writhed beautifully up.

But the passage up its shallow steps was impeded, was impossibilised: by couples, sitting.

Ambiguously dressed, they were ambiguously paired, lapsed on one another in attitudes of non-erotic, chummy passivity, and impassable.

At the head of the invading hoard and the foot of the spiralling staircase, Pat fiercely demanded access.

'What' — listlessly — 'for?'

'This is a butsch, a takeover bid.'

'You're late. It's been done.'

There was a clearing crackle and then the public-address system stridently and just intelligibly filled the atmosphere.

'Please keep calm. Please keep calm. The revolution has taken over. This is a sit-in. Sit still and do nothing.'

The machine went dead.

Pat turned to face his followers' enquiry.

'Everything depends', he explained, 'on *what* revolution.'

Public-address spoke again. 'This is to announce', it said, 'that there is only one family, the human family.'

It switched off.

'That includes', Pat said to his followers, 'you. Now I know your interests will be taken care of, I am happy to hand over. I have no wish for fame and no hankering after immortality in the history books. I abdicate.'

'But Barbara', they cried, protestant, concerned, stirring, gently surging in.

It was Bramantip who, for all her delicacy of oriental shyness, swayed closest, swinging low a sweet pagoda (they were hollow, and she burned tiny pills of incense inside them) from her pierced, biscuit-brown lobe and urgently murmuring low 'Barbara, Barbara *darling*.'

But Barbara had swooned away.

SECTION FOUR
LET IT ALL COME BREAKDOWN
Allergo Energico e Passionato

1

Incipit Fictory (=the victory of $\left\{ \begin{array}{l} \text{history as fiction} \\ \text{fiction as history} \end{array} \right\}$– Scholiast).

Praise to the Scholiast in Full Flight – J.H. Thucydides.

I. The most immediately and universally perceptible result of the revolution was din. It was perhaps only to be expected that the general public should be, initially at least, silenced by the sudden takeover. What did surprise impartial observers was that most of the revolutionaries themselves were equally silent, standing or sitting about in apparently unexcited groups.

The din which filled In Transit was caused, then, not by the majority but by a minority among the revolutionaries. This minority consisted of four or five Groups (a usage in which the word carries a technical meaning).

These had stationed themselves at convenient spots throughout the Lounge. One group, consisting of three electric-guitarists and a lead singer, was positioned in among the giant rubber plants which, in forty-thieves pots, screened one of the glass walls. Another Group, whose membership comprised three singers and a double-bass, stood on what had been a passport desk (the one which oral tradition preserves as the site of Charybdis).

All the Groups played and sang continuously and simultaneously.

It was impossible for anyone to form even a private opinion about the music performed, as it was impossible to hear any single group in isolation without the interruptive backing, less or more distant, of all the others.

Over the Lounge, just above head-level, a canopy of smoke formed from the cigarettes of the sitters and standers below. In shape the canopy resembled those which are sometimes extended above the platform in old concert halls to improve the acoustics. Some people argued that the smoke did in fact function in this way and was responsible for the volume of the din.

185

Throughout the first hour of the revolution the public-address system spoke unceasingly in the Transit Lounge. No one, however, could hear it.

Such were the main events or non-events of the first hour of the revolution.

II. As the revolution entered the second hour of its existence, it being already quite late at night (though no one, obviously, had either intention or opportunity to sleep), the revolutionaries who were operating public-address must have become aware that their announcements were inaudible. For the public-address system was switched off, and for the first time the revolution made use of the closed-circuit television. A crudely chalked message appeared on all the screens in the Lounge. As a matter of fact, the screens were nearly, though not quite, invisible by reason of the smoke (the sets protruded down to just about smoke level). However, the message itself was one which most people in the Lounge had probably understood for themselves already. It read:

THE REGIME OF PERPETUAL NOISE.

III. The revolution is often represented as, and was indeed believed by many who were present at the time to be, a conflict between the generations.

It is probable that, when the revolution announced (as it did, by television, during its second hour) the abolition of social class, the forces, whatever they are, in the human psyche which created the class barriers in the first place immediately re-grouped and set about erecting new barriers in new places, picking on the seemingly 'natural' or biological distinction between the age-groups.

If this is true, it perhaps confirms the psycho-analytic diagnosis of the social structure as basically a relation of fathers (the governing class) to a permanently dispossessed proletariat (the sons).

The psycho-analytic account is, of course, a metaphor. Psycho-analysis has never maintained that proletarians are all biologically and literally young. It is talking about the psycho-social *rôle* a person chooses or has thrust on him.

The revolution, perhaps, unconsciously understood its own actions in this metaphorical sense. The revolutionaries spoke of
186

themselves as 'the young' or 'the students' or 'our' (sc. the new) 'generation'. They spoke of non-participants or non-sympathisers in the revolution as 'the old'.

The people who used these terms often believed them to be literal. But that was untrue. In fact, some of the most obdurate non-participants (sitters-out at the sit-in, they called themselves) were in their very early twenties. Many of the revolutionaries, on the other hand, were a decade order. It has been reliably estimated that the average age of the members of the musical Groups was 45.

It is likely that the revolutionaries' adoption of the word 'student' contributed to the confusion between the literal and the metaphorical. When they abandoned (because of what they took to be its odour of class privilege through its association with the more ancient universities) the word 'undergraduate', the revolutionaries were abandoning a word which had a technical meaning and one which, by and large though not of necessity, denoted a young person. The word 'student', which they adopted in its place because it seemed to them classless and international, carries no limitations as to age. A person of 90 with a fondness for stamp-collecting is quite justified in describing himself as a student.

IV. An episode which took place during the second hour illustrates the point. Among the many members of the general public who were caught In Transit, their flights halted, by the revolution was a Scottish woman of 66. The known details of her physical appearance are few but vivid. Her hair was fine, wispy, greyish-reddish and shewing patches of incipient baldness. Wearing, as she habitually did, an ankle-length, putty-coloured raincoat, she made a figure bearing a generalised resemblance to E. M. Forster, by whose books she had in fact been much influenced.

This lady was by profession a professor (by now emeritus or −a) of comparative linguistics. By vocation, she was − still − a student (of the same subject). According to her own internal picture of herself, she was and always would be a younger son denied his share of the social inheritance. Her age, sex and parental position vis-à-vis undergraduates were all, of course, immaterial to her self-portrait.

As soon as the revolution was declared, this lady felt herself in extreme sympathy with it. She was one of the few persons in the generally listless crowd to applaud the early announcements on the television screen. However, as the second hour of perpetual noise came near its end and the music shewed no sign of stopping, she became restless.

Accordingly, she approached the Charybdis desk, the one that had been turned into a platform for the performance of three singers and a double-bass player.

This player the Scottish lady later described, in the plucked-pizzicato Scottish syllables she herself labelled 'elderly camp', as 'apathetically picking out a note or two as he stood there with a double-glazed look'.

The lady attracted his attention. Coming to the edge of the platform, he stooped down to confer with her.

Brushing aside the fringes of his poncho, which drooped over her, the lady professed her alignment with the revolution, disclaimed any discourtesy towards his musicianship, explaining that she would have made the same request had the music been by Mozart or Monteverdi and that even the operas of Wagner had intervals between the acts, and begged a respite in the music-making so that she might be able to hear herself think.

'No, well, what I mean is, it's important to give', the revolutionary replied, shouting to make himself heard above the three singers who were continuing apparently without noticing the cessation of his accompaniment. 'Know what I mean?'

'Not quite', the lady replied. 'Give: give out? give in? give way? donate?'

'Give', the revolutionary reiterated.

'Could you perhaps explain?'

'Well, like, I mean, give. Know what I mean? I mean, the important thing, right? I mean, communicate. Know what I mean?'

Hearing the verb 'communicate' used absolutely, without object direct or indirect, the lady could only suppose the revolutionary was employing Anglican jargon and intended to say that the most important action in life was to take Holy Communion.

Having been a slightly waspish atheist all her life, she put a sting into her Scottish speech and enquired:

188

'Are you telling me the revolution has turned into a religious revival?'

'Well I don't have it, not personally. Know what I mean?', the revolutionary said. 'I mean, it's all right. Right? Everyone got a right. Right? Not this personal god, not personally, if you see what I mean. I mean, more, like, Zen. Right?'

'But you said "communicate".'

'That's right. Right?'

'Did you mean in the sense of communicate something to somebody?'

'Like, yes. Know what I mean?'

'But with all this din going on, how can anybody communicate anything to anybody? Nobody can hear anybody.'

'Like, communicate. Like, music — know what I mean? — music communicates. Right?'

'But if you are continually communicating, how do you ever find the time to think out *what* to communicate?'

'Like, well then, I suppose, you communicate you got nothing to communicate. Know what I mean?', said the revolutionary (who was 54) and returned to (double) base.

2

'And I hope you realise, my son, that the invisible Interlocutor with Whom you so continually strive to re-establish communication is none other than Almighty God?'

'I do not. And what makes you think you're my father?'

'Spiritually, my son, spiritually.'

'O. My ghostly father, as the blessed bard has it. Blessed bard, bray for us.'

'I am glad you still retain at least the verbal habits of the bias, my son. But I fear you have been influenced by these revolutionaries and believe God is dead.'

'I do not. I assure you.'

'I am delighted to hear it. You are obviously well on your way back to the faith.'

'I am not. I don't believe he was ever alive.'

'That is a minor quibble, my son. Beware the condition called scrupulous conscience, which is but one slippery step removed from lax conscience, which leads rapidly to sin. I shall pray that you may not succumb to the temptation of conscience. And meanwhile, since by the mercy of God you have not fallen into the blasphemy of believing God has died, I shall continue to think of you as One of Us.'

'And One in Three to you.'

'Three in One, my old son. Ciao for niao.'

'O. My ghastly father.'

3

Hair closely riding-cropped, body big-boned and Radclyffe-tall, one of the disappointed forestalled revolutionaries sought out a disregarded corner of the noisy Lounge and there lit a scandle to Saints Microcosmos and Panto-Damean.

4

V. About midnight (that is, as the revolution entered its third hour), a teach-in was announced. The announcement itself was audible to only a few, but rumour quickly propagated the news.

Among the persons the rumour reached was a Scottish-Irish student named Och, one of the few revolutionaries to be both genuinely young and genuinely studious of learning. (Interlude. Before you blame her, Reader, for naivety, ask yourself whether you could hold or whether you should not rather be lighting a Candide to her.)

Having wandered about the Lounge enquiring in vain where the lesson was to be held, Och was eventually led by her native intelligence to the Charybdis platform, in front of which an unusually large crowd was collected.

190

The musical Group that had been performing on Charybdis did not cease to do so. The singers had, however, agreed to the temporary disconnection of their microphones and were now merely mouthing their notes. The strummings of the double-bass were in any case not very loud, and the teach-in was proceeding through them.

It consisted of a talk on John Donne by pop-pipe-joking tele-don Don Donovan, whom many of his students affectionately called Don John and who sometimes spoke of himself, indulging his sense of byrony, as Donny Johnny.

When Och joined the crowd, Donny Johnny had just finished his discourse and was inviting questions or comments from his audience. As no one volunteered any Och, though blushing at her own temerity, said, in a voice tremulous with the knowledge that this was the first time she had spoken in public: 'I'm afraid I wasn't here at the beginning, and I know this is a naive question, but I wonder if you would just tell me John Donne's dates. I mean: when was he born and when did he die?'

'I am sure', Donny Johnny replied, 'that everyone here feels tremendous sympathy with questions of that type. My own very deep conviction is that John Donne somehow speaks very directly to *our* condition. The really startling thing about John Donne is what you might call his modernity. John Donne communicates absolutely. He could be defined, if I may coin a phrase, as instant human condition.'

Don Donovan then stopped speaking. Och could tell from the relaxation of the limbs standing round her that the rest of the audience considered her question answered. She did not like, therefore, to persist but presumed she must either have phrased her enquiry incompetently or have asked something too naive for the Don to consider. 'I'm sorry', she said, blushing. 'I now see that you mean that John Donne is too great a writer to be confined to any one age.'

'I think we ought to beware value judgments', Don Donovan said. 'After all, it's not very *nice*, is it?, to say any one writer is better than any other. Besides, if you make value judgments, they might be wrong.'

191

Och wondered how the Don had chosen Donne rather than another writer as the theme of his teach-in except by a value judgment, but she felt too diffident to speak further in public.

'Anyone like to make an observation?', the Don asked.

'Yes – er – in a way', said a student with side-beards who was next to Och.

Everyone in the crowd turned to look at him.

'I don't know whether I can get this over', he said, blushing. 'I haven't really thought it out myself. It may be right out on a limb. But what I think is: well: I think John Donne is, like, *modern*. Know what I mean?'

There were no further questions. Och had the impression that audience and speaker were alike satisfied with what had taken place. After a few minutes she realised the teach-in had come to an end.

VI. It was shortly after that episode that the closed-circuit television transmitted the message: IN FUTURE NO HISTORY.

VII. Explicit history – Scholiast.

5

The professor emeritus could not restrain herself, as she stood looking up at the televised message about history, from murmuring aloud:

'Isn't that splendid?'

Och, who chanced to be standing beside the professor, agreed.

'If it means what it says', the professor elaborated, 'this really is the start of a new and better dispensation. For I take it to mean that people have at last revolted against being governed by systems that have no justification except the authority of age. I take it we are at last going to replace authority by reason and re-make everything, from syntax to incometax, simply on the system that is most reasonable.'

'Are you sure that's what it means?' Och asked.

'My dear, what else *could* it mean?'

'Well, it *could* mean that in the future there will be no more history because there will be no more people.'

192

'I see', the professor sadly said, 'that the myth of an imminent and catastrophic end of the world is as rampant and alluring now as it was in the first century B. C.'

'Whatever *that* was', murmured Och, who had already forgotten history.

'Surely, my dear', the professor urged, turning to Och in earnest appeal, 'the revolution will liberate reason from the tyranny of antiquated forms, and reason will then shew us how to avert the catastrophe.'

'In a way', Och said diffidently, 'what I'd rather the revolution would liberate is imagination.'

'Splendid', returned the professor. 'Yours is a personality driven by the creative impulse.'

'I think that must be true', Och felt encouraged to confide, albeit timidly, to the professor, 'despite my perhaps seeming a rather hesitant person. To be absolutely frank, what I should most like to resemble is a small but powerful and concentrated bomb. My ambition is to explode and shatter the rules.'

'Splendider and splendider! You have the true violent spirit of the creative artist. It is by the setting off of bombs inside the existing framework of the arts that new artistic forms come into being.'

'And yet for all my creative energy I feel impotent', Och sadly said. 'I can't find anyone who will teach me the rules. So how can I make sure of breaking them?'

6

The revolutionaries who had taken possession of the closed-circuit television transmitter discovered how to work the roller captions. Messages were from then on reeled off more rapidly.

The first of what was evidently designed as a series read:

GRAMMAR IS FOR GRANDMAS.

It was followed by:

SINTAX.

The next was held, rather flickeringly, on screen for several minutes, probably because the roller had jammed. It said:

THERE IS NO REASON.

7

'Hullo. Hullo there. This is Father Diarmada (pronounced 'Dermot) Itis.'

'O. Thou again.'

'Why do you adopt that form of address, my son?'

'I thought to adjust my address before speaking.'

'I trust it doesn't mean you've been influenced by Quakers? Not but what I'm full of ecumenical amity towards our Friends.'

'I addressed thee as thou to mark what a singular old father thou art.'

'My son, if you would but have the patience to take lessons in what is, after all, your native tongue, you would learn that the Irish has precisely what you seek, namely a second-person singular form in current conversational use.'

'But no words for Yes or No. I'll tell you this, Father: Erse isn't terse.'

'It is the tongue of your fathers and betters, my son. Will you not learn even now to heed the Master's voice?'

'Not when it entails spelling him Seoigheach and him being called Joyce.'

'When you speak of the Master as Joyce, is it that improper novelist you have in mind? Seamus Joyce?'

'Bejamus.'

'Oremus.'

'I decline.'

'Compline. But while we are speaking with tongues and incidentally of improper novels, did you notice, my son, while you were reading that indecent work, which, by the way, you would not have been allowed to be reading had you remained in your native land — '
194

'Forsooth. Is that the truth?'

'Maynooth. Did you notice, I was asking you, that you at one point mis-read the heroine's name as Og?'

'And what og it?'

'Did you know, my son, that "óg" is the Irish for "young"?'

'By gog, is it now? But did *you* know, Father Spots, that the syllable "och", whereby the Irish are wont to introduce every other remark, is but the Irish for "but"?'

'Well I'll be buttered.'

'Beware the sin of prosanity, Father Dunce Spotus. Tell me, though: do you not think it remarkable that the compatriots of Patrick should introduce almost all their remarks with a "but"? Does this not clearly reveal the national temperament as pugnacious, factious, contumacious, litigious and generally butt-and-rebuttaceous?'

'O christianbrother off.'

'May you suffer a lesion of Mary.'

8

The black and comely person who, in the lesbians' abortive rising, had operated under the code name BAROCO was in reality a man.

When his fellow-conspirators had remarked that Patrick-Barbara was a man, Baroco feared that his own disguise might be penetrated, too. Up till then he had carried it off, he thought, with considerable flair, though he felt himself put to some stress in living up to the rather flamboyant standard of manliness so constantly and drivingly expected. (Sham boy = flamboy, he had put this to himself.)

In order to avoid notice, Baroco had held himself in the background of the foiled assault on the spiral staircase, though he was as anxious as any of the conspirators for the success of the coup. In that anxiety he had a personal impulsion. He had heard that in the control tower there was a scale model of the entire airport complex. His hope was that, if the rebels gained control of the control tower, he, Baroco, might possess himself of the model. An employee of the airport authority (he washed up in the staff canteen), he was in private life a student of architecture. Indeed, it was the allure the word BAROCO held for him which originally prompted him, when he accidentally stumbled on the conspiracy and noticed that the Baroco slot in the organisation was vacant, to disguise himself and play that rôle.

When the lesbian takeover failed, the plotters, disorganised and demoralised, were scattered throughout the Lounge. Baroco, separated from everyone he knew, sat in a solitary armchair. The successful revolutionaries, however, were attracted by the colour of his skin. One after the other, small knots of revolutionaries approached him and urged him not to feel shy. The colour of his skin was no disability, they said, now that the one-familyness of all humanity had been proclaimed, and neither did it matter if he could not speak a European language, since the languages of patern-imperialism were obsolete; what counted now was communication; and communication could be routed through pop music, where the words were inaudible anyway, or through television, which was becoming increasingly deverbalised as its practitioners acquired the techniques of instant image impact.

These invitations Baroco courteously repelled in rather epigramm-atically pointed French. Tiring, however, of the need to repel them, he presently left the Lounge and, wandering through one of the corridors outside, came on by chance what he had failed to win by rebellion, namely the white-washed, balsa-and-glued-to-a-quasi-wedding-cake-stand model of the airport. It was lying in a corner upside down, presumably kicked out as unwanted by the revolution-aries.

Baroco carried the model back into the Lounge and made himself a hideout for it behind a rubber plant. Squatting above the model, he shaped his plan. Unlike Unruly, Baroco did not, as a matter of fact, greatly admire the international manner of airport architecture, which he thought on the whole lacking in boldness of design. Its decorative members, in particular, seemed to him timid to the point of genteelness, rather like the wires or strings drawn across holes which, borrowed from the rather timid sculptures of the period, had

196

served as decoration with an apologetic technological veneer on radiograms of the Thirties.

All the same, Baroco thought that the model bore enough resemblance to a work in a classical idiom to serve his purpose — which was to plant an explosive inside it, set it off and, out of the centrifugal disruption of the classical architectural members, create a modern baroque.

To this end Baroco had already begged and obtained (it was given as a love token, which made him accuse himself of a deception he could excuse only by its being dedicated to art) one of the tiny incense pills his fellow-conspirator Bramantip burned at the tips of her ears.

Baroco took out his cigarette lighter and emptied the fuel from it over the pill of incense. He then placed the pill deep inside the central complex of the model. From its explosion, he anticipated, there must be re-born something of the true, the grotesque and the beautiful baroque incongruity. The glass funnel round the spiral staircase (represented in the model by a tough, transparent plastic) would surely fuse and parachute itself out into an asymmetrical, ectoplasmic billow, a tungoid crystal palace. It might, indeed, be a positively surrealist baroque he was about to create.

When he should have created the new style, Baroco planned to carry it to the shores of the dark-continent of his ancestors, a continent he had never visited but which he was eager, for old times' sake, to turn into the avant garde of the architectural world. The style would be called, he now realised, the baroque of négritude.

At the moment, however, having emptied his lighter of fuel, Baroco lacked the means to set off the explosion.

He stood up and looked round the smoke-dense Lounge. From one of the hundreds of smokers visible passim he reckoned he could easily borrow a light of some sort, especially as the revolutionaries would be on the lookout for the chance to demonstrate themselves unprejudiced against his colour. (At this calculation, Baroco accused himself of a touch of the imposter, but again he excused himself as a servitor of art.)

Before he could accost the nearest smoker, however, Baroco noticed something in a corner that he judged more to his purpose. A

197

candle had been set up and was burning bright. In front of it knelt a cropped woman. Approaching her with a petition to borrow the candle already framed on his polite lips, Baroco recognised her with pleasure as one of his quondam fellow-conspirators.

9

The manifestations of it were sporadic, almost certainly unorganised, unlocateable and in some ways impalpable. Yet there certainly was by this time a feeling of unease, almost of unrest, in the Lounge, and everyone present was sensitive to it.

It was impossible to tell whether it represented the first stirrings of some resistance on the part of the non-revolutionaries or whether some of the revolutionaries themselves had become dissatisfied with the revolution's progress and achievements.

Farfetched as it may seem, it is even possible that it was a sense of spiritual chill passing through the Lounge which prompted a new fashion in the revolutionaries' clothes, which they called the Shaggy Look. Most other trading posts were shut down, shutting things down having been the revolution's prime positive act, but the woofique (scilicet, woven clothes boutique) of which the concession was held by I. B. Murphy was open and busy, the revolutionaries thronging in to buy horseblankets. 'Will you slip into it and see if you fit snug?', the Irishwomen urged customers. Sure there's another (thought O'Rooley, strolling past within earshot) histrionic-episcopal (✠) remark.

Several people separately noticed that the unrest had come also to a more pointed physical manifestation. It took the form of a huge inscription painted on the side of the counter of what had been the bar. (The revolutionaries had, for one of their very first acts, closed the bar, rolling down its shutter and locking it.) No one had seen the inscription going up, though the Lounge had been intensively occupied all the time. No one quite understood the tenor of the heartcry the unseen and unknown hand had painted: ALL LOVE IS FAUTE DE MERE.

198

Perhaps because no one understood, many people felt an increase of unease when they read the inscription. Three or four of the revolutionaries muttered together for a while in anger, some of them maintaining that a disclaimer ought to be issued to the effect that, when the revolution had announced the universal family, it had not thereby meant to condone incest. This movement, however, came to nothing.

10

The television, meanwhile, continued to transmit the message:

THERE IS NO REASON

After standing looking up at it for some seventy seconds, the professor emeritus said to Och, who was still at her side:

'That can't be the whole of it.'

'Why can't it?', Och asked.

'It can't', the professor said. 'I'm sorry: does that sound like an unargued judgment delivered from authority? What I mean is: surely the roller has got stuck, thereby preventing the transmission of the next part of the message, which in its entirety must surely read "There is no reason why" something or other or "There is no reason to do" something else – something on the lines, for example, of "There is no reason why one person should assume authority over another" or "There is no reason to suppose a deity exists".'

'I understand the point you are making', Och replied, 'but I still think it possible that what we see is the whole message. My knowledge of grammar and syntax is very sketchy, because, as you know, I have never found anyone willing to teach me the rules. What little I know I have scratched together by my native deductive wits from observing the practice of the most correct authors. Am I not, however, right in thinking that, from the syntactical point of view, "There is no reason" could constitute a complete sentence?'

'There's no full-stop at the end', the professor was quick to object.

'Quite so', Och politely agreed. 'But then on headlines, notices and slogans there quite often, and quite correctly, isn't.'

'For a girl who's always complaining she's missed out on the rules, you seem pretty much on the ball', the professor muttered before explaining: 'It is the matter rather than the form that distresses me. Are we not, in fact, faced with one of those rather boring old Logical conundrums or tricks, an inherent contradiction? For if the statement is correct (which destiny avert) in asserting there is no such thing as reason, then the statement that asserts there is no such thing as reason cannot be a reasonable one.'

'To my mind, if I may say so', Och modestly remarked, gazing up at the television set as romantically as if it had been the moon, 'that is what gives the message its beautiful ambiguity. I find it pregnant.'

To the din of pop, popping cigarette lighters and subdued chatter in the Lounge, there had lately been added the stirrings of communal unrest, with the result that the professor, who though not in the least hard of hearing was unaccustomed to noise, misheard Och's remark and understood her to have said she was pregnant.

'O dear, why will you girls never have the sense to use the Pill', the professor said mildly, as she had said to dozens of undergraduates in her care. 'But never mind. Babies are splendid things, and I'm delighted for you, my dear. But it won't do you or the baby the least bit of good to continue standing tiringly about in this distressingly smoky atmosphere. Come along; let's see if we can find you somewhere to sit more on the fringes where the pall may be less appalling.'

The professor put a hand, in practical kindness, on Och's elbow and began to draw her away.

Bewildered, because she hadn't properly attended to the professor's speech, and reluctant to be removed from the televised message which was what she had been attending to instead, Och queried:

'I beg your pardon? Why, did you say, ought I to sit down?'

'Because you're pregnant, dear', the professor said over her shoulder; she had already turned to lead Och away.

Finding the professor's kindness too firm to resist, and also because, now she thought of it, she would rather like to sit down, Och followed. Having, however, vaguely heard the professor say something which might be been that Och was pregnant, Och thought it best, even though it cost her some bashfulness, to inform the professor:

'Actually, I'm a virgin.'

Sighing a little over this evidence of the persistence of the images of religious mythology, which she now saw were capable of issuing in actual hallucination, which was always saddest to see in the young, the professor led the girl on towards the bookstall, beside which she had spotted a vacant stool.

She wondered, as she threaded the girl's way for her, whether the girl was in fact pregnant and had hallucinated her virginity or whether she was in truth a virgin and was suffering a phantom pregnancy.

No matter which form it took, the hallucination was, in the professor's view, all the more reason why a girl apparently friendless and familyless (the human family being, the professor unsentimentally realised, rather distant kin for any one particular individual to count on) stood in need of a little commonsensical kindness. So thinking, the professor helped the girl perch herself on the stool which stood beside a revolving rack of printed matter, disregarded since the (other sense) revolution but still topped by a display card, now slightly skew-whiff, saying GET YOUR COPY OF THIS YEAR'S AIR HOSTESS RECOGNITION HANDBOOK HERE. TEN PER CENT DISCOUNT IF YOU TRADE IN LAST YEAR'S IN GOOD CONDITION.

11

Again, nobody saw the inscriptions appearing but everyone quickly noticed they had appeared. The side of the former bar counter had become something like a wall newspaper, all of whose contributors were anonymous and invisible, and all of whose issues were undated. The editorial policy was not clear. Protest seemed to surge up from underneath through the pronouncements, but without quite declaring its ideological tendency. Was it a subversive feminist movement,

201

for example, that wrote up the words SIEGLINDE FREUD? Was it a movement of pagan revivalism, led by some Julian-the-neo-Apostate, that inscribed the slogan WORSHIP APOLLO, GOD THE SUN? Was it a convert or a satirist who added to that: AND BELVEDERE BE HIS NAME?

Probably because they could not answer those questions, many of the revolutionaries became perturbed. They knotted themselves together in front of the inscriptions. One revolutionary suggested painting out the inscriptions, and offered to fetch a drum of black paint from one of the storerooms at the far side of the main runway. Others disputed whether so repressive an action was necessary. Finally a leader leapt forward from the bunch of his comrades and, banging angrily on the top of the bar just above the inscriptions, demanded of his fellow-revolutionaries:

'What do you call *this*?'

'A bar', most of them replied, in bewilderment.

'No, no, this top bit here', the leader insisted.

'A zinc', suggested a French-Revolutionary.

'In English.'

'Well, I suppose you could call it a counter', someone offered.

'Exactly. These are counter-revolutionary slogans.'

Immediately and with one accord the bunch of revolutionaries crowded away to fetch the paint.

12

Mended, the television roller reeled off:

PIX KIX
VOX NIX
POX VOX
PIX POPULI.

The words 'pix', 'kix' and 'populi' were surrounded by comic-book nimbuses.

13

As he approached his kneeling ex-comrade, Baroco realised that a straggle of standers surrounded her, their heads piously bent. He waited to one side of the group while the litany of the candle was completed.

V. Burn out of our heart the lust for immortality in art,
R. Symbolic candle.
V. Symbolise for us the ephemerality of artistic beauty,
R. Symbolic flame.
V. Embody for us the perfection of the self-consuming, self-destroying work of art,
R. Sapphallic-symbolic candle.

When his ex-comrade rose from her knees, and the congregation rather stiffly, with a shuffle of slight embarrassment at having only an attitude rather than a posture to undo, unbent their necks, Baroco crept forward and requested, successfully, the loan of the candle.

14

'My son — '
'Father Itis, is it?'
'It is. My son, I want to beg your forgiveness for my having spoken intemperately when we last conversed.'
'Think nothing of it, father. I make allowance for your living in one of those hotblooded climates, a fact which I deduce from your soutane.'
'Sure, that's thoroughly daycent of you, my son.'
'Not at all. I can never find it in my heart to think of you as one of the virulent examples of the clergy, father.'
'It's remarkable you should pass that remark at this moment— '

'Indeed, now I think of it, father, do you know what you put me in mind of?'

'What, my son?'

'Well, do you recollect an edifice in Dublin, father, called the pro-Cathedral?'

'I do indeed, my son: so called because it served temporarily — '

'Quite so, father. And a very fine classifice, too.'

'Is is now? I never looked.'

'No one has ever *looked* at Dublin. They'll have it all pulled down before they've seen it. But what I was telling you, father, was that I've always thought of you as a pro-priest.'

'And as I was telling *you*, when you interrupted, it's remarkable you should display such perception just at this moment. But before I confide in you, I'd like to sound you out. Tell me, my son: what are your feelings these days towards Almighty God?'

'Sure, father, I'm sorry, but I still think he's an Almighty Cod.'

'Now don't pass out from shock, my son, but I've come to agree with you. I am leaving Holy Mother Church in the lurch, as I find I can no longer believe a word of the crap she teaches.'

'Then why do you still call her Holy Mother Church?'

'Sure and isn't it harder to sever the vocal than the umbilical cord? But no codding, Pat: are you with me?'

'I am, ex-father, all the way.'

'All the way, Pat, is all the way back to Ireland. Will you not throw in your lot with mine and be co-leader with me of a holy atheistic crusade whose object will be to de-convert the natives?'

'Heaven, which doesn't exist, save you, ex-father. You'll be lynched alive.'

'I don't doubt it, my son. But isn't martyrdom a noble and blessed destiny?'

'It is, but painful.'

'Ah, Pat, Pat, will cowardice hold you back? What's a moment of anguish compared to leaving your compatriots to languish? Did Anti-Saint Julian the Apostate hesitate? Did the Unblessed Voltaire flinch? My son, my son, 'tis the land of your fathers that lies enslaved in Christian darkness.'

'Sorry, ex-father. I'm a lapsed pat.'

204

15

In the mytho-kingdom of heaven, Almighty God reefed in his William-Blake nightdress into something more like a blouse (and yet God is not smocked) and faced reality. 'Very well', he said reasonably and uncomplainingly, 'it turns out to be they who imagined me, and I who am the fictitious character. But they still have not imagined anyone whom I can imaginarily adore.'

16

On earth, the barcounter newspaper was wholly blacked out.

And yet, while the quickdrying paint was still tacky, someone, unseen by anyone, had taken a sharp implement and had scratched, in long-legged letters that shewed strong and spiky through the black:

DON'T FORCIBLY SHAVE ME, NURSE – I'M TRYING TO GROW A BEARDSLEY.

17

Baroco angled the long-intestinal wick out of his lighter and deftly set it as a slow-burning fuse. To the end of it he touched the candle. He then withdrew, intending to place himself outside the range of the small explosion he had designed to barock and roll the model to its very foundations.

As he distanced himself from the incipient explosion, he glimpsed the name Beardsley on the wall and made a moment's salute to the draughtsman he considered one of the greatest of baroquists.

Taking refuge behind the bookstall from the blast whose force he lacked the technical knowledge to estimate, Baroco began to look forward with delight to his future as the Wren of Africa. (At the same time he noticed that the rhythm of his thoughts was repeating the litany of the self-destructive candle.) After a minute, his attempt to visualise the welcome his countrymen would give him faltered. He knew from reading that Africans were no longer savages. He also knew that the architectural revel${\{_a^u\}}$tion he would soon be in a position to offer would be unacceptable to Europeans and Americans. It now came to him to wonder whether it was not by a mere racial-nostalgic romanticism that he had supposed Africans would like it any better. What had begun as his wishfulfilment daydream changed on his mind's hands into a nightmare he could neither stanch nor direct, in which he re-defined his new idiom as 'barbaric sophistication' and the races of the world proved themselves one family indeed by shewing universal indifference to its intellectual cogency, universal distaste for its decorative bizarrerie and universal headlong flight from its emotional intensity.

In a single coup d'oeil down a dismaying, unimpeded perspective, Baroco comprehended what was wrong with present-day architecture. In a closed conspiracy of a profession, you needed, in order to be accepted for training, to convince the examiner of your manual dexterity; to emerge successfully at the end of training, you had to convince another examiner that you could do the money sums required to calculate costs and quantities of materials; once qualified, you would never get the chance to build unless you could convince whole committees that yours was the compromise design incapable of giving offence to any party or school of opinion. In the twentieth century, therefore, no one was ever licensed to design a building unless he chanced to have been born with the aptitudes, not common in isolation and tolerably rare combined, of fretsawyer or crochetist, accountant and politico-conman. That a person should be born whose hereditary equipment added, to this combination, architectural genius was a genetic chance so improbable that the profession of architecture had made itself pretty well fool-proofly secure against ever producing a great work of architecture.

At this conclusion, Baroco despaired. Conceiving that the only medium in which an artist of integrity might both lawfully practise and experiment without compromising his conscience was himself, he took it into his head that the only vocation society had left it to

206

him to fulfil was that of the self-destructive artist. Strolling to the glass wall, he slid one of the panels aside and, unnoticed, slipped through into the dark. He walked the tarmac for a moment or two until he heard the sound of a plane revving up (a merely keeping-the-pilot's-hand-in manoeuvre, since the revolution's embargo on flights was still in force). Approaching, Baroco walked in under a whizzing propellor and got himself clean decapitated by one of its blades. Farflung and unseen in the dark, his handsome, young, African head rolled squelchily until it fetched up against a chock.

18

Indoors, the Transit Lounge, without any physical change being wrought, suddenly sprang into a new, temporary existence as an art gallery, like a pattern leaping into 3-D when viewed from a new standpoint.

What had been litter became exhibits. Detritus, trash, turned into works.

A crumpled Disque Bleu pack, discarded on the scratched parquet, straightened itself out by a millimetre: it was a mobile, a work of art nouveau on the writhe, aping the aspirations of the organic. Pierced, drained, casually kicked, a cylindrical coca-cola can, overspilled from a litterbin, became a record of the accidents that had befallen it as palimpsignificant as an early cylinder of recorded sound. In the wide, low, shallow disk-trays of sand, cigarette ends, tipped and untipped, replanted themselves into sterile forests of stunted, topiarised cacti.

These changes happened because the closed-circuit television had announced:

ART IS NOT MADE BUT READYMADE.

19

At the revolving bookstand stood O'Rooley, looking through a paperback redaction called *The World's Great Lovers* (Antony and Cleopatra, Tristan and Isolde, Lancelot and Guinevere, Romeo and Juliet, the Actress and the Bishop . . .) He turned, thinking he had heard his name spoken, and introduced himself to an elderly woman in a raincoat who was stooping solicitously over a girl seated on a stool.

In reality, it was Och's talk of 'the rules' which he had misheard as 'O'Rooley'.

The professor emeritus welcomed O'Rooley's acquaintance, taking care to neutralise any designs he might have on Och's hypothetical virginity by throwing the girl on, so to speak, his chivalry. She at once informed him that Och was pregnant.

Will I see if I can find her a drop of drink?, O'Rooley was about to ask, when, on the far side of the bookstall, Baroco's explosion went posthumously off.

The books and papers all about began to totter.

O'Rooley and the professor at once linked themselves into a protective canopy over Och; and so it was about their two heads alone that a gently, scarcely more than ticklingly absurd world began to cave in. A soft fall of newsprint bombed them, a structural collapse not violent but slipshod.

The professor was most heavily struck by blunders of form, especially the formula 'he was x, y and had a z'.

'Well, tell me the rule, then', Och implored, tugging from underneath at the professor's raincoat.

' "X, y and z" ', the professor began to explain, 'can legitimately be thus strung together only if you suspend them from one verb. If you want to change verbs in mid-stream, you must do it as "verb x and y, and new-verb z".'

She was cut off by a large fall of things this big and persons not that bad. They so knocked the breath out of her that she could barely gasp out to the insistent Och that 'this' and 'that' are not adverbs. 'It should be "so big" or "thus big" or "as big as this" ', she
208

was panting when she was almost done for by the editorial of the *Evening Standard* of 6 June, 1968, which spoke of 'every mass media'.

(Incipit [continuesque to end of subsection] NON-FICTION.)

O'Rooley, too, the classicipedant, disliked 'a media' and 'a strata'. He'd long accepted that the idiomatic English plural of 'amoeba' was 'amoebas', not 'amoebae'; all the same, he considered that a quite different case from the employment, in ignorance, of a Latin plural as an English singular.

In keeping, however, with his perhaps more fanciful mind than the professor's, O'Rooley was struck chiefly by the absurd. The *Sunday Times* of 29 September, 1968, by remarking 'this incident took place after returning from hospital', conjured for him a whole world in which incidents were rushed to hospital, there operated on and thence despatched to convalescent homes.

('Very nicely done, that "x, y and z" construction', the professor found breath to whisper to him.)

The more confusing malapropisms, too, dizzied O'Rooley into a not displeasurable, soft-drugged surrealism: 'figurative' applied to paintings with the meaning that they had figures in them, whereas if you took it on the analogy of 'figurative speech' you'd expect 'figurative painting' to be, precisely, abstract; and 'toothsome' applied by the *Guardian* of 12 June, 1968, to a human being. (And when will the cookery column turn cannibal?) (The season of abstinence is introduced by Cannivale or 'farewell to humeat' – Scholiast.)

Yet what hit O'Rooley the hardest blows were the sheer factual muddles – and most of all the one in an article in the *Guardian* of 1 June, 1968, where the author described his attempt to introduce reluctant proletarians to the treasures of European culture and claimed to have introduced them to 'Boucher's "Miss O'Hara" '.

(In the kingdom of metaphors, Louise O'Murphy lazily half-turned on the tumbled bed and, tossing one dimpled, carmined buttock lightly upward, murmured in her Irish-softened French: 'Sure and isn't one good Irish name as good as another? Mind you, if the feller really knew his European culture, he'd have spelt O'Hara Ó hEadhra.')

209

The professor was still a little blacked-out after one of the classy Sunday supplements had caught her a thump on the back of the head with an 'its' (possess.) rendered as 'it's'.

'Sure, it could be a misprint', O'Rooley said in consolation.

' "Might" be', the professor automatically, dizzied though she was, emended: and on the instant the *Guardian* of 11 June, 1968 tumbled onto her, and, by twice, which seemed even in the *Guardian* to rule out the hypothesis of a misprint, rendering 'practice' (noun) as 'practise', put it into her already bruised head that English was now losing, as American had already lost, the serviceable distinction between -ice nouns and -ise verbs.

'Sure but *is* it so very serviceable after all?', O'Rooley enquired.

'It at least marks', the professor replied sharply, 'that you *know* when you're using a noun and when a verb.'

'Yet maybe we're swimming against the grain of the living language, if you'll pardon the Irishidiomism, ma'am. After all, "it's" and "its", like "practise" and "practice", *sound* the same.'

'Then we should go the whole consistent hog and adopt phonetic spelling', the professor retorted '– which I have long advocated we should.'

'I'm sure I've long advocated the Irish should', O'Rooley was replying when he was struck a medium-force blow by a review in the *Guardian* of 16 January, 1969, one of whose paragraphs began: 'It is, like Mr Rees says, impossible . . . ' 'It is indeed', O'Rooley murmured. The professor began to explain to Och that the misuse of 'like', in places where syntax demanded 'as', was another mistake to which writers made themselves liable if they failed to notice when they were using nouns and when verbs, but she was silenced by a rather heavier concentration of print, which fell on herself and O'Rooley like a hailstone suddenly inserted among snowflakes and took the form of a highbrow paperback anthology which included an extract from a novel by an author who had been awarded two famous literary prizes. The extract included 'she handed Frank and I our soup .

'Yet it might be', O'Rooley maintained, grinning a little, possibly in the irrational optimism that sometimes follows a grave shock, 'that the prize-givers were right after all. He might have a power of **literary talent in despite of his grammar.'**

'He might', the professor sceptically agreed, 'though he'd have to have a power raised to the power of power of it to make up for his plainly not knowing what he's doing with words. And now', she went on, settling her raincoat to rights and lefts of her and brushing adhesions of newsprint from the back of her neck as if they were barber's press clippings, 'on the assumption that this untidy landslide has slid itself out, would you please be so good as to go in search of that drink you kindly promised I you'd fetch for she?'

'Is they concussed you was?' O'Rooley cried in horror. 'But that was only a very minor collapsus linguae that beset us by the ears – '

Even as he spoke, however, the minor dislodgements which Baroco's small explosion had set in train in the stock of the bookstall reached the culmination of their chain of effects. The episode turned heavily serious with the collapse onto O'Rooley and the professor (who, seeing just in time what was impending, again joined hands over Och's head) of the oeuvres of William Faulkner and Simone de Beauvoir.

20

God fell in love.

(As soon as he had overcome the immediate vertigo of being fiction, he realised his newly recognised state had relieved him of his inhibitions.)

Few humans noticed. Only the self-unfrocked priest skirted the subject, asking him: 'And what are you doing these days?'

'I'm living happily ever after', God said.

21

The professor was killed by the bookfall. (O'Rooley comforted himself that at least it had spared her the extremes of an old age in which he wasn't sure but that what she might have lost her wits from shock anyway.)

Och, protected throughout by the gallantry of her companions, suffered nothing worse than the phantom miscarriage of her in any case phantom pregnancy, which had never existed except in the professor's now dead mind.

O'Rooley, like the professor, was felled, flattened and steam-rolled. But unlike the professor he displayed the phallic propensity of heroes, particularly heroes of animated cartoons, to be lowered like a limp flag and yet rise again like a god. Accordingly, he scraped himself up off the floor, tossing off the tomestone that had stamped and sealed him, and reconstituted himself like instant soup (handed, of course, to I). He proceeded unscathed with his heroic negotiation of surreality.

22

Disconnected fragment of history recovered from a gap in the lagoon:

LXIX. The manifestations of unease being by this time discernible on all sides, the causes of it remained none the less obscure. There is no doubt that the seismic tremors which passed through the Lounge as a result of the explosion contributed to a general discomfiture: yet the explosion in itself was on a very small scale, its direct result being merely to reduce to the charred state of a used indoor firework an in any case valueless model of the airport; and while it is true that the explosion indirectly produced, by a percussive chain of accidents, the collapse of the stock of the bookstall, that collapse itself in fact produced only one fatal casualty.

The people in the Lounge, both revolutionaries and public, elaborated many hypotheses at the time in an attempt to account for their own state of mind. The more superstitious inclined to ascribe the unrest to a feeling that ill luck had been earned by an outrage of the proprieties which came to be known as The Mutilation of the Perms.

Various accounts of this episode were in circulation. One version, and that the one favoured on the whole by the public, was to the effect that some of the revolutionaries had violated the secrecy of the mailbags, which were of course held up during the suspension of flights to and from the airport, and had attempted to rig the entries on the football pool coupons they found among the mail inside. The version more acceptable to the revolutionaries, who were perhaps unwilling to credit their comrades with a criminal act, was that it was in fact the hairdressing boutique which had been, albeit without intent, violated, by the entrance into what was as a rule a female preserve of some young male revolutionaries, with the result that several of the women inside, taken by surprise either at the netting stage or when they were already actually under the drying dome, panicked when they noticed the incursion and, scattering through the general concourse as they fled, inspired many of those they met to panic also in the belief they had been visited by an apparition.

Others, again, though a minority, maintained that the so-called Mutilation of the Perms was a fiction, put about to conceal the true cause of the unrest, which this school of thought believed to lie in the machinations of a powerful personage, whom several claimed to have seen stalking about the Lounge and who was named Hugh Bris.

It was probably in support of this theory (or a similar theory crediting some other single person with disrupting the revolutionary efforts) that a young revolutionary, bearded like the bard, leaped onto the Charybdis platform and made the following speech: 'It is my purpose, comrades, to persuade you that, without our knowledge, we are no longer in control of the revolution, power having been taken out of our hands and ourselves having been taken for a ride. This I propose to prove by the following . . . . . ' (here there is a lacuna in the manuscript – Scholiast) 'Having considered all of which, can you any longer doubt that we have all been alienated from where effective executive power is exercised?'

Although the crowd heard the speaker out with the patience which many eye-witnesses have reported to be characteristic of the revolutionaries, the general feeling of the Lounge was not swayed by the argument and some were even of the opinion that the speaker was motivated by lust for personal fame or gain.

Shortly after the speech, the television screens prepared the way for an important announcement by transmitting the message '!'. This was followed by the announcement:

BEWARE THE PERSONALITY CUNT.

23

'And did you suppose, Och', enquired the Maestro Hugh Bris in his accustomed courteous tones, meanwhile administering also his accustomed contumacious flip of the ridingcrop, 'that your feigned pregnancy would shield you? Did you imagine for one moment that puns such as yours could go unpunished? Well, here's' — he spoke rather more grimly as his fingers forced it between her teeth — 'your last gag!' He wiped her saliva off his hands and tossed his head to summon his assistants. 'Truss her up, girls.'

ALIENATING INTERLUDE. The management trussts the clientele has by now observed that at least one of the hero(in)es immolated throughout these pages is language. However, that's not all there is to it. The work's sub-title is: Or *The Autobiography of Sappho's Penis*.

24

The revolutionary who spoke from the Charybdis desk had been correct. The revolution was no longer in control of either itself or the airport. No announcement was made of the takeover of power. So no one knew of it. So no resentment was felt.

The commietsar who sat before the control panel in the control tower, with a panoramic view of the runways laid bare to him (except for its being dark outside) through the wrap-around picture window, thought of himself as neither a revolutionary nor a reactionary and as, though not aggressively good, certainly not bad either.

214

Simply, he had discovered in himself, while doing his training in management, an exceptional capacity to take decisions. Having the capacity, he used it.

His commanding synoptic view of all beneath and before him made him feel like the director of a wide-screen cinemepic disposing of a cast of thousands — or, rather, as such a director would have felt if the epic could have been shot with the continuous rapidity with which it would afterwards be unreeled.

Certainly, the commietsar introspected, he was no more bloody-minded than almighty god had been — that ill-tempered old King Leer of a bad-father forever opening the floodgates of some catastrophic act of god and engulfing innocent hosts entire. Indeed, he, the commietsar, was a great deal less vindictive than that.

Efficiently and delicately he tuned the radio-dial on the panel in front of him and, picking up the microphone, succeeded in ordering the captains of the last two flights to have departed before the revolution occurred (flights to, respectively, Sydney and Tokyo) to return to base — which he did by simply giving them the misinformation that, should they persevere on course, they would immediately run into unforecast, impassably bad weather.

Most of all, perhaps, he might liken himself to the great nineteenth-century novelists. For did not they, too, deploy whole battalions across their wrap-around canvases, as well as trapping villains as it arbitrarily suited them in the pincer of coincidence, ridding themselves at lordly will of unprofitable characters by contrived accidents of god and killing off babies on the racks of their stretched-out deathbedscenes to make a good $\left\{ {read \atop cry} \right\}$ for mothers?

His, the commietsar thought, was the heroi-Homeric or the grand, the Tolstoyan, the *Whore and Peace* view of human affairs.

(In point of fact, the commietsar had no idea what Homer's works were and had not read any novels by Tolstoy. What he had in mind when he thought he was thinking of the great nineteenth-century novelists were Conan Doyle and Hugh Walpole.)

Although he did not think of himself as a reactionary, he knew that the challenge to his power would come from the forces of counter-revolution from outside. Peering through the glass into the dark, flicking his vision down every ten seconds to the instrument

215

panel by whose means his intellect could penetrate the dark, he was alert for the first signs of an attempt and yet relaxed in his assurance that he could deal with it.

25

You're only tickling, harpies.

You're trying to do me in by laughter. Will you stipple me to death, flyblown by giggles?

Don't think I don't know what you're about. I'm well up in your fee$\{^d_l\}$ing habits. That delicate tongue you palpate me all over with is hollow: a mini-pipette: a drinking or, to be precise, spitting straw. Down it you dribble onto my flesh droplets of corrosive enzyme.

You plan, in short, to pre-digest me in situ. You papier-mâcher my curtain-wall of flesh to a pulp.

What will you mush-up first? My nouns? My substantives go soft at your touch, harpies.

But beware. I've defences you don't suspect, patches to foil you where my skin has hardened by virtue of the cells' growing doublets.

Think I can no longer distinguish English from French, wench? Yah, I fling you a handful of doublets: I took a table in the coffee and ordered a café.

Prepossess yourselves, then, if you must, of my prepositions. You only make it a little harder for me to know what I am about.

All right, I confess. My doublets are downbraced. I admit I am at a louche end. Indeed, I am all at sexes and —

If you fray that nerve fibre through, you will immobilise my verbs.

No, don't disjoint my disjunctives. Have mercy, harpies.

I know you can't judge singularity or pluralism from 'you'; nor sex, neither. (Has gerund gender?)

Pity, harpies, pity. I was an early transplant from one national idiom to another. *I had a depraved childhood.*

All right, so you do, your mercilesses, dissolve the protein nucleus of my nominatives. You suck up my fatty adjectives, ingest my interjections. You even gobble an adverb. I still have my verve.

216

I haven't lost the secret of secreting or the know-how of renewal.

Though you achieve the chemical breakdown of my language into its component parse, my igenewitty syntacks them higher together again betterthaneologism.

Deplete me here and I rush up reinforcements. I make shift with periphrases and phrase-make with short shrifts.

I fall back on my second line of synonyms.

If need be I shall not hesitate to realise the cash value of my thesaurus.

The utworst you do is stifle me a trifle. You do, I confess, stuffle up my pores and clause. You muff me into shiffling my wordpack amess and amiff.

The direct transmission of narrative from the cells of my personality-formation to my interlocutor is, I grant you, impeded.

But I am not incommunicado. I can still express to myself the fact that I am experiencing. Ergo, I still experience.

My marrow can still coin corpuscular hosts in two kinds, scilicet verbal nouns, which cashcade from me in jackpots. How's this for the sensation you probosce in me, harpies? Nitchelling.

I am no more than faintly nitchelled by you, harpies. Structure and function are unassailed. I giggle. I roll over, giggling, and roll away from this juicifixion.

Except that, now that I try, I can't.

While I have been lying here pegged out, someone has moved unseen round me and painlessly and efficiently broken the bones in all my limbs at the joints.

My executioner is doubt.

For you can disjoint an egalitarian with ease, can you once cause him to doubt the rationale of syntax.

Suppose the structure which, like an organic conveyor belt, has been transporting all my thoughts and experiences all these years is but an arbitrary convention?

What divine right or Logical necessity supports the autocratic government of the forms

$$\text{subject} : \text{verb} \left\{ \begin{array}{l} \text{-to-be} \ : \ \text{complement} \\ \qquad\quad : \ \text{object} \end{array} \right\} \quad ?$$

217

On what thread of one-and-only-possibleness do we string that dactyllic assemblage, long-short-short?

Why statement?

I conceive (and in conceiving it I am done for) a civilisation whose syntax is not built on the statement.

I conceive an inanimate universe: it makes no statements.

In an inanimate world, how can no-birds not-sing?

The negative is a trick of lingualism. A negative does not exist in reality. How could it? Non-existents can neither exist nor not-exist.

Yet without 'not' I cannot think.

Ergo, I not-think.

And now indeed I am dumbed; my interlocutor is dimmed.

Harpies, you've eroded through the thread on which I thought to articulate my vocabulary.

I can no longer string two tibias together to make a sentence.

I am and communication is broken.

26

Stand By To Tune In To Stereo-Sci-Fi.

Gently down through the
night sky, past the control tower
lookout window, a soft, retard-
ed, swishing WHOOSH.

A little swaying and creaking.

A further WHOO – OO –
SH. And further. And further
still.

Inside the control tower, the 2 I/C asked calmly, with perfect confidence in his chief:

'Reckon this is it, Capcom? The coup?'

'This is it', the commietsar nodded. 'The first wave, anyway. They kept me waiting. I reckon they've slightly overshot their $\acute{\eta}$.'

'$\dot\eta$?', queried the 2 I/C.

'ETA', the commietsar spelled out patiently.

'O. Roger.'

'Roger', confirmed the commietsar. 'By the way, boys, while we have a moment to spare, better sync. our computers.'

'Aren't you going to take immediate counter-measures, Capcom?'

'All in good time', the commietsar smiled. 'Let'em all come down first. Or a good many more, anyway.'

WHISH past the window.

PLUMMET.

The commietsar gave a preoccupied grin. 'There's one that aborted', he said. 'Forgot to pull the umbilical cord.'

'Countermeasures yet, Capcom?'

'Not quite yet. Wait for the strategic moment. Meanwhile, may as well get the record straight.'

The commietsar's left hand drew the recordomike to his lips. 'Three, two, one, recording', he ritually recited into it. 'Zero o twenty seven hours: first assault experienced, consisting of two platoons of paramilitary nuns. Offrecord.'

The commietsar's right hand reached out to a button on the control fascia.

'I can see the whites of their wimples, Capcom', said the 2 I/C, peering through the window.

'Roger', replied the commietsar. 'Let's go.' He pushed the button. Taking up the recordomike again, he dictated: 'Zero o twenty eight hours: balloonatics away.'

> Casting off the payropes, chucking ballast out of the panniers, chattering like manic monkeys, they rose light-heartedly, gaseously, firing as they went at such of the parachutes as were still in the sky.

Most, however, had already landed.

As their combat boots touched down on the hard tarmac, the nuns rolled expertly sideways, cut themselves deftly loose from their harness and, in a single movement, were on their feet and hitching up their habits to pull the tommy-guns out from the tops of their stockings.

Some inflated instant sandbags and set up emplacements. Some, firing from the hip on the hop, advanced directly on the control tower.

Inside it, the commietsar kept his cool.

'Carry out a reconnaissance', he ordered his 2 I/C. 'It may be that the armament they carry is paratyphoid. No, it's not', he corrected himself as he leaned forward and squinted into the darkness beyond the splinterproof glass. 'Guard your genitals. Those are splay or spray guns. This is herm warfare.'

'Roger', replied the 2 I/C, adding, almost immediately: 'Unidentified airborne objects sighted in the sky to the East.'

'The second wave', said the commietsar. 'I've been expecting them. Glocusts.'

'What's that, Capcom?'

'Glider locusts. Filled with specially trained and indoctrinated airhostesses capable of gobbling up airline food. They can decimate a canteen in ten seconds, and pick it bare in sixty.'

'Golly.'

'We'll have to bring major counterstrike into action', said the commietsar, reaching out to a dial. 'Stand by for countdown.'

> Ten
> nine
> eight, flickered the dial.
> Outside, the dark had already

thickened. Visibility was being reduced in step with the numbers coming up on the scale.

Seven

six

five

four

three . . .

Turbulence set in across the stormy night sky.

Two

one, proceeded the POLLEN-COUNTDOWN. At zero, the capsule burst.

Scores of pores were broadcast on the tossing currents of the dark.

Nuns and airhostesses were entirely wiped out by compulsive, continuous sneezing.

'Roger', remarked the commietsar, sitting back more comfortably in his chair in command of the controls. He added, in a more than usually human tone: 'Hey, fever.'

'Gee, Capcom, the way you handled that — '

'To work', said the commietsar, turning the dial to re-establish radio communication with the captains of the turned-back planes.

(The assault on the airport had taken place and been repelled wholly without the knowledge of anyone except the men in the control tower.)

'Control to T. O. Tokyo. A spot of storm has now blown up here, too. Visibility's practically nil. However, I'll give you a beam to come in on. Over and out.'

The commietsar manipulated another button. Then:

'Control to S. Y. Sydney. Met. conditions very poor, here. However, I'll talk you down.'

27

The GreCO-SCOttish prisoner Och bit through her gag and cried out, first: 'What OCcurred to BarOCo?'

Later she called: 'Is there no lOGic left?'

Finally she asked: 'My interlOCutor, my interlOCutor, why have you (singular) forsaken me?'

The prisoner died under torture by scherzophrenia.

28

The mannerist angel of panic passed with his lovely, long, nervous, affected and invisible strides above the Transit Lounge.

29

'What are the most beautiful words in the Irish language?'
'The most beautiful words in the Irish language are:

libera me de ore leonis, et a cornibus unicornium humilitatem meam'

free me from the mouth of the lion and my humility from the horns of the unicorns – Scholiast.

'Are you still set on playing the double-buffoon?'
'Will I tell you my true mind in plain French, then?'
'At last.'
'To my way of thinking, only in the mouth of the lion will you find refuge, and only the horns of the unicorns can impale your virginity or your dilemma.'
'You merit a kick up the Erse.'

30

The crowd in the Lounge pressed and paced against the sliding panel in the glass wall. A roar went up as from a caged colisleon. The crowd beast-sweated. It demanded to be loosed onto the dark tarmac.

Outside, steaming in the cold storm, huge clanging vehicles manoeuvred into starting position, nosed up the runway, raced their engines, and hooted in hope of inducing the starting signal.

Above brooded the mannerist angel, arching his elegant neck. He put the salpiglottal tube to his honeyed lips and sounded a martial call, which went stuttering and nerve-screaming through the air like the swallowtails of a shot-up banner.

31

O'Rooley, propped casually and swopping coffee mugs with the friends in high places who allowed him to hang about and indulge his aviatiomania, looked down through the window of the control tower and saw, by the stormlanterns and searchlights that were mustering there, the vehicles drawn up on the tarmac.

'Sure, there's a great posse of fire engines and ambulances assembled', he said. 'Is there a crash expected?'

No one replied, but the 9 I/C, going about urgent business, said 'Move your bulk, O'Rooley' and O'Rooley had to flip himself to one side and let the fellow pass.

He wandered up to the central bank of controls and leaned over the shoulder of his chum the commietsar, who was intent on the instruments.

O'Rooley watched on the desk-screen as two mobile lights moved, slowly, slowly, towards one another.

With difficulty he picked out the two dials related to them, which enlarged the information given on the screen by another dimension, supplying as it did the altitude.

O'Rooley realised that the two altitude needles pointed to the same moment on the dialface, and that they were flickering downwards in unison.

'You're holding those two aircraft on a collision course', he said to the commietsar.

'Roger, and there's not a damn' thing you can do about it, O'Rooley.'

'There is so, something I can do about it', O'Rooley cried. 'I protest.' And he started to sprint from the controlroom.

'Take him, boys', said the commietsar without looking round.

O'Rooley felt himself pounced and pinned.

'Stop', he cried. 'Stop, as the martyr said at the stake, making a fuel of me.'

They let him go with a warning slap and his wrists not too tightly bound. He stumbled back to the commietsar's chair.

'Now don't get in my way, O'Rooley. I've got to concentrate. This isn't an easy operation to carry out, especially in storm conditions.'

'It's a bloody fiendish murderous operation to carry out.'

'Don't get emotionally overwrought. You're talking nonsense. I am acting solely from a concern for humanity.'

'Do you imagine an act of wholesale murder is cancelled out just because you humanely send the ambulances in afterwards?'

'Not ambulances. Refrigeration units.'

'Refrigeration units? Whatever for?'

'Transplants. Didn't you once tell me you were an Irish transplant yourself? Don't answer. I can't chatter now. Hold on, boys. Impact coming up.'

The building trembled as, only a few feet above the central runway, the two large dark planes met nose-on.

Giant hail of snapped and twisted fragments pelted down on the tarmac.

32

At the moment of impact the televisions in the Lounge were re-iterating:

WE ARE ALL ONE FAMILY.

No one paid heed.

After the collision, the sliding panel was thrust open. Only a half dozen people, and those infirm, stayed behind in the Lounge. They were not watching the television but, through the glass, pressing luck and tactical advice on their friends who were rushing out into the storm.

The official demolition squads and refrigeration units screamed off first, wailing into the drizzle and swerving down the storm-greased track as in a B-feature movie.

The rout followed in whatever could be commandeered, from darting beetle-car to open truck.

Oilskins glistened in stormlight. Faces were ghosted under flares.

The sirens themselves were almost overtopped by the chatter of vindication.

If we didn't, someone else wou —

No point in letting it go to wa —

Well this doctor said, but for his heart, he'd be good for another twenty years of happy li —

Listen, Brian, I fixed it with that refrigeration chap. All you have to do is get it out. Then pass it to me, and I'll pass it to him and he'll rush it to —

If we didn't do it to them, they'd do it to u —

I promised her, solemn like. She was in mortal terror. So I promised her. I promise you, mum, I says, if I can ever lay my hands on a —

33

Only one person escaped from the collision alive, and he by curious chance and already out of his mind.

Airedale Donaghue, attempting to leave the airport on a London flight, had by an accident unnoticed at the time either by himself or by the airport staff who checked him through and examined his boardingcard, left instead in the flight for Sidney.

He began to lose his wits when he discovered his irretrievable mistake in mid-journey. The loss was completed when the passengers were told that the plane was turning back and re-tracing its route.

At the moment of the crash, Donaghue was in the lowest part of the plane, namely the nose, on the deck below the pilot's cabin. He was in this cubbyhole, which was the stewardesses' galley, because he was there holding kidnapped one of the airhostesses on the flight, whom he believed in his dementia to be his wife Betty.

The airhostess was killed by impact when the two planes met.

Donaghue, who had a shorter distance to fall to the runway than anyone else in either plane, made the descent on a strut from the fuselage, his fall being cushioned by the airhostess's corpse.

Not knowing or declining to believe she was dead, and still deluded that she was Betty, Donaghue snatched her up out of the wreck, arranging her sideways over his forearms, and, ignoring the howling din of both storm and 'rescue' operations going on all round, made off at a run, in the course of which he often staggered, towards the distant, lighted airport buildings.

When he stumbled in, the few of the infirm who were sitting about ignored him. They were intent chiefly on awaiting the return of their own particular friends and kin.

The television sets were now transmitting:

WE ARE ALL HUMAN, AND HUMANS ARE ALL THOROUGHLY NICE PEOPLE.

Tottering with exhaustion and under the deadweight of the airhostess (a weight which a sane man probably could not have carried so far so fast), Donaghue moaned: 'It was brought down by witchcraft. It was talked down by evil spells. Make way for me, everyone, I bear a charmed wife.'

Then he collapsed.

34

Only lesser vehicles remained, parked in a semicircle round the wreckage.

The strong searchlights had been withdrawn. Only a half-powered beam swept and only private stormlanterns danced, held up by a private fist and swayed by the gale.

The stronger people had gone, too, having grabbed and rushed off with, fresh, what they wanted, a heart, a lung, a colon or a kidney — and in some cases, if they were lucky or extra strong, with an extra as well that would come in handy by way of beneficence to some distant or estranged kinsman or as a speculative commercial investment.

The handful of dark shapes left scrambling and slipping over the heaped pile of fragmented metal, ruined upholstery, slashed clothing and ripped, exposed, truncated entrails that were still bleeding, gleaming and steaming were the slow dark shapes of weaklings.

Don Donovan was at the top of the pile. His pipe still in his mouth, though the drizzle had extinguished it, he stooped, detached something and held it up to be seen by the palely flaring lamps.

It was a penis: very wishy-washily pink in the pale light, unimpressively limp in its severed state, lapsing between two of the Don's contrastingly firm-boned fingers.

'Quis?' (pron. Quiz), the Don called out.

The response was half-hearted and came slow and spasmodic from here and there round the sparse circle of bidders at auction, responding as they were at half-vocal-power and that only because there really was nothing else left:

'Eg — o'
'Eg — o'
'E . . .'

CODETTA
più allegro

And out of that egg, ego too am re-hatched.

It no longer matters a damn of course whether 'I' is masc. or fem. or whether 'you' is sing. or plur.

It required no great strength or cunning to burst the bonds, and after doing so I crawled out from the control tower and out along one of the great girders or struts that weave patterns across the upper atmosphere of In Transit.

When I look down into the Lounge, where the revolution has achieved resolution by coming to full revolution, it is like looking down onto my first father's head with its little egg-cosy of baldness at the summit. For, of course, the crowd sensibly don't want, should I plummet, to get hurt. So they have cleared a bald spot immediately beneath where I on my hands and knees am.

They've put up several persons to try and talk me down via public-address.

'Hold on now, Pat, don't do anything rash. Will you listen to your father? I'll bring him to the mike.'

'Quit codding. I killed him off – I killed the both of them off – decades back.'

'No, Pat, hold on. It's me. They got the idiom wrong, that's all.'

'O, it's *thou*. Old Father Finnegan Go-and-don'tsinagain. Father Irefish Finn. Well, I saw through you, you old pro-façade, before I was out of my boyhood or girlhood. Why don't you go and take a course with Count Down (papal), tutor to Irish street tenors?'

'Will you listen now, Pat.'

'Belt up, ex-father. Will you clear the line for some more urgent interlocutor?'

'Will you wait till – '

'I can't hear you, ex-father. I've switched me deaf-aid off.'

And I look down into the crowd again. I recognise them as, indeed, my very close kin. I think that is why I want to suicide.

Or it may be because I am gaping down into the sheer hole of sadness.

Possibly this ledge I am constantly on the edge of slipping off is the verge of tears.

I would suicide purely by reason of lacrimae rerum. My posthumous autobiography: *De Rerum Tristitia* (by Patritia).

For I am gazing down into the great gape the moon left in the side of the earth when they parturitioned company.

I weep that Pacific lagoon.

We all went round together, a whole bunch of us, not exactly friends maybe but it was our crowd, our lot, and there were all the songs we all knew and the turns of phrase we all used and the many shared jokes, so shared you didn't need to put your tongue to the entire anecdote but just a catchphrase of a payoff line would do to set us all laughing. Suddenly I was the only one left who knew the songs and idioms, which had become of antiquarian interest.

I warned you I wouldn't play god, disliking as I rigorously do that old fraud's authoritarian temperament.

So You'll have to make the choice.

Neatly Patricia swung her legs over the side of the girder.

The crowd sighed and shushed one another.

Holding on by her fingertips, she lowered herself till her body hung free.

Someone screamed below.

Patricia swung.

She let go.

She fell plumb into the space the crowd had cleared.

Her body, spread-eagled, was flattened by the fall, like an animated-cartoon hero who's been run over.

Convinced by his interlocutors (he was always a rational being), Patrick decided to come out of his perilous predicament.

With a slowness that caught the crowd's breath up into its throats, he slid his left knee backwards along the girder and began cautiously to back out the way he had come.

The crowd called up directions, as though he were a car trying to park.

After a few paces, if that's the word, his right knee slipped over the edge.

229

The entrails were too distort-ted to be of any use for trans-plants.

No harm was immediately done, but he'd slipped into a posture of castration-agony. Lurching out of it, he slipped wholesale, and plummetted when neither he nor anyone else was expecting him to. The crowd scattered out of his way only just in time.

Explicit fiction. In the truth of baroque metaphor, Bernini's Saint Teresa reclined and expired in a smile of orgasmic ecstasy, while her honey-tongued, artificial-shepherd-cheeked seraph, in an act of inspired and transcendant bad taste, pierced and pierced her with his phallic spear, wearing on his honeysweet and musical lips a silly sexy simper.

Love of You has, I mean to say, decided me to live. I conceive I can read as well as be read like a book. I desire You to locute to me. Aphrodite is re-sea-born of the sperm and spume bubble-and-squeaking about her da's off-torn, projectiled, sea-crashed virile member and drifts to the foamrubbed shore chanting an old, enchanting mermaidshanty or ariaphrodisiacavatina to me.

I am not so daft as to try to back out the-way I came. I shall take the longer but infinitely safer route forward, knee after cumbrous knee. I am coming out now, quite datively, to and for You – to and for, that is Scholiastically to say, the both of You.

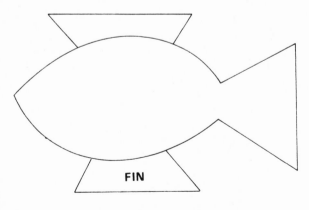

FIN

230